The Fall of America

Book 4 — Winter Ops

WR Benton

LOOSE CANNON ENTERPRISES
Paradise, CA

Ingram Edition
ISBN 978-1-944476-58-8

Author Photos © Copyright 2015, Melanie D. Calvert,
used with permission
Cover Photo by: www.shutterstock.com, used with permission
Book layout and design by W R Benton LLC, © copyright 2015
Edited by: Bobbie La Cour, Juanita Duryea, and Daniel Williams
Logo fonts [*Shortcut, Dirty Ego*] by Eduardo Recife,
misprintedtype.com

www.loose-cannon.com

"Loyalty to country ALWAYS. Loyalty to government, when it deserves it."
— Mark Twain

"I am an American; free born and free bred, where I acknowledge no man as my superior, except for his own worth, or as my inferior, except for his own demerit."
— Theodore Roosevelt

"The soldier is the Army. No army is better than its soldiers. The soldier is also a citizen. In fact, the highest obligation and privilege of citizenship is that of bearing arms for one's country"
— George S. Patton Jr.

Books in this series by W.R. Benton

The Fall of America, Book 4, Winter Ops

The Fall of America, Book 3, Enemy Within

The Fall of America, Book 2, Fatal Encounters

The Fall of America: Book 1, Premonition of Death

— *Also available in Audio Edition*

Visit http://www.amazon.com/author/wrbenton/

for more WR Benton titles.

DEDICATIONS

This book is dedicated to the memory of Edna Marie Benton, August 1931 – May 2015, my mother, who kept me writing when times were rough, because of her guidance when I was a child. Mom taught me to not be a quitter and to work toward my goals. It was through her patient and tender teachings that I am the man I am today.

To Juanita Duryea, who is still fighting a continuous battle for the full recovery of her health. Juanita is true gem, in all senses of the word, a beautiful Southern belle, and wonderful woman. Keep up the fight, we love you.

Foreword

I've had many comments about this series, with some being down right mean and ugly, but make no doubt about it, *when* America falls and not *if*, it will turn mean and ugly, too. Our society will be destroyed as we know it and law, along with order, will disappear, to be replaced by chaos and death. The strong will kill the weak, and our weak will the first ones to perish. It's this author's opinion that over the years, most Americans have become lazy, obese, and soft, so the collapse of our nation will hit most folks hard. Those people who years earlier had strong opinions against gun ownership, will now own guns or die. People will die by guns, knives, and almost any object that *can* become a weapon *will* become one. While robbery, rape and murder will be common, handfuls of people will band together for protection. Cells or tribes will form, and mankind will revert back thousands of years. Rest assured, only the strongest and best armed will survive. Society will be made up of those alive and those who will soon be dead.

Then, major countries who we owe money, and lots of it, will come for real estate since our being able to pay them back will be out of the question. Those Americans who can resist will do so and viciously, too. It will be a war with no quarter given and none expected for either side. In this series I have the Russians coming, but it could be almost any major power, including China. We are now hopelessly in debt and eventually, I feel our overspending by those we elect to serve us will bring about the death of our country. I cannot understand why our veterans are not having their needs met, American children go hungry, our elderly are not cared for, and much more, while we give billions of dollars we don't have to countries that hate us. I say, let our enemies hate us for free, and every child knows you can't buy friendship.

2013 information from the U.S. Bureau of Alcohol, Tobacco, Firearms and Explosives, states there are about 300 millions guns in the United States, but I'm sure there are many more weapons on hand that have never been registered. Out of that number of weapons, 23 million to 43.7 million of those guns are owned by hunters; this estimate came from the 2001 National Survey Of Fishing, Hunting and Wildlife-Related Recreation, which was based on the annual data provided by the United States Fish and Wildlife Service. According to the VA, there are 19.6 million living veterans in 2013 in the United States, of which 1.6 million are women. So, with roughly 23 (using the lower figure for hunters) million men and women, who know how to safely use a weapon and can shoot, our private sector army is huge. Now, in some cases individuals may be both a hunter and a veteran, but regardless, the figure is large. According to Reuters, The United States has 90 guns for every 100 citizens, and that's a fascinating figure. It is obvious now why the United States has never been invaded before, because we have the largest armed private fighting force in the world.

Of those weapons, data from the 1994 U.S. Bureau of Alcohol, Tobacco, Firearms and Explosives figures, shows approximately 65 million pistols of all types, 70 million rifles of all calibers and types and 49 million shotguns. As you can see, this is not even close to the total count shown above, but there is almost a 20 year gap between the information in 1994 and 2013. Regardless of the actual numbers, we have a lot of weapons in this country, and most would be used to fight off an invader.

The biggest threat to the defenders will be technology, which will be difficult to confront, unless all aspects of an attack favor the attacking partisan force. I suspect helicopters alone will kill many, not to mention tanks, missiles, and other weapons. However, the invaders will find one weapon carried by the Americans that no one can defeat; our patriotic attitude. We're a hard-headed people when it comes to our liberty and I suspect our defenders will fight to capture weapons, just to turn them against our enemies. I also suspect all politics will disappear, along with our political correctness, and there will only be one active political party, the American party.

So, sit back and enjoy book four of my series, *"The Fall of America: Winter Ops,"* and see America as it may be one day. I hope and pray this will never happen, but right now I'm deathly afraid of the direction our government is heading. I feel our political correctness, ISIS, and many other threats, as well as our runaway spending, will one day spell the end to a country I love. I care about this nation so much, I spent over 26 years of my life in uniform to help protect her. May God bless and protect the United States of America.

WR Benton
Jackson, Mississippi
July 2015

"I predict future happiness for Americans if they can
prevent the government from wasting the labors of the
people under the pretense of taking care of them."
                                                —Thomas Jefferson

"My reading of history convinces me that most bad
government results from too much government."
                                                —Thomas Jefferson

TABLE OF CONTENTS

BOOK 4

Winter Ops

CHAPTER 1

As the man lay dying, I went through his pockets. He was a Russian, and since we had no prisoner of war camp for captives, we took no prisoners. I'd heard we had some special prisoners held in the swamps, but I'd never seen one. I stuck the long sharp blade of my skinning knife deep under his ribs and then twisted the blade as I moved it quickly from side-to-side. While you may think me cruel, he'd suffered a severe head injury and a large chunk of his skull was missing along with a fair portion of his brain. I felt I was doing him a favor. Since I'm a partisan and bullets are hard to come by, I used my knife. Because he was near death, he'd not even screamed when my long blade entered him. Blood, with a strong scent of copper, quickly pooled under the mans lower back.

"Let's move, and do it now." my wife Sandra said. Once a stunning beauty, the Russians had captured her and while being tortured her face was disfigured, her ears and lips now missing.

"Are the others ready?"

"Oh, yeah, and they're worried about the helicopters we've heard all morning. Did you find anything of value on this man?"

"A map, Bison and pistol, as well as a canvas couriers pouch, and some letters from home. He's a Junior Sergeant, so being mounted on a motorcycle, I suspect he was carrying orders and such. I've not looked in his pouch. I'll do that once back at camp."

"Let's move, and do it now." she suggested, since I really outranked her, but we all know who is the boss in a marriage.

I smiled and said, "Alright, let's move —"

There came a sudden noise and someone yelled, "Chopper!"

We were in a wooded area, with a gravel road running down the middle. The Russian dispatch rider had been moving along the road at a fair clip, when Joyce, my sniper, took him out with one shot. The bullet had struck his head and while he was already dead, his body was taking it's sweet time to shut down. So, I'd killed him.

"Into the trees!" I yelled, hoping we could down a chopper. Once in position, the sound of the aircraft grew louder, which meant it was getting closer. I pulled a LAW from my backpack, extended it and was ready. I place it on my shoulder, glanced around, cleared the area behind me, and listened closely for the aircraft.

The chopper came flying slowly down the middle of the road, hovered over the crashed motorcycle, and then two men came out the aircraft doors using ropes. When the men were about halfway to the ground, I fired the LAW and the bird took a direct hit on the nose. A fireball resulted and the chopper fell hard to the ground where the fuel tanks exploded, sending up a huge fireball of red and black greasy looking smoke. A man ran from the fire, fully engulfed in flames, and after a few feet, he fell to his knees. Seconds later he fell to his side, still burning, but no longer moving.

"Arwood, plant some pressure detonating mines around the crash site and have a couple of others help you. Near the mines, add some toe-poppers as surprises."

He replied, "I hear ya. Walsh, Kerr, and Silverwolf, help me plant some surprises. Quickly now, we don't have much time."

It was then the ammo began to cook off from the heat and other explosives exploded as well, which caused a large black cloud to rise above the crash site.

"Let's move, people, and do it now!" I yelled ten minutes later and then added, "Arwood on point and Kelly, you bring up the rear. Move at a fast clip, but watch for mines."

"Yo!" Arwood said and moved forward. He was a smallish man with a good sense of humor, meek, and had been a music teacher before the fall. There was little about him that was unusual, except his small size and bald head, which sported a little brown hair on the sides. He was thin, but all of us were. However, with that said, he was an excellent scout when deep in Injun country.

Kelly was a tall man, closer to seven feet than six, serious, red hair and beard, and officially my medic. Unlike in previous wars or conflicts, he wore no identifying red cross on a white arm band, and would kill as quickly as most of us. I think he said he'd been a paramedic before the fall and had simply picked up a gun and joined the fight.

We moved cross country quickly and not on any beaten paths. Both sides frequently mined trails and I avoided them, especially when in Russian controlled areas. My primary concern now was avoiding searching aircraft and ambushes. The Russian bear would be pissed, but he'd been pissed before, and at us. My only secret to staying alive was to move faster than they expected me to move so I'd be out of their search circle. The sky was gray with light winds, and the temperature was near freezing. The clouds looked like snow, but we rarely got snow in Mississippi, so I expected an ice storm or rain.

Less than ten minutes later, my questions on the weather were answered, when it began spitting sleet. We continued to move and would move at all costs until I felt safe again. If the weather turned to rain we'd hole up, because in wet weather the infrared imaging equipment on the Russian helicopters failed to work properly most of the time. That meant we could have a fire and warm food for a change.

Arwood suddenly stopped and raised his right hand in a fist; he'd seen danger of some sort. He squatted in the grasses, scanned the area around us and then moved toward me. I moved forward to meet him. Once at my side, he cupped his hands around my ear and whispered, "Smoke; do you smell it?"

I sniffed the air but smelled nothing. He took my arm and moved forward to his old position. I then picked up the faint smell of a cigarette. I motioned for everyone to stay in place, as he and I moved toward the source. If there were other partisans in the area, I had to warn them of the danger since we'd downed a chopper. If they were Russians, we'd kill them if possible.

Less than 100 yards later, I peeked through some brush and watched a squad of Russian soldiers preparing a meal. They were dirty, and looked tired and sleepy. I turned and made my way back to my group. Once there, I moved them forward a couple hundred yards and explained what I'd seen.

"Do we attack or keep moving?" Walsh asked.

"We attack, and at every opportunity." I replied, but since he was a fairly new man, I let his question slide. I then added, "This is what we'll do."

Twenty minutes later, with a Claymore mine positioned toward the group of Russians, I waited until the men moved to look over a map, all but two anyway. At that point I squeezed the clacker and sent them straight to hell in loud explosion. The other two stood, which was the worst thing they could have done and were shot down. I heard screams for many long minutes after the explosion, but still we waited. *Damn*, I finally thought, *I don't need this with the weather bad and maybe choppers looking for us. I'm tired, hungry and need some sleep.*

"Move into them, but if one even twitches, put a bullet in 'em. Let's move!"

We moved forward as a group, but we were well spread out. One man was still alive, with some injuries to his left arm and his side. The rest were dead.

"Kelly, cover Walsh as he checks the man for weapons."

No sooner had the two men moved into position than Kelly yelled, "Pistol!"

I was looking right into the Russian's eyes as Kelly pulled the trigger on his Bison and stitched the man right up the middle. The man's eyes grew huge, he bucked violently as bullets struck him, and then he fell back, dead. Blood, gore, and bone covered the ground around the dead man as his body quivered and jerked as his central nervous system shut down.

"Damn me, that was close." Walsh said as he looked around.

"Too close, but that's why if it's possible, we always check the injured in pairs. Alright, look for any ammo, gear, or food we can take. Let's hurry, folks, the Russians will be on our asses twice as hard once they know we killed some of their men, too." I glanced at the falling sleet and then the sky. It looked to me as if we were in for a spell of bad weather and I prayed it turned barnyard bitch dog ugly. The worse the weather, the more likely we'd make a clean get away.

Ten minutes later, we were back on the trail and moving north. As we moved, the wind picked up and rain was mixed with the sleet. I noticed more rain than sleet and suspected that if the rain froze, the Russians would hunt a hole. I smiled, knowing right now they'd have to see us to find us and that made my day. We were now cutting across a large forest filled with large pine and oak trees, and some looked to be hundreds of years old. It was almost dry where we walked because the limbs on the big trees kept most of the moisture off us. I considered stopping, but knew we needed to cover some ground as long as we could move. The skies were dark, almost black, and the winds were growing stronger.

Arwood, who was walking point, waited until I neared him and then asked, "When do you plan to hunt a hole?"

"Not until we have to do the job. I want us to cover as much distance as we can before we stop. Right now, distance and bad weather is all that is keeping us alive. I think if we can cover 20 miles we can slow down and hunt a place to rest."

"We need someone to scout ahead of me, then. This sleet on the ground and the crackling noise it makes as it hits the ground confuses me and makes it hard for me to check for mines. I don't really expect any, not moving cross country, but they're always a consideration."

"Silverwolf, I need to talk with you." I said and glanced down the line of partisans to see him smile. John Silverwolf was a good looking man of mixed Indian blood, his momma Lakota Sioux and his daddy Pawnee. His hair was black, his skin the color of bronze, and his teeth even and almost too white. His cheek bones were high and his eyes a deep brown, almost black. He was a no nonsense kind of man, but did have his humorous side; it just didn't come out often. Prior to the fall he'd been a cowboy and making good money with rodeos, but now he was about the best tracker we had in Mississippi.

When he neared, I said, "John, I need to have you roaming out in front of Arwood, say three miles, and see if you can spot any potential threats to us."

"Sure, I can do that. Will you be maintaining this heading?"

"For the rest of the day I will, but near dusk I'll swing due west." I said and gave a sigh. I suddenly felt tired and worn out. Years of constant battle, no real deep rest, and absolutely no escaping the constant threat of a violent death, was hard on me emotionally. *Pull it together*, I thought, *you can think about being tired after all of this is over, or you die, whichever comes first.*

John nodded and said, "I'll be out there someplace. If I don't come back at some point before dark, it's not likely I'll ever be back."

Our eyes met and I said, "I hear you. Now go." Then turning to my people I said, "Saddle up and let's move. Arwood, you drop from point for a while and let Kerr take it for the rest of the day."

"I'll be up front, so hold all my calls." Kerr said, grinned, and then moved forward.

Kerr was a tall black man from Jackson, Mississippi, about six feet and six inches; I have no idea what he did before the fall and have never asked him. He's usually a quiet man, causes no trouble, and all our talk has been about how he lost his parents after the pharmacies closed. Seems they were unable to get their medication and eventually died, like so many others, of complications. I feel, each time I speak with him, a deep anger and I think it's related to the death of his parents. If so, he was a loving and caring son, which was rare in the days prior to the fall. Nonetheless, he's a damned good point man, alert, quiet, and with good eyes. More than once he's saved our collective asses by pointing out trip wires made of thin, almost invisible, monofilament fishing line. He had the eyes we needed.

An hour later, just as we were crossing a large field I'd not wanted to cross, but we needed to cover some distance, I heard the high pitch scream of a jet fighter.

"Down, and don't move!" Sandra yelled as we all went to ground.

I heard what sounded like the worlds largest zipper being yanked down and then the area right in front of me erupted into a ten foot high wall of dirt, rocks, and debris as a Gatling gun tore the place to hell and back. I watched the bird pull up and then circle to come back around for another pass.

I called out, "Stay still, because he'll not know, even if he sees us, if he killed us or not. If you pray, now would be a good time to ask the Lord to be merciful."

The jet did not line up for an attack, but flew down low, less than 300 feet, straight and level. When near us, he banked slightly to view us and then pulled his nose up and began a step climb into the dark clouds. In a matter of minutes he was out of sight and no doubt would call his home base and give some exaggerated number of partisans killed.

"Is everyone okay?" I asked as I stood and knocked the sleet from my pants.

"Walsh took a glancing blow from a rock and is bleeding, but he's okay. I'll bandage him up and he'll be good to go in a couple of minutes." Sandra replied.

At that point, Kerr returned at a run and said, "Russians coming in, they're hot on my ass. Y'all move back to the trees and I'll place a mine. Move, I mean they're *really* close to me."

"Everyone to the trees and *now!*" I said and took off at a hard run.

A couple of minutes later, as we entered the trees, I said, "Spread out and watch Kerr. Cover his ass in the event the Russians see him."

I watched the far treeline for the enemy, but saw nothing. Then I saw Kerr stand in the tall grasses and run hard for our trees. It was then I spotted the first Russian step from the woods. The aircraft that attacked us must have radioed a squad on the ground to check our area out and get a good body count, because that's what I would have done.

Kerr entered the trees without a shot from the other side and I suspect they didn't see him. Our man was almost to the trees before the first Russian was seen, their point man. A few minutes later, a larger group of Russians walked from the woods, following. I quickly estimated their size at a squad, almost the same as my force.

They were good, I noticed, as they spread out wide to cross the field.

"Hold your fire," I whispered and heard my order passes around to the others.

The main group continued on Kerr's tracks and at a little less than the half way point, there came a loud explosion, screams, and then yelling in Russian. I saw where there were five men earlier, smoke and bodies littered the ground. One man, I suspected he was the medic, ran for the downed men and when he neared, I heard a toe-popper go off and watched as he fell screaming. No one else moved. I pulled my Russian binoculars from my case and brought them to my eyes.

The medic looked like he'd taken most of the shotgun shell blast in his thigh and he was bleeding heavily. I watched as he pulled his kit near and began to work on his injury. Of the other five that were down, only one was still moving and he was screaming almost nonstop. Adjusting the focus on my glasses, I saw long strands of gray purple intestines clutched tightly in his hands. He was dead, only he didn't realize it yet, and was moving on adrenaline. I expected him to go into shock shortly and then death. One man had his head completely missing, and of the other three, they all looked dead, but that meant little to me.

I pulled Joyce, my sniper, in close and whispered, "Take out the furthest man first, and when you fire, so will we." I looked around and everyone nodded.

Joyce was a short woman with blond hair and blue eyes and about five feet and five inches tall. She loved to joke, until she picked up her sniper rifle; then she turned deadly serious. I watched her Russian sniper rifle come up and she began sighting in on her first target. She made some minor adjustments to her scope and took a deep breath. As she slowly exhaled the air trapped in her lungs, I saw her finger slowly tighten on the trigger.

Her shot was more of a muffled pop than the blast of a high powered rifle, and I saw the man at the rear collapse into a heap. Other weapons opened fire and one by one the Russians began to fall. Seeing all the enemy were either dead or gone to ground, I called out, "Cease fire, cease fire, and now we wait. Keep your eyes open in case one makes a move. Joyce, put a killing round into each body you can see."

Her shots began to ring out.

Finally, a man on the right screamed something, stood and began running back toward the trees. Joyce fired once and the man's head exploded sending blood and gore high into the air. He collapsed as if he'd hit a brick wall.

We continued to wait.

Finally, an hour after her last shot and ending of all cries and moans, I said, "Okay, I want most of you to remain here as Scott and I check them out."

I heard the twenty year old gulp and then he stood as I did. Scott was one of the few in the field that spoke fluent Russian. At a young age he'd been adopted by a Russian couple and raised as their own son. To avoid suspicion and problems, he'd not used his Russian name when he joined us and so far he was proving to be a loyal American. I liked the lad, as did Sandra, but some distrusted him because he spoke the language of our enemies. Both of his Russian parents were killed when they were hanged in retaliation of our attack on the air base at Edwards earlier this year and I feared the man was on a vengeance trail, because he was hard on any Russian taken alive. While only twenty, he had the eyes of a sixty year old man and by that I mean sad eyes, very sad.

"If one moves," I said as we moved forward, "put a bullet in him."

"Oh, trust me, I will."

In the main group by the exploded mine, the five were dead and the medic was fatally injured. Joyce had put a bullet in his head, a large chunk of skull was missing, and his breathing was jagged and uneven. Scott leaned over, pulled his skinning knife and cut the man's throat. We moved on.

Of the others, all were dead, and the one who'd ran for the trees had most of his head missing from the killing shot fired by my sniper.

"Gather up anything we can use, as I pull all the papers and maps from these men. Hurry now, because I want to be gone as soon as we can. Sooner or later the base these men came from will try to contact them by radio."

Twenty minutes later we were moving north and it was still sleeting with a mixture of ice, but I suspected by morning we'd be facing an ice storm. I stopped by the trail and watched my men and women walk by. They looked good, but tired, and it was then I spotted Scott. He was packing the radio from the group we'd killed in the field.

Dropping back, I asked, "What's the idea of packing the extra weight?"

"Colonel, I think I can speak to them enough to mess them up."

"What about your accent?" I asked.

"I was told I don't have one. That was what I was told in college, where I further studied the language, according to the Russian language professor anyways. I'd hoped to get a Masters degree and become a diplomat, but we all know how that turned out, huh?"

"I have a stack of papers in my pack. Do you read the language as well?"

"Oh, yeah, my momma taught me to read with a Russian Bible."

"Good; now let's stop talking and keep moving. We'll be at the safe house by dawn."

Just as it grew dusk, Silverwolf appeared and said, "The woods are crawling with patrols out looking for something, but I don't think it's us. Most were moving at a fast clip east and so were most of the aircraft, but I only saw two birds."

"East? That would be toward Jackson, unless they have some partisans surrounded, or are planning to hit one of our groups hard. How many men total do you think you saw?"

"A thousand, maybe a few more or less. Most all were in company sizes."

I knew of none of our people out that way, but often I wasn't told things. Our security was designed so that you couldn't tell the Russians what you didn't know if taken prisoner. This meant we needed to move quickly to the safe house and pass the word on of what Silverwolf had found.

"Okay folks, listen up. From the information Silverwolf brought us, we need to get to the safe house as soon as we can. This means we'll not stop until we get there. The Russians are moving a lot of men to the east and it must be for a reason. Maybe, just maybe, the maps and other papers taken from our last ambush site will provide some information. If you have to pee, do it now, or take your chances later as you walk. I'll stop for a few minutes every hour, but get ready for a long night."

CHAPTER 2

Lieutenant Sasha Smirnov walked around the blood-stained killing grounds of the open field and grew angry at the slaughter of his fellow soldiers. About half had been shot in the head with a high caliber rifle, from a far distance he suspected, because there were no powder burns to any of the heads. Others had been killed by a mine and one had his throat cut. The long distance shots, likely from the distant treeline, would have been made by a well qualified sniper.

"Lieutenant!" Senior Sergeant Morozov called out, "Our partisans were in the tree line and I've found the empty brass from their weapons. It looks as if the mine was a pressure detonating one with some shotgun shells resting on nails scattered around to confuse, injure or kill any survivors."

"How can a shotgun shell rest on a nail?"

"It's easy, sir. Take a block of wood, drill a hole the diameter of the shell, then drive a nail up into the hole from the bottom. To use, you bury the block and place a shell in the hole. When a man steps on the block the shell is pushed down, the primer resting on the nail goes off and the shell explodes. It almost always causes a serious injury to the thighs or lower stomach. The shot can also take a man's pecker and balls off, too—and I mean in a second."

Smirnov waved him away and ended the conversation. The Lieutenant had been told in Moscow the resistance was a bunch of unorganized farmers and prior military. What he saw here was a well executed ambush and it worried him. He realized he was not facing a ragtag group of peasants, but men who knew well how to kill, and that worried him. His Senior Sergeant had told him the Russian patrol had chased the Americans into the trees, started crossing the field, and then the ambush had been sprung. The enemy hadn't panicked and even had the presence of mind to plant a mine and some shotgun shells before moving to the shelter offered by the trees. That told him this group of resistance fighters worked well under pressure and that meant experience.

"Egorov!" the Lieutenant yelled, "Contact base and let them know we have ten killed and no American bodies found. Also, inform them the Americans have moved away from our direction of travel, moving north, and then ask if we are to pursue them or continue East."

"Yes sir." Junior Sergeant Abram Egorov replied, and then picked up the headset and began talking. Egorov wasn't sure what to think of the Lieutenant, the army, or America. He knew he didn't like America or the Army, because both tried to kill him, and the Lieutenant hadn't been with the unit but a couple of days, so he was unsure of him. Egorov had been in the field for a little over six months and during that time he'd seen Lieutenants come and go, most killed, some wounded, and only one promoted up and out of the field.

"Senior Sergeant! Get these bodies ready to be picked up by helicopter. I am sure headquarters will want them removed." Lieutenant Smirnov said as he walked toward the trees inattentively. The Lieutenant had taken about a dozen steps when he heard someone yell, "Grenade!" Before Smirnov could turn there was an explosion, followed by shrieks of pain and loud cursing.

"Medic!" someone yelled.

Completing his turn, the young officer saw five men down and knew by looking three would never get up again. One was almost blown in half, one had half his face missing, and the last was attempting to hold his intestines in place. It was the man with the stomach wound that was screaming.

The medic, Sergeant Borya Volkov, moved quickly to the injured man's side and started working. He had one of the Privates hold a plasma bag up as he found a vein in the man's arm. After about five minutes, he yelled, "Sir, I need a helicopter for this man or he will die. I have got his bleeding almost under control, but he is torn up inside."

"Egorov, what did base say about us? And get me an evacuation helicopter now!"

"Wait, base." Egorov said and then turning to the Lieutenant, he said, "Sir, they are discussing our moving now and I have requested an evacuation."

"Good, but stress if the man is not evacuated, the medic says he will die."

Now talking on the radio, Egorov waved in understanding and kept speaking. Finally, he placed the headset away and said, "We are to remain here until the bodies and our injured man are picked up. Once they are gone, we are to continue our original mission. Uh, Major Sokolov reminded me, sir, that the terrorists often booby-trap the dead, both ours and theirs. The estimated time of arrival for the helicopter is in fifteen minutes."

"I am aware of booby-traps, Sergeant." Smirnov said in anger. *I should have thought of the booby-traps right off, but I didn't. I need to start thinking clearly, if I want to make Captain and more importantly, survive my tour here*, he thought.

"Damn sleet is hard on my eyes." Private Mikhailov said as he pulled his forage cap down so the bill better protected his eyes.

Senior Sergeant Morozov said, "If the sleet hurts the Private's eyes, wear your goggles. Why do you think they were issued to you? Where in the hell does Moscow find you fools they send me to use as soldiers?"

Egorov said, "I have the helicopter on the radio and he is asking for us to give him smoke when he nears, so he can see the wind direction."

"He will have it as he nears our location." the Senior Sergeant said and then added, "Private Pavlorov, have a smoke grenade ready and pop it when I give the word. The rest of you clowns, circle us and at least look like you are in the Russian army. Fools, I am surrounded by damned fools. Move, now!"

Men scurried in all directions and a crude circle was formed just seconds before Egorov said, "I see you and guess your distances at less than three kilometers. Continue on present course. It is hard to see you in this sleet. Pop the smoke now, Pavlorov!"

The private pulled the pin on the smoke grenade and dropped it by his foot. The winds quickly blew the smoke to the East.

Once the aircraft was on the ground, a crewman ran to the group and explained that all movement toward the helicopter was to be made from the very front, so the pilot could see them at all times. He then had the dead loaded on the floor of the aircraft and the injured man was placed on a stretcher that strapped to the wall. In a matter of a few short minutes, the helicopter was gone.

"Get the men up and moving, Senior Sergeant." the Lieutenant said.

"Efreitor Bulgakov, you take the point and Private Mikhailov, I want you to bring up the rear. Now, Private, keep us in sight at all times. Also as we move, stay alert at all times. It is not unusual for a partisan to pull the last man into the bushes and cut his throat."

Damn me, Mikhailov thought, why did I ever join the army? I was milking cows on the farm a year ago and now I have to worry about some American cutting my throat.

Tonight as they sat around a small fire about the size of a dinner plate, Private Mikhailov asked, "Why have we not seen the snakes I was told about? In Moscow they made it sound like there were snakes covering the ground here."

"It is too cold, you fool." someone said, and it sounded like Bulgakov.

"I know little of snakes, but much about wild boar, bears, wolves, lynx, and wolverine."

"You will not run into any of those animals here, except maybe a wild boar. The biggest threats here, in my opinion," Senior Sergeant Morozov said, "are snakes, alligators, and partisans. Of the three, you are more likely to be killed by a partisan."

"The sleet is changing to snow." Lieutenant Smirnov said, and then grinned like a kid as he held his hands out to catch the falling flakes.

The Senior Sergeant stood and then said, "I am off to sleep. I want the same guard shift we have had from the start. If you start to get sleepy, wake someone. If I make my rounds and catch one of you asleep, I will kick your ass."

Morozov moved to his sleeping bag, climbed inside and used his backpack as a pillow. He was an old military man and was asleep in minutes.

The snow began to fall heavily and within an hour, a good inch covered the ground. The guards moved back under some large pine trees and stood their shift wrapped with wool blankets.

Morning dawned with it still snowing, but falling less now and the flakes were smaller. The men coughed, hacked, and moved into the trees to do their morning toilet. The Senior Sergeant had to tell the men to quiet down and shook his head as he pulled out a ration to eat. Most of the men were disgusted by the grease found on the rations, but the old NCO didn't give it a second of thought.

Minutes later, his meal complete, he stood and moved for the trees, his stomach growling as he walked. He passed Lieutenant Smirnov along the way and nodded at the man. He placed his Bison on the leaves, glanced up at the sky, and hoped his stomach wasn't going to bother him again. He removed his webbed belt, unbuckled the belt to his trousers, and then unbuttoned them. He unzipped his pants, let them fall to his boots, and was bending over when a huge explosion filled the morning air. He heard screams and gunshots for a few minutes, then silence except for one wounded man, who was shrieking loudly. He heard a single shot and the screaming man stopped instantly.

Damn it, he thought, *I need to see about the Lieutenant. I think the camp was overrun by terrorists!*

He pulled his pants up, grabbed his web belt and Bison, and then moved toward the officer. Lieutenant Smirnov was kneeling, a pistol in one hand and a knife in the other. As Morozov neared, the young officer swung his pistol toward him.

From where the Lieutenant was in the brush, a quick glance toward the campsite showed Americans ransacking the place. All gear was being collected and weapons, with ammo, gathered up.

The Senior Sergeant whispered, "We will both toss a grenade and then run. Follow me, because I just reviewed the map not ten minutes ago, as I ate breakfast."

The Lieutenant nodded and Morozov pulled a grenade from his belt. Both men pulled the pins at the same time and then tossed the grenades toward the camp. The Senior Sergeant saw them land less than two feet apart and as he started to stand, he heard an American voice scream a warning. Three seconds after the scream, both grenades exploded, and as Morozov began moving, screams of pain were heard.

The woods were dense, with vines, logs and other obstacles scattered all over the forest. The Senior Sergeant knew once clear of the trees in about a mile, he'd find a swamp. By following the swamp to the west, he'd eventually come to a macadam road, where they could flag down a Russian convoy or walk to the nearest Russians for help. The Russians now had roadblocks, tanks and even machine-gun crews watching all major roadways. Sooner of later, he'd find help.

At the swamp, which was an ugly and nasty looking thing to the two Russians, Morozov said, "Sir, if we follow this swamp to the left we will come to a road."

"What's to the right?"

"I don't really remember, but more woods and some small villages, I think. I suspect it would be smart to avoid all Americans right now and try to get back to our lines."

"I was briefed this whole area is friendly."

Morozov gave a light chuckle and then asked, "Sir, if that is true, then who killed all our men back there? We own this area in the day, but at night, the ownership changes hands."

"Good point, Senior Sergeant, so lead us to the left, please." the Lieutenant, now extremely nervous, said.

"Neither of us have our packs, so we are facing lean times for food, sir, unless you have something in your pockets."

"Maybe a half-dozen hard candies, but that is it, because I was going to the bathroom when they hit us."

"Well, we can be sure, we are the only survivors." Just as he spoke, a twig snapped and both men went to ground. The Lieutenant, having left his Bison with his backpack, pulled his pistol.

They heard two voices speaking in Russian. Without getting up, Morozov called out, "State your names! And where you are!"

"Huh?" one voice said and then moaned.

"We are Junior Sergeant Egorov and Sergeant Borya Volkov, survivors of an American ambush. We are both wounded, with one being severe." Volkov said.

"Come to me, but make no sudden moves, keep your weapons in the air, or I will shoot." the Senior Sergeant replied, in case the Americans were forcing the two Russians to lead them to the others.

"Listen to me, Senior Sergeant, Junior Sergeant Egorov has a bad wound to his chest and I am almost packing him. I am coming to you, but rest easy, no one is with us and I am almost packing our radioman. If you want to shoot us, then shoot. I am tired, bleeding, and had enough of the damned army."

"Come to us." Lieutenant Smirnov said and then meeting the Senior Sergeant's eyes, he nodded.

The two men walked out of the snow and the Senior Sergeant recognized both, so he moved forward to help. He helped lay Egorov on the ground and then asked, "Do you have your medical gear?"

"Yes, but he is not going to live, unless we can get him back to the base and quickly. He is bleeding on the inside, too."

Smirnov said, "Make a litter and we will pack him out, if we must."

"Sir," Morozov said, "I do not think you understand. Unless we stop him from bleeding on the inside, he will never last the trip, not if we walk back to the base. He will run out of blood before we even see the main gate."

"I am not sure how to handle this." the Lieutenant said.

"The bullet has pierced his lungs, but I sealed him front and rear so he can breath. We can wait here and hope a helicopter flies over or I can put him to sleep."

"Put him to sleep?" Smirnov asked.

"Give him too much morphine, sir, so the overdose kills him. It is a pleasant death and he will feel no pain."

"Then, why did you bring him all this way?" the Senior Sergeant asked.

"I am a medic, Senior Sergeant, and I do not have the authority to kill a man. Oh, I would if half his head was missing or if there was no hope, even in a hospital. This man would live, if we had a way to get him to a hospital."

"End his life now. I will not have one man endangering all three of us as we move. I am not a cold man, but he will, or could, cause the death of all of us. If I were him, I would expect the same thing."

"I agree, Sergeant, so consider it an order, Sergeant Volkov." the Lieutenant said.

"Was that his radio I saw on his back a few minutes ago?" Morozov asked.

"Yes, but it has been shot."

"Did you try it at all?" The Lieutenant asked.

"No and I did not have time to remove it either." the medic replied and then started removing his shirt. He'd taken a bullet burn on the chest, which had taken his right nipple right off, and then burned a furrow across his chest. He'd bled hard, but a compress quickly applied took care of the bleeding, and a couple of painkillers had kept him able to move.

Looking in his medical bag, Sergeant Volkov said, "Damn me, I am out of morphine. The vials I have are all broken. I took a bullet to the bag and do not have a one left."

The Senior Sergeant pulled his knife, walked to the downed man and said, "Move out of the way, Volkov. I will kill him, since we lack the medications."

"With a knife? My God, what pain." the medic said, his eyes large in disbelieve.

"I cannot afford a gunshot, or I would shoot him. I want to keep all noise to the minimum."

The medic stood and moved out of the way, as the Senior Sergeant knelt beside Egorov. A religious man in his own way, the Sergeant prayed, crossed himself and placed his hand on the injured man's chest. One quick slash of his sharp knife blade and blood shot into the air; as Egorov's eyes popped open, they grew large. Soon the smell of bright cerise blood filled the air as it pooled under the man's neck. His fingers clawed at the dirt and his feet kicked at the soil as his life's blood spurted high into the air. The medic and Lieutenant turned their heads, but Morozov met the dying man's eyes and said, "It had to be done, son. If you were able to walk, you would still be alive. Go to God as a brave soldier." He then wiped his blood-stained knife blade on the dying man's trousers.

"Medic Volkov, bring the radio to me." the Lieutenant said, as he squatted in the snow covered grasses.

Picking up the radio, but still in shock at the brutality of Egorov's death, he carried it to the man and handed it to him.

"Senior Sergeant, bring any spare batteries you can find when you strip the radioman of useful items. Hello, any station, this is Bobcat 1, over."

"This is base, Bobcat 1, and you are late reporting in. Is all well with you?"

"It works!" Lieutenant Smirnov said almost in a shout, but caught himself at the last minute. He then spoke with his base camp about the ambush and the fact three were needing helicopter pick up.

"I thought it was ruined by the bullets that hit it." Volkov said and then added, "Killing Egorov was wrong. They will send a helicopter to pick us up now."

Shaking his head, the Lieutenant said, "You are wrong. All aircraft have gone to Jackson to be ready for our massive push in the morning. We have orders to return to base. We will not be part of the coming fight."

"I imagine, sir, they need all helicopters to assist with the coming wounded, and there will be many. I will lead us back to camp, but I want Volkov to bring up the rear and to carry the radio. I estimate we are about twenty miles from the nearest Russians, so we will walk all night too, if we have the need."

"In this snow and sleet?" the medic asked.

"Yes, and in any weather that we run into. We do not want the partisans to capture us, Sergeant, or they will torture us to death." the Senior Sergeant warned.

"Why the hurry, Senior Sergeant?" the Lieutenant asked.

"At night, once this sleet and snow stops, if it does, sir, there will be aircraft moving east and if they pick us up on their thermal devices they may just kill us. My main reason is I do not like being out here surrounded by the partisans. If they catch us, we will all die a horrible death."

"Let us move then." the Lieutenant said and then blinked rapidly, realizing his Sergeant was correct and it was a foolish way to die.

Most of the day was uneventful and no one was seen as they moved. They'd just left the edge of the swamp and were moving north by west, when the Senior Sergeant heard metal hitting metal. He waved his small group into some brush. The three Russians went to ground.

Minutes later, a single partisan walked by and then about five minutes later over forty walked in front of the Russians. Senior Sergeant Morozov prayed neither Russian would be dumb enough to shoot. His stomach turned and a small animal came alive deep in his gut. He felt the urge to soil his pants and to puke, but did nothing. Silence.

When the Lieutenant started to stand, Morozov pulled the man back down and pointed. Following the main group was their drag man. Once the last man was well out of sight, the Senior Sergeant took the radio and called base, reporting over forty Americans.

Handing the radio back to Volkov, he said, "We are to proceed as ordered and some jet aircraft will attack the Americans."

A few minutes later as they crossed an open field, right at dusk, the three heard a roar in the sky and glancing up, the Senior Sergeant yelled, "Give me the radio, now!"

Volkov handed the headset to Morozov and heard the man yell, "Russian fighter plane, overhead now, you are lining up the wrong targets. The Americans are south by east of us! Do you read?"

"He is lining up for an attack!" the Lieutenant screamed.

"Pull off now! Break off the attack! You have Russians on the ground! I do not have his radio frequency, sir!" the Senior Sergeant yelled, his fear obvious.

"What to do?" the medic asked.

"Split and all run in different directions, now!" the Lieutenant said, and then began to run back the way he'd come.

The ground in the field suddenly erupted with clumps of dirt, rocks and grass being thrown ten feet into the air. Suddenly, Sergeant Volkov flew apart, with his arms, legs and torso ripped to pieces by the Gatling gun. His whole body disappeared leaving behind a thick bloody red fog hanging in the air and very little of the man or his gear seen.

While this was happening, Morozov was running and talking to base in an attempt to get them to abort the attack. Once in the trees, he heard the pilot had just called in confirmation of over twenty dead Americans.

Livid, the Senior Sergeant yelled, "The sonofabitch killed just one man, base, and that one was a Russian! Yes, sir. I wish to re-port Medic Sergeant Volkov, Borya, as killed by friendly fire. I am

Bobcat 2, base, and I have no idea if the commander still lives or not. I will look for him and have him contact you. Out."

The Russian aircraft flew over, along with his wing-man, and they rocked their wings in friendship. Senior Sergeant Morozov had to fight the urge to fire on the fast moving aircraft. Soon they pulled up, and were out of sight in seconds.

"Lieutenant! Are you alive, sir?" he yelled.

"I am here, in the woods, but have sustained an injury."

"Can you move?"

"Yes, but I cannot see. I am blind, Sergeant."

"I will come to you, sir." Morozov said and then thought, damn me, this army life is out to kill me. Once this tour is over, I am retiring, finding me a small apartment in Moscow and will drink myself to death. I am getting too old to keep doing this crap.

CHAPTER 3

I continued to move my group overnight and most were understanding, but a few younger members complained about no food or sleep. There was about an inch of snow on the ground and it was cold, but the winds were slight. Corporal Kerr told the youngsters to shut the hell up and to keep moving.

Finally, Private Kelly asked, "Corporal, when will we stop to eat and sleep? I'm dog tired and need both."

"We'll stop in the mornin', Private, just as soon as we reach the safe house. Right now the intelligence we have from the Russians is more important than when Private Kelly gets his beauty rest or eats his next meal. Grow up some, son, and do the job fast, or you'll not be around next year. Now, close your mouth and don't open it again unless I ask you a direct question. Do you understand me?"

"Yes, Corporal."

"Good, son, now saddle up, we've some miles to cover." Kerr replied, and then shook his head.

All went well as they moved, until around two in the morning, when Silverwolf neared and said, "Armor ahead, and I counted three Russian tanks. They're blocking a crossroad and I think about now, while everyone is asleep, is the perfect time to take them out. They had three guards, but my sharp steel blade took them out. I suggest three of us move in, toss two grenades in each of the open hatches and then beat feet out of there."

"See any infantry?"

"Yep, but only a couple of squads that I could see. I crawled in close to kill the guards and not one of the men in the foxholes looked awake to me. I say hit the tanks and then run down the western road, because it's lined with big oaks. Then our attackers and the rest of the squad could meet, oh, say a mile west on the road."

"Joyce, slip a night scope on your rifle. I want you to take out any machine-guns, officers, and NCO's for sure. Got that?"

"Simple, and I'll do the job right."

"Sandra, I'll take Kerr and Scott with me. Since Scott speaks Russian, he might come in handy if someone challenges us." I then looked at Scott and said, "Leave all gear except your weapons and three grenades. If you can, puncture the gas tanks and spare Jerry cans they always have on the sides of the tanks. Let the gas leak for a good two minutes, then climb up, drop your hot eggs and then get the hell out of there. No one climb on a tank until you see me on one. I want the rest of you to provide cover fire in the event things turn hot for us. Any questions?"

Silence, because there were none.

"Okay," I said, "Let's move, people, and now."

It was snowing a bit harder now, which I hoped would help mask our movements to the tanks. If even one machine-gun opened up, we were dead meat. I parted the brush, got down flat and crawled toward the Russian perimeter. I could see they were too far apart and unless I sneezed or farted loudly, I'd get through them. I soon wiggled my way past a fox hole where both men were asleep and even snoring. I shook my head at their lax security, but suspected after tonight, that'd all change. I'm sure some Russian Lieutenant or Captain would be shot or sent to a gulag for his poor performance here.

I took the center tank, so I'd be easily seen in the bad weather by both of the other men. I wanted our grenades dropped close to the same time. I was growing apprehensive as I pulled my hunting knife and stabbed into metal containers holding diesel. I then climbed on the tank and from within the iron beast, I heard snoring and heavy breathing.

Glancing to my left and right, I spotted my men ready to drop their explosives. I then raised both hands, which held grenades, and then lowered them. I pulled the pins from my grenades one at a time, held the levers down, and then centered them over the open hatch of the tank. A split second after I dropped them, I heard both give a loud ka-clank sound as they struck the metal floor.

As I was moving from the tank, I heard a voice scream a warning in Russian, saw the front hatch for the driver open, and then heard the explosion. I ran as hard as I could and then dropped to the ground and began to crawl fast. Four other explosions were heard and then the ammunition and gas in my chosen tank exploded, sending a huge fireball high into the sky. One-by-one the tanks blew and the last one blew its turret high into the air, where it tumbled as it fell back to earth. Three gigantic fireballs filled the sky and for hundreds of yards around the tanks, it was almost as bright as day. What saved our asses were all the Russians watched the tanks burn and few looked away from the fire. Then, thinking the attack had been from outside the perimeter, our enemies began firing into the woods.

I saw one man, an officer by his movements, move up and out of his hole in the ground to direct fire. No sooner had the Russian fire slowed a few minutes later, than I heard the loud bang of my sniper's rifle and the officer fell to the ground unmoving. Three more times Joyce shot and each time a man died. Finally entering the woods, I stood among the trees, and saw four bodies sprawled out on the snow-covered ground near the tanks. I then ran toward the road on the north side, where I'd meet everyone else.

When I arrived I discovered the other two were already there, along with rest of my squad. I moved them into the bushes as we waited for Joyce. Less than five minutes later, she joined us. Without speaking, we moved north by west, using the stars to guide us.

It was during out first break, an hour later, that Joyce said, "Four confirmed kills for me tonight. One was a Russian Captain, one a Senior Sergeant, and the other two were Privates that manned a machine gun. Head shots for each of them."

"Great shooting, Joyce, and that's four less Russians we'll to have face later." Sandra said and then added, "It's not often we destroy three tanks and kill their crews without the loss of a single fighter. It's been a good night for us."

I stood, adjusted my pack and said, "Let's move, our break is over."

It was an hour after dawn when we spotted the safe house back in some thick trees in the middle of what was once a national forest. The house was once occupied by the senior park ranger for the area and it was isolated. What worried me was it showed on all maps, but so far the Russians had not visited.

"Silverwolf, take Scott and the two of you make contact with those in the house. I think walking to the door as a group is a good way to get our butts shot off. Once they confirm who you are, return for us."

"Will do; come with me, Scott." Silverwolf said as he moved toward the building, his rifle held at the ready.

Twenty minutes later, he returned and said, "Colonel Lee is in charge down there, and he said for you to get down there pronto, because the Russians are up to something, and he needs to look at the intelligence you gathered."

"Alright everyone, let's move to the house and in a single file. Once we get there, you'll be given food and a place to sleep. I suggest all of you eat and then rest. It may be a long day, depending on the Russians."

Once in the house, there were a good twenty other partisans inside. I knew there was a sniper or two hidden outside, but where I had no idea. Colonel Lee was a short man, just a little over five feet tall, thin, brown eyes, bald and wore black framed glasses. I extended my hand and we shook.

"Welcome to the group, again." he said and then smiled.

"Glad to be here, sir, and I have some Russian documents my man who speaks the language thinks are attack orders. I personally removed them off the dead body of a Russian dispatch rider. There are other documents as well, but we didn't go through all of them well. Since the one paper looks like an attack order, I rushed to get here."

"Very good, John, and I have plans for your group, no matter what the Russian papers say, but we'll discuss them after you've had something to eat and then some sleep. You look like hell warmed over."

"Yes, sir." I said and then turned and walked toward Dolly and Sandra. Dolly had remained here while we were gone and she was very happy I'd returned. My last dog hopped and jumped on me when I neared her. All my other dogs had been killed years before. I sat on the floor, with my back against the concrete wall.

Top walked over, tossed me an old MRE and said, "Colonel Lee, a direct descendent of General Robert E. Lee, is using one of General Lee's old plans against the Russians. When Grant was riding Lee's ass hard toward the end of the war, the Confederate General sent out troops to raise hell, which meant the Union had to release some troops to find and fight the hell raisers. Each group Lee could muster into service and release was sent out to make the Yank's think many large groups were involved, when in reality, they were few in number. These groups would hit, move quickly, and then hit again in some unexpected location, which kept the Yanks off balance."

I looked at Top and asked, "What does that have to do with me?" I tore the plastic MRE package open and pulled out the entree.

"Your squad is going to be one of those groups."

"How do we stay supplied and fed?" I asked, then opened the pouch that held my beef patty.

"We'll send four extra men with you and they'll carry your supplies on bicycles. During the Vietnam War, the north Vietnamese used bikes to pack supplies, and you'll be surprised how much can be carried by just two wheels. They'll pack it to a spot you desire, dig a hole, and bury it for you. When you need food or ammo, dig it up. I suggest you dig three or four holes, away from each other, so if one is found you don't lose it all."

I took a bite of my meat, chewed and then asked, "When is this to start?"

"You'll leave in the morning, but we want you near the old town of Pearl, Mississippi. Roam, kill Russians, and stir the pot up as much as you can. With over a dozen squads doing the same thing in central Mississippi, we hope the Russians will pull some troops to hunt for y'all. If possible, terrorize the enemy and be as bold and nasty as you can."

"How many Russians stationed at Pearl?"

"Our last estimate was five thousand, but we know some were pulled for the operation the Russians are running southeast of Jackson. While we don't have a clear count, I was told by Colonel Lee just a few over two thousand are still there. Truth be told, your guess is as good as mine."

"Any special targets?"

"No specifically ordered targets. Of course, any fuel tanks, supplies, or storage facilities should be taken out if you can do so with minimum risk."

I thought for a moment and then asked, "Avoid gulags?"

"I've given them some thought and think if you can, attack them hard, because they'll use up manpower hunting for all that may escape. Again, weigh the human cost to you very carefully before any major attack."

I spooned the last of my meat into my mouth, opened up a bag containing cookies and as I pulled one out, I said, "Top, I'll do my best. Are we to come back here after a certain amount of time or meet someplace else? How long am I to operate alone like this?" I took a huge bit of the hard cookie, which was a rare treat. I gave the other one to Dolly.

"You will stay for one month, or until the Russians stop their operation. Return here, but if we need you before then, one of the men with the bicycles will know where you are, so we'll fetch you. Also, mark your location on a map one of the bike men will carry, so we'll have it on file."

I was tired and not just physically, but emotionally as well. I asked, "Top, do you see an end to this bullshit, or are we going to fight forever and all of us die in the end? Do you honestly think we can beat the Russians?"

"I think we'll win, but it may take years. Look at the length of the war in Vietnam or when the Russians invaded Afghanistan and you'll see it didn't happen overnight, but in both cases, the larger and stronger army eventually left. Will you and I see it happen? I honestly don't know, but as an American I'll be damned if I will let anyone invade my country and do nothing. I think most Americans want to resist, but some are too old, some have no military skills, and others may not be healthy enough to fight."

"I hear you. You know, I often dream of America like it used to be, the land of plenty, and now we either fight or we're dead. The Liberals are all dead or have changed their method of thought. I was told most of the prisoners in a gulag last an average of three months. Hell, they have no clothing, some lack shelter, 900 calories a day, no blankets, no doctors and no medical help at all. I read in a report that over five hundred a day die in the Jackson gulags alone, most from sicknesses. That's almost 200,000 people a year and from one prison alone."

Top nodded and replied, "I read the same. Look, we can't save them all because it's impossible, and we both know it can't be done. However, we should try to free as many as we can and when we can, if for no other reason than it pisses off the Russians."

My eyes felt like they had sand in them, so I said, "I'm going to catch some sleep. Is there anything else I need to know about tomorrow morning?"

Top lowered his head and replied, "Yep there is. Last week two partisans were captured by the Russians, but instead of taking them as POW's they burned them to death with a flamethrower. When you leave tomorrow you'll have six captured Russians to take with you. At some point, those six are to be tied to trees or posts and killed the exact same way. Colonel Lee wants you to do it on a hill near interstate 55, which as you know, leads to Jackson, so their charred bodies can be seen from the road."

"Burn them to death? Damn, Top, that's a rough order. I . . . I don't know if I can follow this order."

"The Russians must learn that for every captured American they kill, we will execute three of their men, and we'll kill them exactly as they do our people. We have only recently started taking enlisted captives and we keep them deep in swamps in wooden cages. See the order is carried out. Now, you get some sleep." Top turned and walked away.

The next morning the sun was out, but it was still cold and the snow had stopped. Dark gray, almost black clouds, were off to the west, holding a promise of more rain, sleet or snow. As we prepared to leave, Corporal Scott neared.

"Something on your mind, Scott?" I asked.

"Yes, sir, there is. Are we really going to burn the Russian prisoners we have?"

"That's my orders. I don't like the idea much either, but the Russians did the same to partisans they captured a while back. They have to be shown that for every American they murder, we'll kill three of theirs, and the same way."

"I . . . I can't think of a more horrible way to die. Do you think we have to stoop to their level to win this war?"

I had a map in my hand, so I placed it on the table, met his eyes and said, "The Russians are animals in this war and they have absolutely no compassion for our people, none. But, to answer your question, no, we don't need to stoop to their level, we must go lower. We must show them such barbaric behavior so that they become panic-stricken of us, and leave our country. Now, if you have a problem with your orders, Corporal Scott, feel free to speak with Colonel Lee. I have my orders and I will carry them out. Now, either prepare to leave with us, or find the Colonel."

"The Russians are humans too, sir, and I don't think our orders are lawful."

I laughed loudly, sobered, and then said, "Robert, don't you understand there are no laws now? Not a one! Oh, perhaps the laws of humanity apply, or NATO's laws, but NATO can kiss our asses, because where are they now? Since day one of this fight, NATO has said nothing condemning the Russians and has made no effort to even assist us. Think of the billions, or maybe trillions, of dollars our country gave NATO over the years and it pisses me off that they've made no attempt to help us. I'm actually a compassionate man, but when it comes to my country and its freedom, I'll do whatever it takes to get the Russians to leave. I will burn these prisoners to death, and I will burn more and more, if it helps rid our country of the Russians yoke."

Scott was quiet, looking at the floor, and then raised his head and said, "I was raised, sir, to love this country above all things in life. My father changed his Russian name to Scott, so he'd fit into American society better and he considered himself, as did my mother, an American, not a Russian. My home had American flags all over it, inside and out. The proudest time in my father's life was when all of his kids chipped in and bought him a flagpole, so he could raise and lower the American flag each day. While he never served a day in the United States Military, he saluted that flag twice a day. He was a good man, sir, and some of these men we'll burn to death are good men too."

I put my hands on my hips and said, "Scott, you either speak with the Colonel or grab your gear, because I leave in five minutes. I have nothing else to say to you."

"I'll go, but needed you to understand my view. I'll do what I'm ordered to do, but don't expect me to pour gas or light those men up, because I can't do it. I can't burn any person alive."

"No, I won't ask you to do that, because I feel as the senior man, that's my responsibility. Now, grab your gear and let's go."

Ten minutes later, we were moving down the trail with six Russian captives and each looked terrified. I hardened my heart toward what I was about to do and moved toward the front of my line, so I didn't have to see them.

At the first break, Sandra walked up to me and Dolly wagged her tail as she approached with her. Sitting beside me, she said, "The Colonel is not well. From his symptoms, I think he has cancer and, of course, we can't do anything for him. Oh, I can keep his pain level down, but he'll eventually die on us."

I scratched Dolly's ears and asked, "How long do you think he has to live?"

"I can't answer that, because it would take extensive testing and we have no way to test the man. I'm afraid he needs more than we can provide. To be honest, I'm not even a hundred percent sure he has cancer."

"Baby, there is nothing we can do for the man, so he'll either recover or die on us. I hate to sound so cold, but that's the way things are these days. I know some who've stood by and watched their loved ones die for the need of a simple medication, like blood pressure pills, heart medications and even antibiotics."

"About all we have are painkillers and some antibiotic medications, but they've only been available recently."

I shrugged and replied, "You know I'd help him and thousands of others, if I could, but I can't. Now, how are you holding up?"

"I'm okay, I guess, just tired. I would love a romantic evening with you, only that won't happen anytime soon. I know I'm not the same woman I used to be on the outside, but inside I've not changed much."

"I didn't fall in love with the outside of you, and you know that." I pulled her to me, looked into her eyes and said, "I fell in love with your soul, baby."

She started crying, I guess because the Russians badly mangled her face and removed her ears when she was a captive, which prevented her from ever being beautiful again. She was a mass of scar tissue, but she was alive and that's all that mattered to me. I love her as much now as I did the day we married, so her face mattered little to me.

Silverwolf neared and said, "I just discovered an ambush site, but with no blood."

"No blood?" I thought for a moment and then said, "Dead partisans?"

"Yep, about a dozen and not one drop of blood. I've never seen anything like it before."

"Pull your gas mask and lets check the area out. I suspect the Russians used poison gas." I said as I pulled my mask from the canvas pouch I carried on my left leg.

It was when we neared the site and I saw squirrels running over the ground, I knew we didn't need the masks.

"The gas has dissipated, or the squirrels would be dying or dead." I said as I pulled my pistol.

Glancing around, I added, "Don't touch anyone, but if you see any gear we need, take it, but check for booby-traps. I don't see any weapons or ammo. The Russians may have booby-trapped some of these bodies."

A few minutes later, Silverwolf said, "I don't see a single weapon in the bunch and most of the gear is gone, too. They did that to keep us from recovering anything."

"These folks died rough from the looks on their faces. Every one has a grimace with teeth bared."

"Gas, Sergeant. Looks like nerve gas to me, but it must have been released with a bomb or artillery round."

Silverwolf began circling and about ten minutes later, he returned and said, "Looks like a bomb to me, and it's not far from these folks. It left a crater, but I honestly can't tell the difference. I thought gas had to be sprayed out, like they used to do crops."

"The Russians have a number of ways to deliver it. What's this?" I asked as I bent over and picked up a map. On the map, one of our safe houses was circled and the map was in Russian. That in itself was not a big deal, but it was laminated and grease pencil notes written in Russian were on the map as well.

"Looks like a map, but we see them all the time."

"Not like this one we don't. Let's get back and have Scott take a look at this."

CHAPTER 4

Senior Sergeant Morozov led the Lieutenant down the trail and then moved into some thick pines and oaks to look the man's injuries over. Blood was pouring between his fingers, and growing impatient at not being able to pry the man's hands from his face, he said, "Damn, sir, let me see your wound or you may bleed to death before I can do a thing for you."

"It hurts."

"Of course it hurts, it is *supposed* to hurt. That is good; that means you are still alive. Now, lower your hands and let me see what has happened."

The Lieutenant slowly lowered his quivering hands and Morozov said, "It does not look too bad, and I think your blindness is caused by blood and debris. I am no doctor or medic, but I have seen my share of injuries."

As he reached for the medical kit the Lieutenant wore, the Senior Sergeant thought, *The left eye has been blown out and the right doesn't look much better. I need to keep his spirits up or he will go into shock. It will be hard enough to travel with him as it is. He needs morphine, but if I inject him, I will have to carry him and I cannot do that.*

Once the bandages were on tightly covering both eyes, Morozov said, "Okay, sir, we can move now. Listen to me. I can give you a light painkiller in a pill, but no morphine. If I give you morphine I will have to leave you."

"Oh, dear God, do not leave me, please! The pills will be enough." The Sergeant saw blood seeping through the thick bandage.

"I will not leave you as long as you continue to move. Can you walk if you hold onto my belt?"

"I . . . I think so. I do not have much of a choice, do I?" The Lieutenant stood and reached out with his hand.

Removing the belt to his trousers, he looped it and then buckled it closed. Handing the loop to the Lieutenant, he said, "If I come to a big rock or other obstacle, I will let you know. Now, if I tell you to get down, drop to the dirt right then, sir. We can do this, if we stay calm and work together."

"Do not leave me, Sergeant, please; the partisans will tortured me for hours, because I am an officer."

"We are comrades and I have never left anyone alive on the battle field yet, sir." Morozov said and then thought, *Except those who were dying anyway or slowed me down. Let us both pray, for your sake, Lieutenant, you are able to keep up with me. This is a walk for life and I will not be held back by an injured man, but do not worry, I will kill you before I leave you. War is about survival and I fully intend to retire.*

"Good, Sergeant. When we return, I will see you are given a medal."

Medal? A worthless piece of cloth and some tin? I would rather have a quart of vodka, he thought and then replied, "Why thank you, sir. Now, we need to be moving. Let me know if you have problems, the first mile will be the hardest."

"I will move, and thank you, Sergeant."

"Enough talk, sir. We do not know who else is in these woods. We need to be quiet, and let us move now."

The first quarter mile was rough, but after that, the Lieutenant seemed to gain some trust and walked much easier. At first he seemed hesitant to take a step, but with time he moved much faster. The day passed uneventfully, with no one seen and nothing heard. As dusk neared, the Senior Sergeant was near a small lake, so he stopped for a few minutes.

"I am hungry." the Lieutenant said.

"We have no food, sir. There is a lake near, which I'm sure has fish, only I have no way to catch them."

"Is there a stream?"

"Yes, there is one leading from the lake, why?"

"Often fish will swim from a lake, enter a stream and then be trapped when the water level drops. You can find them by feeling with your hands in the water under rocks, logs, or stream banks. You must use caution, because at times snakes will be found instead. Or you can make a fishnet from a limb shaped like a 'Y' and use your undershirt to make the net portion. You can use it to catch small fish or minnows."

"It is cold now and I will need a fire, if I am to fish the stream. Let us move deeper into the trees and find a good spot. I think I have about an hour of light left and then it will grow dark."

"Good luck, Sergeant."

It was cold and the Sergeant didn't really like the idea of getting wet, but they were both hungry, which meant he had to try. He stripped completely naked and entered the cold waters of the stream. He glanced at the sky and cursed the falling snow.

An hour later, after catching four large fish under the banks, he had them cooking over the flickering flames of the fire. He knew fresh water fish carried parasites, usually worms, so he cooked the fish well. He didn't know the locals called the fish bass and would not have cared anyway. His hunger was acute and he also craved a strong glass of vodka, but knew that would have to wait until he returned to the base.

As soon as the meal was finished, with two large fish left over, he wrapped it up in some cloth and attached it to his belt. At least now, they'd not starve to death, because there was enough fish left for a couple of days. By his estimation, they should be close to the base by morning.

"Lieutenant? Can you walk?"

"Yes, but I thought we would stop for the night."

"Sir, we cannot take that risk. With partisans moving around us, we need to return to the base as quickly as possible. If we are caught out here, I would fight hard, but the battle would not last long. We need to continue to move until we reach safety."

Standing, the Lieutenant said, "I understand; I am just hurting and tired. My mind is not working well."

Pulling his first aid kit open, the Senior Sergeant handed the officer a small white pill, placing it in the man's hand.

"Take the painkiller, so you can continue to move."

Lieutenant Smirnov pulled his canteen, placed the pill in his mouth and washed it down with a swig of tepid water. He screwed the top back on the container and said, "Let us move now."

In the darkness the officer tripped often, until Morozov realized he was moving too quickly for the man, so he slowed his rate down. Deep inside, the Senior Sergeant was afraid, because he'd seen what partisans did to captured Russians, and it filled him with apprehension.

All went well, until half way through the night, and the Sergeant smelled smoke. Moving forward carefully Morozov hoped to see the fire before he saw a guard. It was directly up wind and strong, which mean the men with the fire were to their west, or left side. The Senior Sergeant would move forward about ten feet, stop, listen and smell, only so far he'd seen nothing.

The Lieutenant said, "I —"

The Senior Sergeant slapped him hard and then whispered, "Damn, Lieutenant, keep your voice down, sir. Do you not smell the smoke? It is probably partisans and we do not need for them to catch us."

"I was not thinking." the Lieutenant whispered back.

"Sorry I hit you, but you endangered our lives. Now, we are going to slowly move forward and hopefully not see anyone."

"Okay, I will keep quiet."

You had better stay quiet or I will stick a knife in you. You, the big offi-cer, will not get me killed. Morozov thought and then slowly moved forward.

Suddenly, on his left he spotted a light and guessed it was a couple hundred feet from the trail. *There is always a chance they have mined the trail to give them advance warning,* he thought, and then moved toward the trees to his right, hoping to circle the trail for about a hundred meters. His heart was pounding in his chest as he moved and hoped the Lieutenant wouldn't draw attention by falling or talking. He slipped the safety off his Bison as he moved.

Twenty minutes later, he was back on the trail and moving toward the Russian camp. The Lieutenant had remained quiet and other than having to hold onto the belt to lead the injured man, it was hard to believe the officer was injured. While still snowing lightly, the moon was out and it looked as if the bad weather would soon be gone. The moonlight made for faster travel, but the Sergeant knew it would allow his enemies to spot him faster too.

Near dawn, he stepped around a curve in the trail and came face-to-face with a partisan point man. The confrontation surprised both men and as the American brought his gun up, the Senior Sergeant fired from the hip. The slugs of his sub-machine gun stitched the man up the left side, barely grazing him, until a bullet struck his left shoulder. The round exited the man's back, blowing

bone, blood, and gore out behind him. The partisan fell unmoving, but Morozov knew he had seconds to escape. Either the wounded American would fire or his comrades would come to investigate the shooting.

Jerking the belt he said, "You must run now, Lieutenant, or we both will die."

When the Senior Sergeant cut to the left and started running, he felt no resistance on the belt. Looking back the officer was keeping up, which was good, because Morozov would leave him in a second. Bullets knocked down leaves and small twigs as they moved, but the NCO knew hitting a running man in the woods was hard to do for most soldiers. It was then he felt a blow to his right leg and he fell, taking the officer down with him. Once he glanced down, he knew they were in trouble, because the round had struck bone; the front of his kneecap was missing.

"Sir, I cannot walk."

"I will carry you then. You will have to tell me how to walk; now hurry, before the Americans come to see if we were injured. Once away from here, you can splint your leg and be able to walk again."

Bending down, the Lieutenant had Morozov climb on his back and after he picked him up, he said, "Whisper to me as we move."

"Straight ten steps and then turn sharply to your left."

Taking the steps was slow, but once done, both men knew they could do this for a short distance.

"How far do we need to move, Sergeant?"

"Maybe one kilometer. I do not see them looking for us long, because the temperature is too cold, and it is still snowing. Also while the moon is out now, the clouds are moving closer. The moon will soon be covered and once the clouds do that, it will be dark again. I think in another hour, we will start to have sunlight. Go straight about forty steps and I will tell you when to turn to your right."

An hour later, the two men were under a large oak tree as Morozov trimmed a limb to use as a splint for his leg. The limb was long enough that he'd removed the branches and then cut the stem in half. He'd already cleaned and wrapped the injury as well as he could, so once the splint was in place, they could move. He had taken two of the white pills; his pain was almost gone, but enough remained to remind him of his injury. He wondered how painful it would be to move.

He wrapped the splint in place using his cutup tee shirt, and then with the help of the Lieutenant, he stood. He took a single step and then winced in pain; it hurt badly, but what choice did he have? To remain meant death and that wasn't an option for him.

"Is your pain severe?"

"Bad enough, but we must move, do we not?"

"Yes, so hand me the belt."

Ten minutes later, Morozov was in such pain he was crying silently as they walked. He wanted to take another pain pill, but knew too much of the medication would harm his liver, so he kept moving.

More than once over the morning, he felt faint and he knew soon he'd have to rest for a few hours. His mind was clouded with painfulness of such a level he worried about passing out. He gritted his teeth and kept moving. The snow had stopped, but the temperature dropped a great deal, and now he grew concerned about freezing to death if they stopped without a fire. He didn't want to build a fire, because any partisans in the area would either see the smoke or smell it, and that he couldn't afford, so they kept moving.

It was as they crossed a small clearing that he heard the helicopter and felt a knot in his stomach suddenly come alive. If the crew thought they were partisans, they were dead meat, because there was no way they could move fast enough to avoid being killed.

"Lieutenant, stop and wave your arms and I will do the same. We have to convince the helicopter crew that we are Russians or we are dead! Wave, and do it now!"

The helicopter approached, circled and finally after many long minutes, it sat down in the field and four men ran to the two. Two men guarded them, as they were asked their names and units. Realizing the two were Russians, the crew escorted them back to the helicopter. Once inside, they were strapped into their seats and handed hot cups of tea. A highly trained medic began working on both men, inserting an IV, but he started evaluating the most seriously injured first, the Lieutenant.

They'd raised about fifty feet in the air, when someone screamed and Morozov saw something fly by the door of the aircraft. There came two loud explosions, just outside the aircraft, causing the helicopter to roll violently and then shudder. Two machine-guns opened up and the noise was loud. The gunner on the left side screamed and most of his backbone, blood and bone fragments, flew from his body to land on the back of the other gunner. The spattered gunner ignored the mess and kept firing. A few minutes later, the single gun grew quiet, and gun smoke from the cabin disappeared into the slip-stream.

The medic moved to the downed gunner, looked him over and said something in his microphone. He then met the eyes of the Senior Sergeant and shook his head. The gunner was dead and all that was holding him in the aircraft was a strap of nylon.

Three bullets entered the cabin from the floor with loud pings. One bullet struck a piece of metal and ricocheted around the cabin, until it struck the medic in the left leg. The medic fell to the floor and screamed as he opened his pouch, and removed a syringe of morphine. He injected the drug into his leg and began dressing the wound. One of the other bullets must have pierced a line, because a thick oil like substance began to flow steadily to the floor.

The helicopter climbed to a higher altitude and moved toward the base.

Just as the base was in view, the aircraft began to smoke and thick toxic fumes filled the rear cabin. When Morozov looked up, sparks were flying and he wondered if the liquid pouring from the ruptured pipe was flammable. The lone gunner handed out smoke masks to those still alive. The Senior Sergeant pulled his mask from a small red canvas bag and donned it quickly.

The pilot turned and yelled something that no one heard. The aircraft began to shake violently, then a piece of tin from the aircraft flew past the door where the dead gunner lay, and the helicopter started descending. Morozov tightened his seat-belt, crossed himself, and then grasped the mounting bracket of his red canvas seat firmly. *Damn me, go through all that shit in the field, and then get killed in a helicopter crash. My luck has not been good on this mission. I hope when we hit, I do not cause more injury to my leg. If not for the morphine, I would be crying now,* he thought as he clinched his teeth and waited for impact.

Impact was bone jarring hard and Morozov quickly unbuckled his seat-belt, grabbed the Lieutenant by his ankles and ran from the aircraft, not caring if he caused the officer more injuries or not. When he reached what he thought was a safe distance, he turned, saw the gunner and one of the pilots run, and a split-second later there came a loud explosion. As the red flames and black smoke rolled into each other, they formed a mushroom cloud overhead; one of the men still in the helicopter stepped from the flames. He was totally engulfed in fire and was shrieking loudly as he stumbled away from the inferno. Morozov raised his bison and put half a magazine in the man.

"No one should be allowed to burn to death, no one!" he screamed when the weapon clicked, empty.

The survivors gathered together and discovered they were inside the perimeter of the base, so all felt safe. Emergency response teams were moving toward them now so the Senior Sergeant asked, "What happened? That was a flight from hell."

The co-pilot was on the ground screaming with an injured back and the Lieutenant was unmoving. The surviving gunner said, "I am not sure. I heard the pilot say the fire warning light was on and then smoke began filling the aircraft. I think the fire burned it's way to our fuel, or the crew did not turn the electrical switches off when we crashed. We will know in a few days."

Morozov shrugged and watched the rescue crews nearing with lights flashing. He then saw the gunner looking the two injured men over.

As the fire trucks neared, he asked, "How is my Lieutenant?"

The gunner shook his head and said, "Dead. He must have taken some of the bullets from the ground fire, because he took one in the spine and another near his heart. I am sorry, Senior Sergeant."

"It is nothing. People get killed in wars." The smell of burnt bodies was strong and the Sergeant had a strong desire for a glass of vodka, a big glass.

CHAPTER 5

Scott looked the maps and other papers over and then shook his head. He met my eyes and said, "Sir, the Russians are gathering, well, at this exact spot circled on the map." He pointed and then added, "They've decided to try poison gases in Mississippi, county by county. Their plans are to gas a place, then send in specially trained units to kill any survivors, and it very well may work."

"Do they say what kind of gas?" I asked. I didn't like the idea, because it would end up killing a lot of civilians and very few partisans. Most of us had masks and atropine to counter the effects of most agents, but especially nerve gas.

"Nerve gas, and lots of it. It's to be delivered in many different ways. The orders list bombs, artillery shells, and aircraft as ways to release it, and the operation starts one week from today."

I thought for a minute and then said, "Okay, we need to make an example of the Russians we have with us and then beat feet to the Colonel. Once we contact him, we'll take it from there. If he wants us to still go to Pearl, we'll do so. He may decide to attack some installations while they're lightly manned to stop the whole Russian operation. The commander of the Russians troops tried poison gas before, except it didn't work then, and it'll not work now."

"Why is that, sir?" Scott asked.

"The partisans have gear we've stolen from the Russians and most civilians have either been rounded up and placed in Gulags, killed, or died years ago during the fall of America."

Sandra neared with Dolly, handed the dog's leash to me and said, "Let's complete our mission and get out of here. I know some people will be killed if they use gas, and I want to keep the casualties down if we can. A nerve agent is a hell of a rough way to die."

I said, "Saddle up, folks, and let's move. Private Walsh, you bring up the rear and Kerr, you are my point man. Joyce?"

"Yo?"

"You stay near the prisoners. If we're ambushed, kill 'em all."

"I understand." she said and then looked at the Russians and smiled, in case one or two spoke English.

I figured, by looking at my map, we had only about two miles to the highway. So I called out a compass heading to Kerr and then turning to Kelly, my medic, I said, "You keep track of our pace. It should only be two miles to the highway."

We had no difficulty reaching a small hill, easily seen from the highway, so I had six poles cut and stuck firmly in the ground. I sincerely dreaded this task, but saw no way to avoid carrying out my orders. The Russians would only understand brutal reprisals and this was as brutal is they come. Once the poles were in place and secure, I had the prisoners tied in place using wire and not rope.

"Scott!" I called out.

"Yo!"

"I want you to speak for me. Now I know you don't like this, but translate my words and then you can move down the back trail and keep watch." I handed Dolly's leash to Sandra.

He thought for a moment and then said, "Okay, and I appreci-ate you taking my feelings about this in consideration. I am firmly against this act as being cold-blooded and in violation of the arti-cles of war for most civilized nations."

"I'll not argue with you, but since you'll translate, tell them they are to die because the Russians have taken to burning cap-tured partisans."

Scott spoke and the Russians grew pale and more than one had large eyes. One spoke and then Scott said, "He wants to know how he is to die."

"By fire."

"No!" one prisoner yelled, "You should not do this thing. We are simple soldiers and not responsible for the killing of any partisans or your people."

"Oh, but it's okay for your people to burn my countrymen to death or spray nerve gas over areas populated by civilians? I'm sorry you are caught up in the actions of both nations, but you will burn to death, and in just a few short minutes."

The Russian yelled something and when I turned to Scott he said, "He called you a bastard."

I took a five gallon gas can, moved to the first man and drenched him from head to toe. While pouring gas on the man who spoke English, he spat in my face and said, "You are a sono-fabitch!"

I wiped my face clean, moved to the next man and covered him in gas, too.

Finally, I said, "Scott, move to the back trail and guard. As soon as you leave, I'll end this mess."

As soon as Scott was out of sight, I said, "You, the one who speaks English, tell the others they have one minute to pray, because in two minutes you'll all be standing in front of God."

"Go to hell, Yankee, because there is no God!"

"If there is no God, Russian, then there is no hell either. You now have 45 seconds." I replied as I looked at my watch, taken off the wrist of a Russian Colonel I'd killed years before.

I pulled a piece of paper from my pocket, folded it and lighted the end with an old lighter. As it flared, I heard two or three of the Russians praying. Still watching my watch, when it indicated a minute had passed, I tossed the burning paper to the nearest man.

With a loud *whoosh* the gas ignited. I watched in morbid fascination as the flames moved down the line from man to man. I noticed it burned almost clear and was tempted to extend a hand to see if the flames were there. However, the look of horror in the doomed men's eyes told me the flames were there. Men began shrieking in pain and terror as the flames licked and bit at their flesh. Clothing burst into flames, and all of them began an almost comical dance as the fire consumed their hair and melted their flesh. Then, one by one, the screeching ceased and all movement ended. Six brave soldiers of the rabid Russian bear were now dead.

I said a short prayer for the men I'd killed, wiped my eyes clear of tears, and then said, "Let's move, because I want to be with the Colonel by the end of the day."

Sandra neared, handed me the leash to Dolly, and said, "I know what you did was hard on you, because inside you're a kind man." Then she touched my cheek.

My eyes watered again. I fought back tears, and said, "A kind man doesn't burn innocent prisoners of war in reprisal for atrocities his enemies commit. This war has turned me into something I don't want to be, a cold-blooded killer." I scratched Dolly's ear, knew the nasty deed was done and added, "May God forgive all of us, on both sides, for what we've done. Place some booby-traps and let's get ready to move."

The smell of burnt flesh was strong as the flames rolled skyward, with the smoke dark and the charred remains hanging loosely on the badly blackened poles. I'd followed orders, but at what cost to me emotionally? I now had to live with the fact I'd burned six helpless men to death, and there isn't a more horrific way to die.

"Let's move, folks, we've miles to cover."

As we began to move my medic, Kelly, leaned to the side and puked.

The Colonel looked weak as he walked around the 55 gallon oil drum where the Russian map was laid out on top. His hands were behind him, his head down, as he gave serious thought to what Corporal Scott and I had told him. Scott was now gone, but he'd read all the intelligence we had, and informed the Colonel of the contents.

Finally, he turned to face me and said, "We must prevent the Russians from using nerve agents because of the potential to cause a large number of civilian fatalities. Granted, there are fewer people now than when the fall happened, but even the loss of a single life is too much. We need to hit them, and hard, too. I want you to continue to Pearl, but once in place, try to take out costly items. Hit their petroleum and gas storage areas, supplies, vehicle motor pools, and if you can, take a train or two out as well. That'll be all."

I knew I'd just been dismissed, but I asked, "Colonel Lee, are you ill?"

"I have some minor pain is all."

"Would you mind if my wife looks you over? She may be able to help you with the pain."

Shaking his head, Lee replied, "No, John, I have cancer, and less than a year to live. I have pain medicines, including morphine, but I've not needed it yet. Upon my death, or when I am unable to continue my work, I have requested you be promoted to my leadership position."

"I'm sorry to hear this, sir."

"No more than me, I assure you. Now, enough talk about me. See to your mission and do it now."

I saluted and replied, "Yes, sir." I then did an about face and left the building.

My squad was outside and gathering gear. Rations were collected to replace those consumed, and ammo and other needs were being seen to, which pleased me. Joyce was cleaning her sniper rifle and Silverwolf was putting an edge on his knife. It was comforting knowing I was leading a professional bunch that took minimum supervision. The men who handled the bikes were still with us, not sure what their orders would be.

"All of us, including the bikers, are to continue to Pearl and complete our mission. While I know most of you are tired, I suggest we all eat, rest and we'll leave in an hour."

Pearl was once a nice small town a few miles east of Jackson and it was quiet compared to the big city, with a much lower crime rate. I'd spent a lot of time visiting my grandparents there and knew the area well. I'd also dated a few girls from the small town, had enjoyed talking with most of the occupants, and it presented a small town atmosphere. Now, however, it was a ghost town, with most of the people sent to gulags, dead, or in the resistance. I selected a dense patch of trees and brush by the Pearl River to establish our main camp. Then, taking the men with the bikes, I'd hidden our supplies at night in different locations near the town. Once the gear and supplies were buried, I ordered the men to return to the Colonel.

Gathering my people in close the first night, I said, "We'll all pull guard, two people at a time, and no fires, unless the weather turns super rough. We're just a few miles from the Jackson International Airport, so air traffic will be heavy. If the Russians hit us, follow the Pearl River south and we'll meet at about five miles distance. Corporal Kerr, later tonight you and I will check the area for threats to our security. Keep in mind to the north of us is highway 80 and to the south is interstate 20, so we've many secondary roads around us. Our best chances, if we have to escape and evade, are the river. If you want to eat, do it now."

"Gag me." Joyce said with a grin, "Russian rations are bad enough hot, but they're pretty nasty cold."

"Well, that's all we have right now, so it's Russian or nothing."

The rest of the evening was quiet and Kerr left with me at 2200 hours, moving almost dead east. Our faces and hands were camouflaged, so if we ran into Russians, we'd never pass for civilians and the Russian weapons in our hands made it clear we were here to fight. There was no traffic at all and in town the only vehicles I saw was an occasional motorcycle. When I neared the old Pearl police station, I noticed many men walking in and out of the building. There was a tank parked outside in the driveway, and two guards near the entrance.

We made our way to the elementary school and junior high school, finding both in use as barracks for the Russians. Both facilities were big, but I only counted 4 guards at each. They must have felt secure with a large number of men inside, not realizing sleeping men took some time to wake up and respond. It was obvious to me the Russians had poor security at Pearl, and we'd hit some nice targets over the next few nights. It took until almost dawn before we located their fuels storage area and it was in an old semipro baseball field. I saw a lot of flexible rubberized fuel bladders, just right for some well placed explosives. The bladders were huge and the resulting explosion of just one would claim them all.

It was nearly two hours before sunrise, so we took a shortcut I knew through some trees. As usual when moving, we did so slowly, covering our flanks, front, and rear. Looking forward, I saw a couple of men with a dog moving right for us and they were outlined by distant lights. If not for the dog, we could have just slipped into some brush, only the dog worried me a great deal. The guards would probably walk right by us, except I knew the animal would smell us and alert the handlers. I decided to wait and see what the dog did, then take the German Shepherd out first, and finally the men. I disliked killing a fine animal that reminded me of Dolly, but survival comes first.

About twenty feet from us, the dog alerted and looked right at me. I didn't think the animal could see me, but the dog handler said something to the other man and guns were made ready. I pulled my pistol as I prayed the dog wouldn't be released. I watched as the handler reached down to release the animal, so I fired once, dropped the dog, and heard Kerr open up with his Bison.

The Russian on the right shrieked, grabbed his face and with good reason. Kerr's Bison sub-machine gun had sent bullets up the man's right leg, blowing flesh and blood out behind him. Then the bullets continued on, striking him with lead all the way to his head. When his head was struck, it flew apart, sending skull shards and blood high into the air. As the man fell, all that remained of his head was a fine carmine haze from flying blood.

I fired two shots from my Russian pistol and the other man was struck in the middle of his chest. Two long crimson fingers flew from his back and then he dropped without making a sound. As his body twitched and jerked, his central nervous system shutting down, we moved forward to strip the men of anything we might need. It was then I noticed the snow falling.

"Hurry and grab what we need." I said and then took the dead man's weapons and ammo. He carried a portable radio, so I took it, hoping Scott could listen to Russian transmissions. I then added, "Quickly, because someone must have heard our gun-shots."

"I'm rushing the job. I hated the dog dying."

"I can kill an enemy soldier in a minute, but love animals. The dogs was the only innocent here, but he had to die. No way he was a pet."

Kerr suddenly gave me a serious look and replied, "We're pretty stupid to be talking while deep in Injun country."

I gave a dry chuckle and said, "Uh-huh, and we both know it. Let's cut the chatter until we return." We knew better than to talk.

It was dark and still snowing less than five minutes later, as Kerr said, "Vehicles on the road on the east side."

I glance in that direction, saw headlights, and then said, "Go, and now. Let's move north some and then later, we'll move to the group."

"If this snow sticks even a child will be able to track us." Kerr said as he stood upright and adjusted this gear.

"Slow jog for a mile, then we'll drop to a walk." I said, and then started north.

Dawn found us moving slowly over about an inch of new snow. It's still snowing and it's coming down hard. I glanced behind us and knew our tracks were being filled by snow almost as quickly as we made them. The wind was gusting too, which aided in our escape. Between the blowing and falling snow, we'd not be found. The temperature was dropping and I knew it was well below freezing.

"Move to the right and then back into the oaks. We need a small fire and something to eat." I said as I changed directions.

"Good, it's cold."

Twenty minutes later a small fire was burning, Russian rations were being heated, and we both held our palms toward the fire to feel the heat. It's surprising how little a person needs to feel human again, but warmth when it's cold, hot food and a little rest always works for me.

"What were those dog handlers doing out in the woods like that?" Kerr asked as he pulled his ration from the fire.

"The Russians have patrols out randomly covering the area is my guess, and we just bumped into them."

Kerr chewed a few minutes and then asked, "What now? I mean, do we keep moving north?"

"I think we can safely move toward our group now. The snow is covering our tracks and I don't want to still be moving toward them when this stuff stops. If we are, our tracks will even be visible from the air."

Kerr nodded and then said, "That makes sense to me. What did you do before the fall?"

"I spent a few years in the army, got out, and went to college on the G.I. Bill. I then owned a security company, was married and living well. How about you?"

The black man smiled and said, "I spent four years in the army, went to school at night, and after I got out I went to dental school. My parents were so proud of me the day my dental office opened. Then a year later, I lost my ass in the fall, including both parents. I was married, had two young twin boys, but they were all murdered one day while I was out looking for food. I returned home to a house spattered with blood."

"My first wife was killed, too."

"My parents were both in their late sixties, with my dad on blood pressure medication, and mom a diabetic. When the pharmacies closed, they were both dead within a few months, and my anger was so great, I started killing. I didn't just kill anyone, but when I found some worthless bastards, I took them out."

"I think you missed a few."

He gave a low chuckle and said, "Yep, I surely did. In Jackson, where I lived, some groups were eating people, but keeping them alive until needed. They'd pull the victim out, tie them up, and then decapitate them with a machete. I watched them a few nights and it was the sickest damned thing I'd ever seen. When they murdered a young girl, no more than ten years old, I did my best to wipe that whole bunch out. Then one day I ran into an old army friend and he told me about the resistance. Now, this was before the Russians were here, but they were coming, or so he claimed. You pretty much know the rest of the story."

"There are still some sick —"

"Do you hear that?" Kerr asked.

CHAPTER 6

From his bed in the hospital, the Senior Sergeant could look out the window and see men and women scurrying around like ants. He'd been questioned so much by intelligence his patience was thin and temper mean. They'd asked him a zillion questions about all sorts of things and made an attempt to make Lieutenant Smirnov look bad. Morozov had finally grown mad at the men questioning him and ran them from his room. *They're a bunch of damned paper pushers and not a one of them has ever been shot at. Any combat soldier knows at times there is nothing you can do but die,* he thought as he moved and then winced from pain.

Suddenly he heard a loud voice, "Taras, you lazy bastard, what are you doing in bed?"

"I needed a short nap." he replied as he met the blue eyes of Master Sergeant Stas Fedorovo.

The Master Sergeant walked to the bed, pulled a pint of vodka from his coat and slipped it under the mattress. Smiling, he asked, "Are they treating you well? And, what are the extent of your injuries? I heard you were the only survivor of your squad, but how can that be?"

Master Sergeant Fedorovo was short, just five feet and four inches, but every inch of him was a fighter. He weighed 120 pounds, or 54.55 kilos. He'd joined the army at 17 and quickly found a home. His brown hair was cropped almost to the skin and he looked mean most of the time, but he was a compassionate man inside.

"Ambushed us as we woke at dawn. Lieutenant Smirnov and I were in the bushes doing our morning business when it happened. The fight did not last more then two minutes and then we started walking back to base. I then —"

The Master Sergeant patted Morozov on the shoulder and said, "I read the report, Taras, but did anyone screw up?"

"Not that I can remember. The Americans must have watched us bed down and then moved in close during the darkness. Then, at first light, they began killing." Suddenly, Morozov began to cry silently as his body quivered.

Pulling the bottle out from under the mattress, Fedorovo broke the seal, unscrewed the top and handed the bottle to his Senior Sergeant. "Take a long deep drink of this; it will help you feel better. Men die in wars, my friend, and we are leaders of the men who will die. At times it will be one of us, but most often it is those who follow us. I like to think God selects who will live or die."

Morozov took a long pull on the bottle, handed it back to the Master Sergeant and nodded. After about a minute, he watched Fedorovo take a drink. Then he said, "All of them dead. But I know I could not have saved them if I had been with them."

"Well, I have come to tell you the bodies have been recovered. From what I read, the ambush was completed by a squad size unit and they were well equipped and trained, or their leader was prior military. That is the problem here that Moscow does not understand. They think we are battling a bunch of ignorant peasants and we are not. There are more guns here than in all the armies of the world combined, and most of the men here are hunters, hobby shooters, or prior military. Hell, we were insane to come here to start with."

Sitting up, the vodka meeting his pain pills, the Senior Sergeant said, "So, what can we do?"

"We are soldiers and we will follow orders. Many more men will have to die before Moscow realizes the cost is too great. By that time, you and I will either be dead and buried, killed here, or retired to mother Russia. We are a hard-headed people, but this time the American eagle has a good solid bite on our arses and won't let go. Just like Afghanistan years back, we will have to learn the hard way, and how many men and women will be sent home to momma in a box?"

"I should have been a farmer like my father wanted me to be."

"Perhaps, but this way you have seen much of the world, have a chest full of cheap tin and ribbon, along with a small pension. No, you are right for the job, but every professional has bad days and you, my friend, had one. Now, I am going to leave, but I will be back later to talk. Sleep now."

By the time the Master Sergeant mentioned sleep, Morozov was already gone. The combination of the alcohol and pills had put him out.

Seeing his good friend sleeping, Fedorovo smiled, wiped his eyes and said, "God, protect this brave man, he is like a brother to me. Keep him safe in the coming battles." He then left the room.

"So, Lieutenant Colonel Vasiliev, if I understand you correctly, over four hundred Russian troops have died this month, while the Americans have lost less than one hundred! Explain to me how this has happened!" Colonel Ivanov screamed as usual during his staff meeting. He then continued, "How can these damned peasants murder Russian troops when they choose? You are the chief of Anti-terrorist Operations and I want answers!"

"Sir, I hav —"

"You *stand* at attention when speaking to me, Vasiliev, or I will have you *shot* for disrespect! Now, tell me what *you* are doing to stop this killing."

The Lieutenant Colonel shot to his feet and stood ramrod stiff as he replied, "We are using state maps and plan to eventually drop poison nerve agent on the whole state. We will do this county by county. We will then follow up with specially trained units, who will be dropped by helicopter or parachute to check suspected safe houses or areas we think have partisans."

"Why think or suspect? You really do not know much, do you? If not, then why not? I want answers, or I will send you packing back to Moscow in shame, for a courts-martial!"

"Sir, these Americans are not talking. Most die before they give us information or they hold out long enough the information is no longer any good."

"Then, by God, use reprisals on them."

"We tried that, sir, and over 150 of this month's dead were killed in reprisals to our killings. On the ground at each site of the murders was a poster that claimed for every American murdered, six Russians would also die. So far, they have lived up to their promises."

"I want a thousand Americans dead by morning. There is no way they can kill six thousand Russians soldiers in retaliation."

"Sir, I would like to sug—"

"Do not push me on this, and I want it done! By morning, I want to drive through the streets of Edwards and see body after body of dead lining the streets. Do you *fully* understand your orders?"

"Yes, sir, and it will be done."

"Good. Now weather, tell me what to expect this week."

As the weather man stood, Vasiliev thought, *My commander is a damned fool! He has no idea what this order will do to the American resistance. They will come for us and him, because they will be filled with such anger. Oh, I should have taken the job at Jackson, but this one offered me a promotion. I have made a terrible mistake.*

"Did you not hear me, Vasiliev?" the commander asked a second time.

Standing, the Lieutenant Colonel snapped to attention and said, "I am sorry, sir, I was organizing your orders in my mind. I do not know if I have that many captured partisans in the camps to execute."

Looking at Colonel Kuznetsov, the gulag commander, Ivanov asked, "How many do you have, Colonel?"

"At last count this morning, a little over 900 are suspected partisans."

"See, Vasiliev, that was not hard and make up the difference with civilians, male or female, and any age is fine. The Americans do not like to see their citizens killed and it is time they learn we

Russians will kill any American we wish. Now go back to your office and see my orders are carried out. Dismissed."

"Yes, sir!" the Lieutenant Colonel said, saluted, did an about face, and left the conference room. As he walked to his car, he thought, *things in this American War are about to heat up. We have never killed this many people at one time. I think the war is suddenly going to swing against us and we will have partisans coming out of the walls like cockroaches, all looking for Russian blood.*

Nearing his driver and car, Vasiliev yelled, "Get your arse in the car and take me back to my office."

His driver, a Private, tossed his cigarette to the soil, stepped on it with his boot and pulled the keys out of his pocket. As he started the car, a glance in the mirror showed the Lieutenant Colonel drinking from a silver flask. *Must have had his ass chewed hard this morning*, he thought as he slipped the car into gear.

The drive to his office was uneventful but stressful for the Commander of Anti-terrorist Operations. Once in his office he called a meeting with his junior officers and senior NCO's. When all were seated around the table, he explained his orders and waited for questions.

"Sir, do you have any idea how long it takes to execute a hundred people?" Senior Sergeant Silin asked.

"Not, not really, because I have never done the job. I suspect how they die determines how much time it takes. Shooting is quickest, but what do you suggest?"

"I suggest a mixture of shooting and hanging. Take, let us say, half the group to hang and the other half to shoot. The hanging victims can be loaded on flatbed trucks, ropes thrown over telephone poles, limbs on trees, light posts, and then pushed off a truck. No need to wait and watch the victim die, just shove them from the truck and move on.

For the shooting, place the victims in an open field and position tanks at the corners. Bullets from our machine-gun crews will bounce off the armor of the tank, but kill anyone in the field. Any that the machine-gun crews miss, the tank machine-gunner can take out in seconds. Send them out to the field a hundred at a time."

Captain Pasha Blinov said, "That is nothing but murder."

"This is war, sir," Senior Sergeant Silin said and then added, "and reprisals are part of the game."

"Game?" the Captain almost yelled, "Damn it, Sergeant, it is cold-blooded murder in my book."

A Private stuck his head in the smoke-filled room and said, "A patrol just discovered the remains of six of our troops, all burned to death with petrol. They found the empty petrol containers."

Lieutenant Colonel Vasiliev smiled and said, "Captain, I want you and Senior Sergeant Silin to go and recover the bodies. Private, radio the patrol leader that we are coming to recover the remains. I think, Pasha, you will see shortly why we 'murder' Americans. Now, Silin, gather your men and tell the motor pool to give you the number of vehicles you think are needed. If you have any problems, let me know. Pasha, you go with him and watch a true professional in this man's army, and learn, my dear Captain."

The recovery convoy left Edwards two hours later, just as the Lieutenant Colonel had the first 100 of the soon to be murdered people pulled from the gulag. There were five vehicles in the group, plus two motorcycles, who rode in the front and rear of the trucks. The ride was short, less than five miles, and from the road they could see the bodies tied to the posts.

Jumping from the cargo truck, Senior Sergeant Silin yelled, "Watch for trip wires and mines. It is very likely they have mines planted near the bodies."

A Sergeant neared, the squad leader of the unit that found the dead, and said, "We have not gone near the bodies, because our mine detector is not working properly." He then noticed Captain Blinov and saluted.

"How do you know they are our men then?" the Captain asked, his hands on his hips.

"With my binoculars, I spotted bits and pieces of Russian clothing on the ground. I spotted a forage cap, a helmet, and even a shirt. I know partisans could have left the gear, but that is not likely, so I assumed the men are ours."

"Maybe they are traitors and were executed." the Captain said.

"Sir, with all due respect, but partisans usually hang or shoot traitors. Also there looks to be a poster or something nailed to a tree near the bodies. No, those poor dead bastards are Russians, sir."

"Senior Sergeant, take charge of the men and recover the bodies. I am sure the graves registration unit will identify them."

Silin snapped to attention, saluted and then yelled, "Men, form on me and step where I step. Look for tripwires and any discoloration in the grasses or soil." He then started for the hill, with a squad of ten men behind him.

Near the top of the hill, the Senior Sergeant said, "Wait for me as I check for mines or booby-traps." He then moved forward, found nothing and ten minutes later, waved his men forward.

The stench was horrible and even in the cold weather it was overpowering up close to the bodies. Each man's head was back, mouth open, and all of their fingers were crooked, like claws. A new man, Sergeant Avilov, took one look, inhaled the foul odor and stepped to the side to puke.

"Sergeant, get back here becau—" Senior Sergeant Silin warned.

There sounded a loud noise, like a shotgun blast and Avilov, was knocked to the ground as blood spurted from his groin and thigh. He screamed, grabbed at his injury and thrashed madly in the grasses.

The medic ran for the downed man, even as Silin shouted a warning, and a few seconds later a wall of flame shot up as a pressure detonating mine exploded. The medic all but disappeared with his legs and arms, as well as his head, gone. A maimed torso was all that remained, and it was smoking.

"No one move!" the Senior Sergeant yelled. Avilov was still screaming as blood spurted from between his fingers and pooled on the ground under him. His back was arched and he was shrieking continuously.

Ten minutes passed as everyone stood in place and then the Sergeant said, "I am going to check the pole around each body for booby-traps, recover Avilov, and then we will carry the bodies to the trucks. I want none of you to move until I give the word." The

Sergeant then moved to the first pole and it was clean. He was near the third before he saw shotgun shell buried in the soil. He knew the primer of the shell was resting on a nail, and as Avilov had discovered, the detonation often caused serious injury and blood loss. Using his bayonet, he dug the shell up and tossed it aside. At the fourth and fifth poles he found more shotgun shells and dug each up. The smell of the bodies was getting to him, so he stepped back.

There was a split second, just a small flash of time, when he realized he'd just made a terrible blunder. He felt the light fishing line on his boot grow tight, knew it was a booby-trap, and also knew he was a dead man. *Oh, I just made a very stupid mistake*, was the last thing Senior Sergeant Silin thought before the Russian MON-50 mine blew him apart.

When the red dust and smoke cleared, very little remained of the six burned bodies, or the ten men who were sent to retrieve them. Arms, legs, and heads were scattered over the knoll and Sergeant Avilov was no longer screaming, because the blast had caught him in the face. An eerie silence filled the air.

Down by the road, Captain Blinov was in shock, until the patrol leader said, "Sir, I have called the explosion in to headquarters and they have ordered all of us to look for survivors."

"Yes, uh, of course, Sergeant, so lead the way. Once near the explosion, secure the area."

"Yes, sir. Let us move, men. The sooner we recover what we can, the sooner we will return to base. I need three men to stay here and help the truck drivers provide security for the vehicles. Private, bring the radio and stay by my side."

"I will be within an arms reach." the tall lanky Private said.

At the top, there was nothing really to recover. Body parts were gathered and placed in body bags, except it was impossible to tell which arm went with which leg, so they filled three body bags and then moved back to the trucks. Once at the vehicles, the Captain walked from the men and puked a few times. He was looking pale when the squad leader said, "Sir, Headquarters wants us on the road as soon as possible. It seems we suffered a number of terrorist attacks on small patrols last night and we have another forty to fifty dead. The exact words from Lieutenant Colonel Vasiliev are, 'return here and now.'"

"Let us leave immediately then."

Walking to the motorcycle in front, the squad leader gave the order, and within just a few minutes the convoy was returning to Edwards. The Captain was a changed man, only he didn't realize it yet. He would no longer question the executions of Americans and a small seed of hate had actually been planted in his mind. As the big truck bounced and shook as it moved over the highway, his mouth grew tight and his eyes narrowed, as he remembered the bloody Russian bodies. Captain Blinov was learning to hate Americans.

As the trucks entered the small town of Edwards, machine-gun fire was heard and the convoy contacted Headquarters by radio. Captain Blinov grew anxious at the sound and slowed the vehicles down to about half their normal speed.

"Sir!" the radioman, a Private, said.

"What do they want us to do?"

"Lieutenant Colonel Vasiliev has ordered the trucks be returned immediately to assist in transporting more prisoners from the gulag. He wants the remains taken by one truck, dropped off at the hospital, and then it needs to join us at the gulag."

"What did he say of the gunfire we hear?"

"It is the reprisals he has ordered."

"Tell him I will obey his orders and will be with the trucks at the gulag."

"Yes, sir."

As they rolled down the streets in town, the Captain noticed ropes hanging from telephone poles, light poles, and tree limbs, on both sides of the street. Near the center of town, he had his driver stop as two long trucks with flat beds had Russian soldiers placing nooses around the necks of the prisoners. He expected the Americans to be screaming or crying, but most were not. Each male prisoner fought hard to avoid the noose, except it did them little good. Once all were ready, the condemned were given a minute to pray. One man, a tall lanky man on the end of the first truck began to yell, "I pledge allegiance to the Flag, of the United States of Amer—"

"Driver, go now!" a Senior Sergeant on the vehicle yelled and banged on the side of the truck. The vehicle shot forward and the victims were left dancing madly on their ropes.

The man on the end met the eyes of Captain Blinov and the officer felt a chill run down his spine. As the lanky man was dancing as he gasped for breath, the short fall not breaking his neck, and his eyes were huge. As the man's face turned deep crimson, the Captain thought, *What kind of people are these Americans? Do they not fear death like most people? Why was he pledging allegiance to a flag that is no more? I do not understand this.*

"Sir," the radioman interrupted his thoughts and said, "the Colonel wants to know your estimated time of arrival. What should I tell him?"

"Driver, go on. Tell the Colonel the roads are filled with the hanging crews and I expect to be at the gulag within seven or eight minutes."

"Yes, sir."

The squad leader, who was seated beside the Captain said, "It is always the same with these Americans when we execute them."

"What do you mean, Sergeant?"

"They are defiant to the very end, sir. The tall man back there was actually pledging allegiance to the flag of a country that no longer exists. I could be here a hundred years and not understand these people. Do they not fear the might of the Russian army?"

"He was a fool and now he is a dead fool, Sergeant."

"Maybe they are determined to beat us, sir."

"They cannot force the Russian army to run, because we are too powerful. How do they think they can make us leave with our tails between our legs?"

"I know little of Americans, except I do not care much for them." the Sergeant said.

"Many will die as they resist our power." the Captain replied and pulled a small metal flask of vodka from his coat pocket. Taking a drink, he handed the container to the Sergeant.

"I neither like or dislike them individually, sir, it is that I do not understand them. We are the ruling authority over the whole land and yet they fight us. Why? Have they no respect or fear of authority? They must know they cannot win in the end."

"I am just a soldier, Sergeant, like you, and follow orders. I suggest you leave the heavy thinking to those appointed over you and worry about the welfare of your men. I think you have enough to keep you busy."

"Yes, sir."

The ride was quiet the remainder of the trip to Edwards where the Captain stopped the convoy, sent the bodies to the hospital, and then led the other trucks to the gulag. As he rode, he kept hearing the voice of the tall lanky man on the flatbed truck pledging allegiance to a country that for all practical purposes, was no more.

CHAPTER 7

K err and I moved from the fire and blended into the bushes around our small camp. We'd both heard something, but exactly what I couldn't say. We waited; as we did so, I watched the snow fall. The flakes were small and I figured by morning, if it snowed all night, we might have half of an inch on the ground.

Silence.

After about thirty minutes two filthy looking men with beards walked into our camp and then scanned the area. One was tall, well over six feet, while the other was of average height, but both were thin. The short man picked up an empty Russian ration can, ran his finger along the inside and then licked it clean.

"I'm tellin' ya, I saw a couple of men here a few minutes ago."

Neither man was well armed, with one carrying an ax and other armed with what looked like an old .22 caliber pistol stuck in his waistband.

"They left their packs and I saw two, so they've not gone far."

Gripping his ax tighter and with both hands, the short man said, "They might be watching us right now."

"Uh-huh, I suspect they are, too."

The short man called out in a low voice, "If ya hear me, we mean ya no harm. We saw your fire and we're hungry."

"Who are you?" I asked as I carefully watched the men. If they started going through our packs, I'd shoot to kill.

"I'm Tim Mullins, and the tall man goes by the name Trace."

"I want both of you to place your weapons on the ground and then move to the fire and sit on the side opposite your arms. After you do that, we'll step out and talk with you."

"We can do that, huh, Trace?"

"Sure."

The gun and ax dropped to the ground, but I suspected they had some knives or other weapons too, so I said, "All your arms, and I mean down to the last knife."

A straight razor was dropped by the big man, while the smaller threw a butcher knife to the grasses. I still didn't stand, so a the tall man dropped a hand grenade and the other man dropped a small caliber pistol. I then stood.

"Hell, you're a Russian." Trace said.

"No, I'm not. See the yellow armband? I'm with the resistance. Kerr, cover me as I talk with these two and see if they're a threat or not."

"You're dressed like a Ruskie." Mullins said.

"I've answered that already." I stepped near the flickering flames of my small fire, sat in the grasses, and lined my Bison submachine gun up on both men.

"No need to point that thing at us, because we're no threat."

"I'll decide if you two are threats or not. Where do the two of you live and how have you survived since the fall?"

Trace said, "At first we were with a small tribe that lived in the empty houses behind the shopping mall on the south side of Old Brandon Road. Then our group turned cannibal and we left that night, without eating. I will steal, fight and even kill to eat, but I'm no man eater. I was shocked that they'd caught a family and planned to eat them one at a time."

"Since then, well, we've lived like rats. We only come out at night to look for food and sometimes we kill Russians to get their rations or other foods." Mullins said.

Something about the two seemed out of place. Few lived these days in towns or cities without a regular source of food and killing one or two Russians might feed both of them for two days, maybe. I suspected I was looking at two cannibals, but had no evidence.

"Why didn't you two join the resistance and fight the Russians?" Kerr asked from the bushes.

Trace said, "No way. The resistance will get a man killed and for what? I owe this has-been of a nation nothing. The politicians were spending money like water, billions of dollars were given to our enemies, our rights slowly eroded under the bullshit lie of national security, and even ammunition was hard to find and almost impossible to afford. By the time most Americans realized what was happening the President and his family were gone, dead as hell, and then one coup after another followed until no one was left that wanted to run the country. I'll hide and take care of me and that's enough to keep me happy."

"Kerr, I want you to come to the fire and frisk these men, both of them." I said as I slipped the safety off my weapon.

"What gives you the right to frisk me?" Trace asked and I could tell he was a loudmouth that was used to being in charge.

"As you said, this is a has-been nation, so I have any right I am man enough to back up right now. Since I have a fully loaded automatic weapon and you don't, that means I call the shots."

Kerr neared and said, "Stand up, one at a time."

Mullins stood, opened his legs and Kerr found little on the man. He'd just had the shorter man sit and Trace stand, when the tall man suddenly turned and I saw a knife in his hand.

"He's got a knife!" I screamed and the saw Kerr take the blade deep in his thigh. The man fell to the ground and screamed with the bloody knife still in his leg.

Trace ran about three steps before the bullets of my Bison caught him down the back and he fell screaming and clawing at the dirt. I moved the muzzle toward Mullins and asked, "Do you want to run too?"

"N . . . no." he replied, his eyes wide in fear.

"Kerr, can you move?"

"I can move." he said and it was then Trace gave a loud sigh and died.

"Move to me and keep Mullins covered as I doctor your wound."

It took the man a few minutes to stand and then move to me, but he had grit and was a strong man. Once by my side, he pulled his weapon, flipped the safety off and said, "Run, if you want. I've got a real strong urge to kill right now."

Raising both hands with the palms open, Mullins wisely said, "I ain't no threat and I'll not run."

I cut his pant leg, removed the knife, tossing it into the flames and wrapped him tightly in clean cotton material. I handed him a painkiller in pill form and then patted his shoulder.

I then said, "Keep an eye on him and if he even passes gas, blow 'em away. I'm going to check Trace's body and see why he ran from you."

I found little on the man, until I pulled his coat open and on an inside pocket I found a human hand and it had been boiled and eaten on. I brought it with me to the fire, placed it on the grasses in front of Mullins and asked, "Is this how you two stay alive?"

"No! I don't know where that came from."

"You know where it came from, because you saw me pull it from Trace's coat. Now I want to know the truth and maybe I'll let you live."

The man began to shiver and lowered his head.

"You'd better answer me, because I don't have a hell of a lot of patience right now."

"Yes, that's how we survived. We'd kill a lone Russians or civilian and eat them. A body would feed us for a week."

I heard a loud pistol shot, saw a long finger of blood fly from the back of Mullin's head and he collapsed like a rag doll. Looking to my left, Kerr was holding a smoking pistol.

"I told him he might live if he told the truth." I said, somewhat angry, but no overly so, because few had tolerance for cannibals. I was more frustrated than anything else because the dead man had information I needed. He'd known where and when Russians patrols moved and he'd also known of other civilians in the area.

Meeting my eyes, Kerr said, "I gave him no such guarantees. I hate a cannibal and will kill all I find. Anyone that will kill others to live is the lowest form of human being on earth."

"I can't argue with your logic, but we need to saddle up and move. I'm sure Russians will come to see what brought the gunfire."

Moving to his pack and putting it on, Kerr said, "I didn't say anything earlier, but when I went to bury my parents, both were missing their legs. I kicked in every door on their street and finally found a group of two men and one woman roasting my fathers leg over the flames in a fireplace."

"Let me guess, you killed them all."

"Oh, I did that. I secured all three with wire and then set the house on fire. I stuck around just long enough to hear them screaming and then left. I have no use for a damned cannibal and just so you know, I'll kill all I find."

"You lead and get us back to the group."

I grew edgy when I neared where my squad should be located, because I saw no light nor heard any noises. I flipped my safety off on the Bison and approached cautiously. It was almost dusk and Kerr had slowed me due to his injury. His leg was bleeding again and I hoped to have Sandra stitch his injury and doctor him. I can do combat first aid, but she's a nurse and much more gifted than I am or ever will be.

"Stop! If you take another step you're a dead man." I heard a voice just a little above a whisper say.

"Silverwolf, is that you? It's me and Kerr. He's taken a knife to the leg."

"Yep, it's me. We have a hell of a problem. I was out scouting the area, per Sandra's orders, and when I returned, I saw a group of nasty-assed people herding them away like cattle. John, I hate like hell to tell you this, but I think they were man-eaters."

"We just killed two of them and one got a knife into Kerr. Let's get a small fire started, let me sew him up and dress his wound. After that, we'll talk."

I heard a rustling of the bushes and when I swung around with my Bison, Dolly moved toward me and I saw blood on her rear right hip. I called her to me and looked her over, but the blood wasn't hers, so one of the attackers was likely hurt or killed.

"Well, I can show you where they were taken, if that helps. I followed them to Pearl and know exactly where they are."

"Let me care for Kerr and we'll decide how we want to do this. I'm afraid if I don't fix 'em up, he'll bleed to death shortly. He lost a lot of blood getting here."

"Well, they're safe enough for right now. Private Wamsley was on guard duty and they cut his throat. Once they secured everyone, they quartered his body to take with them, and I heard one mention he'd feed them for a few days. I don't see how in the hell people can carve folks up and eat them like a Christmas turkey."

"Get a fire started." I said and didn't need the gory reminder of what cannibals did to their victims.

"I'm feeling weak and dizzy all a sudden." Kerr said as he plopped down in the dirt where Silverwolf was making the fire.

"Symptoms of blood loss. I'll have you wrapped up in a bit." I replied as I pulled the Russian first aid kit from his belt.

I opened my pack, removed a curved needle and threaded it quickly. I then tore an alcohol pad open and wiped down the needle, thread, and my hands. Removing the old bandage, I wiped the area well with another alcohol pad and started sewing his stab wound close. I know I hurt him, but other than an occasional grunt I heard nothing from him.

As I worked, I said, "Tell me what you know of the ones who took our troops."

"Nasty looking bunch, filthy and they were over on the side of town where the high school is and camped in the woods there. I suspect they used to live in vacant houses or apartments, but Russians likely ran them out or scared them off."

"Which side of the school?"

"South side and in the trees."

"Okay, we'll go for them, but they have a lot of firepower since they now have the explosives and weapons our people had. How big a group?"

"A bakers dozen. I counted six women and seven men."

"We'll hide Kerr and we'll leave in a few minutes." I said as I tied the thread using a surgeons knot and then placed a square knot on top.

"H . . . how long will you be gone?" Kerr asked.

"I have no idea, but long enough to free those we can. It's not far, say an hour and half there, free our people, then the same time back. So, guessing, I'd say about four hours. I'll leave Dolly with you, so you'll be as safe as it gets."

"Were any shots fired here?" I asked Silverwolf.

"I think not, or I would have heard them. I didn't find any blood spots or signs of any of the others being injured or killed. The first thing cannibals do after a killing is to cut the throat of their victim, so they bleed out."

I shouldered my pack and said, "Let's move. If you have to move for any reason, Kerr, remember we'll be back in four or five hours." Then, meeting my big dog's eyes, I ordered, "Stay, Dolly. Stay."

"Good luck and kill a few for me. I have no use for man-eaters."

I gave him a thumb up and we moved into the darkness.

Once moving toward the high school, we broke into a slow jog that was just a little faster than a fast walk. It was something we did often in the field and it was a jog that could be maintained for hours without tiring the jogger.

A little over an hour later, I spotted a fire back in the woods and off north near the ruins of the school. It was as dark as a bankers heart, the moon hidden behind some thick snow or rain clouds as we moved toward the group. We'd agreed to circle the group and then meet north of the school to discuss what we found.

As I circled the group, I saw no sign of prisoners, but I did see them roasting human body parts over the fire. One complete leg was cooking, as well as an arm, and I found the smell offensive. I held my anger in and then moved toward the school. When I neared, Silverwolf was in the darkness and called my name softly, just above a whisper.

I moved to him, squatted and whispered, "I counted twelve, and you?"

He replied, "I counted thirteen, with one a guard near some shanties they likely sleep in. I suspect they keep prisoners in there."

"How do you want to handle this?"

"Use a couple of grenades, then rush them and kill the survivors. I think after we toss the grenades, my first shot will be the guard. You can back me, in the event I miss the shot."

"Okay, but I don't want to leave any alive, understood?"

Giving a low chuckle, he replied, "No one has much love for man-eaters, so I'll not complain about killing all of them."

"Let's move and try to toss the grenades in the middle, near the fire."

"I figured as much. Let's get this over with and I hope you understand, something will probably go wrong."

"I've thought of that. No matter what happens, we have to get my squad free. They'd try if we were prisoners."

He nodded, which I could barely see in the dim moonlight. Clouds had been moving overhead for hours and it'd snow, then stop, and then continue again. Right now, the snow had stopped, but it was still cold.

Finally, after thinking about the situation, I said, "Stay close to me at first, then once we enter camp, you move to the shanties. Let's pray they're in there."

"Let's get this over with." Silverwolf said and turned toward the cannibals.

We moved to the side nearest to the shelters and I could see some people in them, but with no light, they were just dark forms. We both pulled a Russian grenade and pulled the pins.

"Now." I whispered and toss my grenade almost into the fire and saw his land almost beside mine. Only one man near the fire seemed to notice anything and he seemed confused. A few short seconds later one grenade exploded, followed a split second later by the other. Along with the blast I heard loud screams and saw people falling. As soon as the smoke and dust from the explosion cleared the air, we both ran into camp, shooting anyone that moved.

A huge man and heavy too, ran right at me, holding a large butcher knife in his right hand. I swung my Bison toward him, gave the trigger a slight squeeze and saw long fingers of blood burst from his back. The man collapsed, his screams loud, but short lived. As I moved past him, I fired a couple of rounds into his head, splattering the ground behind him with brains and blood. The grenades had killed most, but three died hard, taking bullets into their fat bodies.

"All are here, except Wamsley and I suspect that's his leg roasting on the spit, because he was killed earlier."

My people moved from the shelters and Sandra ran into my arms, her relief clearly seen on her face.

"Oh, am I happy to see you, baby." she said and then kissed me.

"Are you okay?"

"I'm fine, but they raped Joyce a few times. I suspect they left me alone because I've been mutilated."

"Look her over and let me know if she's okay to move. I have no idea who heard all of this noise." I ignored her comment about the mutilation, and just because she was no longer beautiful didn't mean I didn't love her. I would talk to her about it later this night.

Silverwolf called out, "It looks like all of our gear and weapons are over here, covered by canvas. I also discovered a pit where bones and skulls were thrown after being eaten. Must be twenty folks in this pit."

"Everyone, look around and see if there is anything we need. I doubt there is, but you can never tell."

A few minutes later, Sandra neared and said, "She's pissed, but no serious physical damage was done to her."

"Alright, everyone, find your gear on the ground in front of the canvas, saddle up and let's move. I expect to have visitors any minute now. Hurry!"

Minutes later, Kelly called out, "I have headlights of three or four vehicles near the school."

"Let's go, and now!" I called out and moved for the woods.

We'd gone perhaps a half a mile when I heard the barking of a dog. I moved to Joyce, who had a night vision scope she could mount on her sniper rifle and said, "I want you and Arwood to remain behind to take that dog out. Take out as many Russians as you can too, but don't stay long. Remove the dog, raise some hell and then leave. Understood?"

She gave me a weak smile and said, "I'll do it. Arwood, you're to come with me."

As soon as she moved away with the Sergeant, I said, "Slow our pace down some and let her do her job."

We moved at a slower pace and few minutes later I heard the sharp crack of her rifle, followed by 5 more shots, all within about 15 seconds. Then silence.

CHAPTER 8

Ivanov paced in his large office, and was livid that a small group of armed peasants had forced him to remove some of his men away from the staging area for the pending chemical attack. Trains had been attacked, warehouses broken into; supplies stolen, Russian soldiers murdered and three small convoys were completely wiped out, with the soldiers all dead and all supplies taken. His frustration level was high, but knew the mass killing of Americans he'd ordered was probably what caused this mess to start with. It all started the day after the mass murder of the prisoners from the gulag.

Private Popolov stuck his head in the door and said, "Colonel, a Senior Sergeant on Colonel Vasiliev's staff just phoned and they found the remains of about a dozen civilians, man eaters is what he called them, in a small village called Pearl."

"Tell them to track the killers, if they can. I am sure no Russian troops attacked the man eaters. The more they eat the less we will have to fight and kill later."

"Uh, sir, they did track the attackers, but lost a dog, and five men, one of which was a Captain. The only survivor of the dog team reported they were all killed by sniper fire."

"You mean to tell me, a single person with a rifle, killed five of our men? Killed five highly trained Russian soldiers? What in the hell is going on? Call Vasiliev and tell him I want his arse in my office in ten minutes!" Then realizing he was asking a Private to give an order to a Lieutenant Colonel, he said, "Never mind, Private Popolov, I will handle this. Continue with your duties."

"Yes, sir." the Private replied, and then closed the door.

Opening his top right drawer on his desk, the Colonel pulled out a bottle of good vodka and poured a water glass half full. Then placing the opened bottle on his desk, he picked up the phone and said, "Give me Lieutenant Colonel Vasiliev's office."

Sitting in his overstuffed chair, he placed his feet up on the desk, held the phone to his left ear, and his vodka glass in his other hand.

"This is Colonel Vasiliev's office, Senior Sergeant Blankov speaking. How may I assist you?"

"This is Colonel Ivanov and I want to speak with your boss. Tell him it is urgent that we speak."

"Yes sir, please hold for a moment as I get him, sir."

A minute or so later, "This is Lieutenant Colonel Vasiliev, sir."

"Pasha, we have a problem. I consider it a big problem and I want answers."

"Ask, sir, and I will tell you what I know. However, keep in mind my information comes from my chief of intelligence, Major Sambor Borisovich, and I feel he is on top of things."

"I will judge how well your Major is doing, Colonel, by the answers you provide me."

"Yes, sir. What are your questions?"

"How in the hell did we lose five men and an expensive tracking dog to only one American?"

"This one American was a highly trained sniper and the shots were all made from a tree, and at a distance well over a thousand meters."

"Have our men not been trained to kill snipers? I can understand a sniper killing one man, but not five and a dog! I want you to get with Major Sokolov, the troop commander and find out what in the hell went wrong! Have the bodies been recovered?"

"Oh, yes, sir and each of the dead had an ace of spades in his mouth. Borisovich told me the partisan unit has been active since we first arrived here, sir."

"I have been briefed on them and I want all of them dead. Now, I want you and your staff to get off your lazy asses and start earning your pay, or so help me, Pasha, you will either end up missing or be placed in a gulag with the rest of the prisoners. I am sure, in a gulag, the prisoners will tear you apart in a matter of just a few short minutes. Do you fully comprehend what I want?"

"Yes, sir!"

"Then see it and do the job now."

"I will, sir." Vasiliev said and then the phone went dead. *That sonofabitch kills a thousand people and doesn't expect the resistance to retaliate?* he thought, and then called for a staff meeting.

An hour later, numerous squads were headed to the field, looking for the resistance group now called 'The Aces' by the Russian grunts. The weather was terrible, minus 12 degrees Celsius, snowing and with wind gust to 60 KPH. In the helicopter, Captain Vanya and his men were fighting to stay warm. Both doors were off the helicopter and the slipstream was cold. His group was to be the point for a much larger force searching for "The Aces," and he did not look forward to meeting the Americans. Like many of the lower ranking Russians, he was tired of this war, and while a veteran of many battles, he saw the American War as not winnable. Except as a professional soldier, his job was to follow orders and not question politics.

One of the gunners turned to him and held his hand up, showing 3 fingers. That meant in three minutes they'd land in the old football field at the Pearl High School. The Captain nodded in understanding.

As the chopper started it's descent a couple of minutes later, Vanya yelled for his men to lock and load their weapons. As his troops prepared for the landing, the Captain pulled his pistol and chambered a round. While he didn't expect any resistance when they landed, a smart soldier was always prepared for a fight.

When the wheels touched the long grasses of the field, the ground troops poured from the aircraft, and went into defensive positions once past the rotating blades overhead. As soon as all the men were unloaded, the helicopter pilot applied more power and the aircraft slowly rose into the air. Within a couple of minutes, it was quiet. Sergeant Ilyich and his dog, Anton, were waiting orders.

The radio man neared and handed the handset the Captain, who said, "That is correct, we took no ground fire and the landing zone is cold. I repeat, the landing zone is cold. Copy. Out." He handed the radio back and said, "Private Iona, you are on point and Private Melor, you bring up our rear. I want both of you a good 100 meters from the main group. Move to where the dog was killed first, Iona, and once we look around we will try to track the killers."

Iona moved forward, his eyes scanning the ground for trip wires, vines and mines, as he also attempted to scan the surrounding area to prevent ambush. His stress level was high, but after a few hours, someone else would rotate to his position and he'd be able to semi-relax. For right now though, he stayed alert and moved slowly.

The move to the spot where the dog was killed was uneventful and Iona was glad to take a small break as the Captain looked the area over closely. After a few minutes, he said, "Let us move now, but I want Private Melor beside the point man. Melor, I understand you were a trapper before you joined the army, correct?"

"Yes, sir."

"Can you track well?"

"Yes, I can track anything that lives. Do you have need of my skills, sir?"

"Soon you will see the tracks of the murderers who killed our men. I want you to follow them."

"If it can be done, I will do it, sir."

"Do the job professionally and you will not only get a quart of vodka, but a promotion to Junior Sergeant too. Our mission is important, so you may even get a medal from this, if you do it well."

Smiling, Melor moved forward with Iona, and together they moved down a little used trail. After a few hundred meters, Melor said, "There are nine of them all total, but here, one moved away from the group. I suspect this was the sniper. They are moving on this trail for a reason, so they must know the area well. We must use caution now, because they are at the point they will start to plant mines and booby-traps."

The Private grinned a little later when he saw the tracks of the sniper return to the others. By the shoe size, he knew the killer was a woman or a very young man, because the foot prints were small.

Half a mile later, Iona pointed to a thin fishing line stretched across the trail. Like he'd been trained, he stuck a stick in the middle of the trail for others to see the line and kept moving. Five minutes later he heard what sounded like a shotgun blast, followed by a piercing scream. As the team medic, Iona, left Melor on point and returned to the main unit.

Junior Sergeant Pavel was on the ground and blood was spurting from his groin area. The man had both hands over the injury, but wasn't even slowing the flow of crimson. Moving to the man, Iona gave Pavel a shot of morphine, pulled his medical bag forward and removed some bandages. Taking his scissors in hand, he began cutting the man's trousers off from around the wound.

He applied a bandage, wrapped the injury tightly and said, "He needs a helicopter to transport him to the hospital or he will die. I cannot stop the bleeding. He has lost both his penis and balls, as well as taken some buckshot in his lower stomach.

"Radioman, contact base and let them know we have a seriously injured man and require a helicopter now." Captain Vanya said.

"Yes, sir."

"How was he injured?" Iona asked.

Melor said, "The partisans had a trip wire across the trail, remember?"

"I still see the wire."

"The wire is connected to nothing except tied between two trees. Buried in the ground on the other side of the wire there were 12 gauge shotgun shells, resting on nails. Pavel stepped on one. Most of the time the shells have small pellets but this one had a buckshot. He took the blast in the groin area and you see the results." Melor said and then shook his head.

The Captain said, "Primitive at best, but it damned sure works."

The radioman said, "Base is diverting a helicopter to use and it should be here in about ten minutes. We have been requested to move to a clearing."

"Tell base we will be in a clearing off our left side."

"Yes, sir."

As they moved for the clearing, the dog alerted and Ilyich said, "Anton smells or senses danger this way. We need to move away and then approach the clearing from a different point."

"Move down about 30 meters and lets try there."

This time, the dog didn't alert and a few minutes later, the morphine now working, a sleepy Pavel was placed in the grass. It was then the *whop-whop-whop* of the helicopter blades were heard.

The radio man said, "They have us in sight and are coming in for the Sergeant."

When the helicopter was about 10 meters from the ground, a tree on the edge of the clearing seemed to explode and the chopper wobbled a bit and then continued down.

The radioman said, "The blast was caused by a mine with fishing line strung across the clearing. When the helicopter pulled the line as it came down to land, it exploded. Minor damage to the aircraft but they want Pavel loaded now."

The injured man was quickly loaded and off the helicopter flew.

"Melor on point and Ilyich, you are to be second. I want Private Varlam bringing up our rear. Let us move, we have spent too much time here." Senior Sergeant Yefrem said.

Senior Sergeant Yakovich Yefrem was a bear of a man, near 240 pounds, standing six foot six inches, and solid muscle. He mostly controlled his men through intimidation, because of his huge size. While always wearing a mean expression, he was a mild man on the inside and always took excellent care of his men. More than once in this war he'd prayed or talked with a much younger man, as he held his head in his lap, waiting for death. He'd lost a little of his heart as each man died. On the other side, he was a typical Senior NCO and allowed little nonsense in his unit. He was tough on his men, but always fair. His fairness had earned him deep respect from his subordinates.

"Move as the Senior Sergeant ordered." the Captain said as he realized he should have thought to give the order first.

The next few hours were uneventful but stress was hard on the man in front as they found a number of booby-traps. An hour before dusk, just as the Captain was about to stop for the night, Private Dima, who was on point returned and said in a whisper, "House about 30 meters from the woods; I see smoke coming from the metal stove pipe in the roof. Someone is in there."

"How many levels is this house?" Yefrem asked.

"Up and down. Two floors, Senior Sergeant, but a small house."

"You," the Senior Sergeant said to Melor, "take Private Varlam and circle the place. Take your time and look for any sign of ambushes. Once you return, if all is clear, we will check the house out. Now, move."

"What do you think?" the Captain asked as he met the Senior NCO's eyes.

"The place is likely occupied or booby-trapped. Either way, we must check it out."

"Do we just kick the door off the hinges and barge in?"

"Sir, no disrespect intended, but you were not going to knock were you?"

The Captain laughed and replied, "No, of course not, but I have little combat experience in this country."

"Have one of the men lob in a grenade and once it explodes, kick the door open and start killing. It is bloody sick work, but it kills well enough."

Ten minutes later, Melor returned and said, "Saw some tracks leading from the house to the woods, but it was not possible to tell how many people made them."

"Okay, when we get to the front door of the house, I will toss in a grenade. Once it explodes, then I want Private Yakim to kick the door in. Once the door is open, I want Ilyich, Iona, and Melor to check the second floor, while the rest of us will clear the bottom floor. Questions?"

Silence.

"Okay let us move and watch your distance between men. Hurry, it will be dark in about thirty minutes." the Captain said and then moved forward.

All went well going to the house, with no sign they'd been sighted. Yakim moved to the door, gave it a hard kick and a wall of fire erupted, with an explosion that knocked all of the men to their backs. Yakim lay on the porch screaming in pain as his blood spurted high into he air. Some men moaned, another screamed with the Private, and as the dust started to settle the Senior Sergeant stood. He moved toward Yakim and yelled, "Medic!"

He squatted beside the mangled man and knew at first glance the boy would soon be dead. Iona moved to the downed man, met the Senior Sergeant's eye's and shook his head. *Damn me*, the Senior Sergeant thought, *why did he not wait for me to throw a grenade in first? Why was he in such a hurry?*

"Give him enough morphine, so he feels no pain." Yefrem said and then moved to another downed man.

Iona gave Yakim a double dose of morphine and knew he was killing the man. His arms were blown off, one leg was gone and his intestines were loose ropes on the ground around him. He was whimpering like a wounded animal and calling for his mother. *This is another man Mother Russia will soon get home in a metal box*, Iona thought as he moved to the next man.

"Private Varnava!" The Captain screamed, "Take Private Varlam and check this house out and do the job properly. I suspect you will find no one, but for God's sake, watch what you touch and where you step. I am sure there are other traps."

"Y . . . yes, sir." Varnava said and then tapped Varlam on the shoulder.

The radioman neared and asked, "Should I contact base?"

"Wait until the hou—"

A loud explosion was heard on the second floor, followed a minute later by a pitiful warbling scream. The Captain and Senior Sergeant exchanges glances and then the officer said, "See what we have in there, Sergeant."

"Yes sir."

"How many men do you want?"

"None," The Senior Sergeant replied, "I only want to watch out for me and I do not need a beginner along."

Five long minutes passed after the Sergeant entered the building, but finally he called out to be heard over the screaming man, "Varlam is on the walls upstairs and not enough left of him to bury in a matchbox. Varnava is impaled in the chest with four vicious and long prongs. The ends are barbed, so I cannot just pull them out of him. He will bleed out shortly, sir."

The Captain said, "Iona, see that Varnava dies with no pain."

"Yes, sir."

"Senior Sergeant, I am sending the medic in to administer morphine to Private Varnava."

"Get in here and now, Iona, or he will not need you." the Senior Sergeant yelled to be heard once more.

"Radioman, contact base and let me speak with the ranking officer on duty."

"Yes, sir!"

Later this night, as the group ate rations around a small fire, the Captain said, "Colonel Vasiliev was very angry and grew madder when I reported we had yet to see a partisan. Three men out of action, dead, and one seriously injured is not good. We must think smarter if we are to win this war."

Senior Sergeant Yefrem laughed and then asked, "May I speak openly with you, sir?"

"Yes, of course and at all times, Sergeant. I respect you and value you opinion."

"We will not win this war and do you know why?"

"No, why not? I mean we have all the advantage."

"We lack the total dedication, sir."

"What do you mean?"

"I am sure you know military history and this will be our Vietnam War or more like our war in Afghanistan. The body count of dead Russian soldiers will continue to rise and then at some point a big bug in Moscow will say, enough is enough. It happened to the Americans in Vietnam and to us in Afghanistan. We will not lose the war, but the politicians will give it away. We cannot in my opinion, ever control this land until every American over the age of six is killed. These people have something that brings them together and allows them to put aside their differences and fight as a team."

"It is patriotism, Sergeant, and Lieutenant Smirnov was telling me of a man saying the pledge of allegiance to the American flag, just seconds before he was pushed from a truck to hang. They still hold on firmly to the belief their country will recover."

The Senior Sergeant spat into the flames of the dancing fire and said, "It very well might, sir."

"I do not see patriotism winning a war."

"Oh? They do not need to beat us, sir, just kill enough of us and we will be brought home. It is all about the cost in Russian lives and not financial cost. The partisans started this war fighting with hunting rifles, bows and arrows, clubs, and even rocks. Over time, they have stolen gear from our warehouses, supply convoys, and our dead. Except for aircraft and armor, they are almost equal to us in gear, because it is our gear they are using. They are experts at booby-traps, fearless, and totally dedicated to killing us."

"Moscow presents the partisans as ignorant peasants and psychopathic killers."

"And, sir, some may be, but most are prior hunters or military veterans and a hard bunch for some Russian kid off the farm to deal with. I have nothing against Americans as a people or individuals, but I am a soldier and go where I am told. I also kill those I am ordered to kill, but I do not do the job out of hate."

"Then, why are you a soldier?"

Senior Sergeant Yelfrem gave a weak smile and said, "I grew up in the country, sir, and did not want to spend my life as a farmer. Of course, my parents lacked the money for me to attend college, so my only option was military service."

"You have done well, with many promotions and medals."

"In the army, along with promotion comes additional responsibility, which most fail to understand. I have both a legal and moral responsibility to my men and women."

"Moral? I do not understand that aspect." the Captain said and then opened a can of goulash.

"Most of these young men are how old, sir? Eighteen to twenty?"

"I would guess about that, yes." He placed his can near the hot coals of the fire.

"I have been in the army longer than most of these people have been alive. I consider myself both a mother and father to my troops. I teach them, worry about them and I am happy when one of them does well. I am proud of most of them, but take today, I am deeply saddened by the deaths of Varnava, Yakim, and Varlam, because they were my boys. Each time one is killed, I cry over it, because maybe in some way I might have prevented their deaths. I wonder if I failed to teach or tell them something that might have kept them alive."

"Men and women are killed in wars, Senior Sergeant." The Captain began eating the greasy meal with a plastic spork.

"Yes, sir, they do, but in most cases it is because we, we in leadership, have failed to teach them what they needed to know to stay alive. Just a few short years ago, these men were still in school, sir, but now they are making decisions that can cost them their very lives, as well as the lives of their fellow soldiers. War is no game, it is for keeps."

Finishing his meal, the Captain placed his empty tin in his pack, turned to the radioman and asked, "Did you call in our exact over night location?"

"Oh, yes sir, and over an hour ago. I got the coordinates from the Senior Sergeant, Captain."

Yefrem said, "Men, we keep the same guard roster as before, but with the number of dead we had today, we will add an extra hour to each shift. Now, let me warn you all, if I catch you sleeping on guard duty, I will have your ass sent to a gulag or cut your throats. Your buddies will be depending on you, so do the task properly. Now, get to your sleeping bags and get some sleep. Iona, since you are my first guard, move into the shadows and try not to move much."

The medic, tired after a full day of trying to save lives, cursed the army in his mind as he moved under a large pine. He sat un-moving for a long period of time, but nothing ever happened on the first shift, it was always in the middle of the night, so finally he relaxed. It was about an hour after everyone went to their sleeping bags that he heard a faint noise. *There it is again and it is big*, he thought. He brought his AK up and waited.

It was bitterly cold, but the moon was up and while it helped a little, it wasn't bright enough for him to see much. Then he saw a patch of brown. *It has to be a partisan sneaking up on us, so I need to shoot him. If I save us from ambush they will give me a medal and momma will be so proud*, he thought. He aimed at the brown color, took a deep breath, and as he released the air, he began to squeeze the trigger. His shot was loud in the still night air, so he fired twice more. There was no returning fire.

In camp, Russians were flying from their sleeping bags and donning their night vision goggles, NVG's, in order the meet this threat. The Captain was shouting orders and troops were running in all directions.

"Iona, are you safe?" yelled the Senior Sergeant.

"Yes Sergeant! I saw something brown moving."

"Brown?"

"I am not sure what the brown was, but I saw a partisan."

"Why no return fire?" the Captain asked.

Standing, Yefrem moved to Private Iona, and then asked, "Where did you see it?"

"About forty meters in front of me."

"I will look and see what you have killed. Remain here and do not shoot again, unless attacked."

"I understand."

Ten minutes later the Senior Sergeant returned laughing. Once in camp he said, "Our guard killed a very nice whitetail deer. I suggest we all take some meat so we will at least have something different for supper tomorrow. The meat will keep well at this temperature and last for days."

Private Iona lowered his head in shame.

CHAPTER 9

I'd heard the explosions when the booby-traps in the house went up and knew we'd cost the Russians some men. I didn't care if we'd hurt them or killed them, as long as I created casualties for them. I didn't know any Russians before the war, don't hate them, but they want my country and I will not allow that to happen. Until they leave, I'll kill and maim as many as possible to show them the tenacity of the average American. I'm no Rambo or John Wayne, just a normal man who is tired, hungry most of the time, and sick of killing. I'd love to have my old country back, but when we started borrowing money from other countries, knowing we couldn't pay it back, we determined our fate. Within four years, we were gone as a nation.

"Crossroad ahead of us and a machine-gun crew, along with a big ass tank. Do I go around or what?" Silverwolf asked.

"Go around. We have one injured and the rest are too tired to fight."

"Sure," he said with a smile, "because I don't like tangling with tanks. One mistake and they'll turn us into hamburger."

"They'll not bother us, because Private Walsh is carrying a flamethrower and no one wants to burn to death."

Grinning, he said, "I'd still bet on the tank. I'll take us to the left and then back about a half a mile to cross a macadam road. I don't think it would be smart to cross where they can see us."

I glanced at the sun, saw it was almost dark and said, "Get a wiggle on and lets get this done before it's completely dark."

"Will do, so follow me." Silverwolf began to move.

As we moved, I gave thought to the tank and machine-gun and decided that later tonight, *I'll return with the Russian speaking Corporal Scott and Private Walsh. If I can get close enough, I need to take the gun and tank out of action.*

Crossing the road was easy and we weren't seen. I then moved into some trees, pulled out my binoculars and scanned the cross-roads. I counted three men with the machine-guns and three with the tank. With a lot of luck we might be able to pull this off, especially if we attacked at night. Since we were mostly dressed in Russian uniforms anyway, that might confuse them just long enough for us to

get close enough to kill them.

I moved back to my people and said, "If you want to eat, eat it cold. No fires and yes, I realize it's cold. From what I saw earlier, snow is likely before dawn, so I suggest you crawl up under a tree to keep dry."

No one grumbled much, so I walked to Scott and said, "Near midnight you, Walsh, and I will try to take out that machine-gun and tank."

"Have you lost your mind?"

"Not at all, why?"

"Hell, the machine-gun alone will shoot us to rag dolls."

"Not if you call out to them in Russian first. Once we get close, take the machine-gun out and then the tank."

"I know you're in charge, but what if I don't want to do this? Damn it, this is insane."

"You'll follow orders," I said and then pulled my pistol, "or I'll shoot you now."

He glared into my eyes and something convinced him I was serious, and I was. I thought we had a better than average chance of pulling this off. Every time I found a tank, I attempted to take it out.

"You would kill me, wouldn't you?"

"Oh, yeah, and not think much about it either. See, I don't have much use for a coward and I've been watching you, Scott. In every battle or fight I've seen you in lately, you hang back just enough to be a little safer. Well, tonight my friend you'll lead us right to the Russian gun and if you don't, I will shoot you, if they don't."

I then moved to Sandra, squatted, and asked, "How are all of them?"

"Fine, except Joyce, who as you know was raped, so her mind is wasted. She's a strong woman, but it'll be years before she can put this behind her, if ever."

"I don't understand, because she's doing all that's expected or asked of her, and I don't see her acting strange or depressed."

"It really hasn't hit her yet, or I don't think it has. Keep her busy and then she'll have a better than average chance of not losing her mind over this. Yes, it happens to some women. Then, she may be pregnant, too."

Standing I moved to Joyce and said, "Tonight near midnight, I'm going for the machine-gun nest and the tank. I want you to come along to help protect us from a long distance. Are you up to doing the job?"

"You bet, and you can be sure if one of them makes sudden move, he's a dead man."

"Good, I suspected I could count on you, now get some rest."

"I will." She pulled a sleeping bag from her pack.

It was a little before midnight when Scott yelled out something in Russian to the machine-gun crew. At first the three men moved behind the stacked sandbags and made the gun ready. Scott kept talking. Finally, a tall thin Russian replied.

"What did he say?" I asked.

"He said for us to come to them and not to make any sudden moves."

"Agree with him and tell him there are only three of us."

Scott called out and a few seconds later the Russian replied.

Standing, Scott said, "Come on, it's okay."

I was apprehensive, but stood beside him, and then Walsh stood. The Russian called out and Scott whispered, "He said come on, he has some vodka for us."

We then moved slowly toward the machine-gun nest. I relaxed a little when the gunner stood and leaned against the tank.

The walk was short, barely 25 yards, but it felt as if it were miles. I started sweating, my palms itched, and I could hear my heart beating in my chest.

When we were close, Walsh raised the barrel of the flamethrower and sent a short spurt of flame toward the three men. One man gave a loud scream, followed by a hideous cry, and moved around engulfed in flames. One man fell unmoving, but afire and the last man moved for the machine-gun, his left arm in flames. I heard nothing, but suddenly his head snapped back and almost exploded as a high powered round from Joyce took him in the face. Blood flew in all directions.

As the last man fell, we ran forward and climbed onto the tank. I found the top hatch closed, but not locked and pulled it wide open. Walsh leaned over the sent a long string of flames into the tank and we could hear the crew screaming.

"Run for the woods!" I yelled and then heard another shot. Glancing down at the drivers hatch I found it open and the dead driver laying halfway out, his upper torso in flames. Joyce had killed again. I jumped from the tank and took out running as fast as I could for the wood line. Just as I reached the trees, the ammo and fuel started cooking off in the tank. We continued moving once in the trees and I wanted some distance before the tank blew.

There suddenly came a bright light, followed a split second later by a loud explosion. When I looked over my shoulder, I saw a red and yellow ball of flames rolling into each other. I kept the men moving and a few minutes later, Joyce moved in beside me.

"I shot two." she said, her joy obvious.

"Two confirmed kills."

"Good, only fifty more to go."

"Fifty more to go? What does that mean?" I asked. I tried to see her eyes, but it was too dark.

"After I was raped by the cannibals, I promised fifty-two men would die for my pain. I have no idea where the number fifty-two came from, it just entered my mind."

"Those men were Russians, not cannibals."

I heard a low laugh and then she replied, "If it has a penis and is our enemy, he's a dead man, if I can get the cross-hairs lined up on him. I want fifty-two men to die for my rape."

"Enough talk, let's move a bit faster," I said. I could understand her rage and urge to kill all men, but let's hope that's all there was to it or trouble would come. Some women want to kill all men after being raped, while others withdraw completely. I didn't want or need any problems with her over something the cannibals did. *I need to have Sandra talk with her and feel her out*, I thought and then glanced at her. She wore a determined grimace on her face and it worried me.

Two days later, we were lined up about a hundred feet from Interstate Highway 20, on the north side, just prior to the last Pearl exit. Kerr was with us now and was healing nicely, but walked with a crude crutch made from a tree limb. Dolly was at my side. I had word a small convoy of two trucks and a motorcycle would be along just before dark, coming from Alabama. I had been instructed to stop the trucks and take all the supplies I could, or destroy what I couldn't take.

Arwood neared and said, "They'll be here in a bit. I just caught a glimpse of them in the binoculars as they drove over an incline." I scratched my dogs ears absentmindedly, and for a second thought of my other dogs, killed years back.

"Wait for me to take the cyclist out before you all start firing." I reminded my troops.

A few seconds later, I heard, then saw the motorcycle nearing. The driver was moving slowly, just a bit over 25MPH would be my guess, and I wanted him slightly past me before I killed him.

When he was right in front of me, I raised Joyce's sniper rifle, and the cross-hairs were lined up in the center of his shoulders. I fired. He fell from the bike, but it kept moving for another twenty feet before it fell on it's side and sent a shower of bright sparks in the air as the foot pegs dug into the pavement. I handed her rifle back to her and said, "Cover us, and if a man moves down there when we approach, take him out."

"Will do." she said and then smiled.

Rifles barked and grenade launchers coughed, as automatic weapons zipped bullets into the cabs of the trucks. Screams were heard and a squad of men jumped from the second truck only to be cut to pieces by our machine-gun fire. The first truck, I suspected the driver was already dead, suddenly turned sharply on it's side and slid down the highway.

"To the trucks, now!" I screamed as I stood.

Moving toward the vehicles, I heard little resistance from the enemy, and at the first truck I found the men in the cab dead, with one fatally injured man soldier under the rear wheels. I could see his lower body was broken and twisted and the wheels were on his chest. I shot him in the head.

Silverwolf soon approached and said, "Seventeen dead Russians, while we had two injuries. Joyce took a slug to the thigh, except it just burned her, and Kelly took a round through his left arm. Sandra is doctoring them up now."

"What's in the trucks?" I asked.

"Crates, but I can't read Russian."

I yelled, "Scott!"

"Yo!"

"I need you to find out what's marked on the crates in both trucks, then let me know."

"Will do, but it may take some time."

"Sure, you have ten minutes."

"I can't read all the cra—"

"Ten minutes, understand?"

"Yes, sir." He then moved to the first truck.

"Strip the dead of anything we can use." I ordered as I looked at the damage my troops had done to the trucks. A few stray rounds had struck the cargo areas, but a good 90% of the shots were in the cabs. Silverwolf walked to me and said, "I have a couriers pouch from the dead motorcyclist and maybe Scott can make heads or tails out of this stuff."

"Bring it with you and Scott can read it to the Colonel, because I'm sending him back later with some other intelligence paperwork. I don't think he's cut out to be a field soldier and besides, his language skills are needed more at headquarters. There is more to being a soldier than hating our enemy."

Crates were being unloaded as Scott walked to me and said, "Most of these crates are shoulder fired missiles. There are cases and cases of the 9K32 Strela-2M missiles or as the Russians call them Arrows. All I know about them is; they are a portable, shoulder-fired, low-altitude surface-to-air missile system with a high explosive warhead. I think they have an infrared guidance system of some sort, but they should each come with information on them. Most of the boxes are simply marked, **9K32 Strela-2M Arrow**."

"I don't care about anything else now, but we must have the missiles. Can the truck that remained upright be driven?"

Walsh replied, "I was an auto mechanic for a few years, let me check it out and see."

"Hurry, because I suspect if the Russians were notified by radio from one of these trucks, we'll soon have Black Shark Helicopters overhead. I want to be a long way from here before choppers arrive."

I heard the engine grinding, prayed it would start, because we could raise real hell with surface to air missiles. *Start, damn you, start*, I thought.

The engine gave a loud backfire and the engine started.

"Load all the crates into the truck and let's move, and now!" I yelled, happy the truck would at least take the heavy load part of the way.

"Better hurry too, the radiator is leaking a bit and I'm not sure how many miles I can get out of this thing before the engine quits!" Walsh said.

Five minutes later, we were bouncing over a rough field moving toward a tree line. I wanted to get as close to Colonel Lee as I could, without compromising his location. I'd already sent Silverwolf ahead on the Russian motorcycle to inform the Colonel of our discovery, asking him to send more men to move the missiles away from the truck.

We'd just entered the trees when I heard a chopper fly over us, then two more, obviously moving toward the ambush sight. I couldn't see what kind of birds they were, but the whop-whop-whop of the blades told me they were helicopters. We were now on a badly rutted logging road and while the ride was rough, I smiled. *Missiles; we can start downing choppers now and do the job right. If the missiles did have an infrared guidance system we might even be able to take out a low-altitude jet or two*, I thought and it filled me with excitement.

"The temperature gauge is going up, so the radiator is hot." Walsh said.

"If we had some duct tape, we could fix it." Sandra said and then added, "It's the redneck in me, because you can fix anything with duct tape." She then laughed.

We all laughed and then Walsh said, "There's stream about a quarter mile from here. We'll stop and I'll top off the radiator with water. That should allow us to get a few more miles out of this thing before the engine seizes on me."

"Try to park under the trees, if you can. I know the tracks of this thing can been seen clearly from the air. The trees shield us well, but on a field we leave a trail even a child could follow even from the air. And, Walsh?"

"Sir?"

"I think your effort today earns you the rank of Sergeant, effective right now. These missiles are extremely important to the resistance and will hurt the Russians dearly."

"I just got lucky and knew how check a few things, and can drive this truck. Not many can drive them due to the frequent gear shifting that's required. Hell, most folks these days, or just before the fall, couldn't drive a stick shift to start with."

"Steam is coming from under the hood now." Sandra pointed out.

"She's hot, see the gauge? But I see the stream in front of us, so I'll pull over under those are pines and oaks."

"Good. We need a few miles more out this truck and then we can relax a little." I said as I opened the door and stepped out onto a running board. I pulled the canvas back and yelled, "Silverwolf, Walsh is now a Sergeant. We'll stop in the few minutes and refill the radiator with water.

"Not a problem, sir. We'll be ready and there are two metal buckets filled with sand back here, being used as as butt-cans, that should work fine."

We no sooner stopped the big deuce and half, and I had security established, than Scott neared with a Russian radio in his hands. "They want to know where we are, sir."

"Tell them when the partisans attacked we drove off the road and into the woods. Hell, they can see that much from the air. Tell them we'll circle around and return to Edwards as soon as we can."

"I'll try but they may want us to stop in some field and wait for them."

"Stall them, Scott, and do the best you can."

"Yes, sir."

Walsh opened the hood and then said, "Everyone move back. I'm going to loosen the radiator cap and the damned thing might fly into the air. If it does, scalding water will fly in all directions." He gave the cap a half twist and steam instantly shot into the air, from around the still in place cap. As I listened to the hiss of the steam, I noticed Silverwolf returning from the stream with both buckets filled with water. He sat them on the ground by the front bumper and said, "Plenty of water in the creek, so that's no problem."

"I'm not sure how well I fooled the Russians, but I know I've stalled them for a bit. They wanted the name of the truck driver, so I gave them my Russian name, Ivan Bulgakov. It's a somewhat common Russian name. When they said I wasn't listed on the manifest as a driver, I told them the normal driver got sick and I was unlucky enough to get selected."

"Good," I replied.

"But, once they call Jackson and learn there is no driver by that name assigned to the unit, they'll know I'm a Russian speaking American. Eventually, they'll come for us and this truck."

"That'll have to work then and we'll worry about the Russians later, after this truck dies."

Taking a rag in hand, Walsh removed the cap and water bubbled up and over the radiator. In just a few seconds it receded but the bubbling was still clearly heard. Water was slowly added, which stopped the gurgling and within a few short minutes we were once again moving down the logging road, being jarred in all directions inside the blood-stained cab.

CHAPTER 10

A week later, Senior Sergeant Morozov was up and moving around now, his injury painful, but not overly so. He kept a full flask of vodka on his person at all times, but used it only when his pain grew to be too much for him. He was standing at attention during a staff meeting as Colonel Ivanov pinned a couple of medals on him and promoted him to the rank of Master Sergeant, back dated to the day of his unit's annihilation by the American partisans. While the medals meant little to him, the promotion would result in his retirement pay jumping up considerably.

"Gentlemen, you see standing before you a true hero of Mother Russia. As the citation I read stated this brave man, then Senior Sergeant Morozov, tried very hard to return his leader to base alive, but was unable to do so, and his efforts were in vain. Lieutenant Smirnov was later killed. Good men like this man are hard to find and we need many more like him. Gentlemen, our newest Master Sergeant."

From the back of the room, when everyone applauded, Master Sergeant Fedorovo gave a loud whistle. He then broke into a big smile. *By God, he deserves higher ranking medals, but the promotion is a good thing too*, he thought as he waited for the ceremony to end. He had a bottle of vodka back in his room, just waiting for two Master Sergeants to celebrate.

As the Colonel moved toward the door, Fedorovo yelled from the very pit of his stomach, "Teeen-huuut!"

Everyone in the room stood at attention and once the Colonel was gone, they lined up to shake hands with the units newest Master Sergeant.

Soon, since it was early evening, they were in Fedorovo's quarters, with Morozov sitting in the lone chair and the Master Sergeant seated on his bed. The quart bottle of vodka was open and both men held a glass of the clear alcohol in their hands.

"So, when do they say you can come back to work?"

"They have said nothing to me at all, but I am not to return to even limited duty without the doctor's approval."

"You, Taras, are Master Sergeant now, and can do what the hell you want to do. However, with that said, only an order or an emergency should make you return to duty. You will soon retire and you do not want to live in pain from not following some doctor's orders. Also, you will only go into the field when something serious comes up, so most of your time now will be much safer than at any point of your career to date."

"What am I to do until released for duty?"

"Wait for me to find you a spot first. I know you want to run a combat unit, and right now all are full, but some are run by Senior Sergeants, and I will not give you a problem position either. I will try my best to give you a good unit."

"Thanks, Stas." He poured them both another drink.

"Taras, let us get you back in shape and healthy, and then I will find a good spot for you. Only about 2% of all enlisted become Senior Sergeants, and only 1% of the total enlisted force become a Master Sergeant. You currently have more power and authority than most officers, but keep in mind, you have a responsibility to use both carefully and properly."

Throwing his drink back, Morozov stood and said, "I need to get some sleep. The drink and my pain pills make me tired."

"Well, welcome to the world of a Master Sergeant, and I am proud of you. Let me walk with you to your new quarters, because I need to check my mail."

They stepped outside and it was cold, but both turned to see a Black Shark helicopter raising into the air. As they watched something flew from the grasses around the base and struck the aircraft, which exploded into a huge ball of flames.

"My God did you se—" Morozov started to say when a black dot instantly appeared on the bridge of his nose and the back of his head exploded, sending crimson blood and shards of bone flying out behind him. Before he struck the ground another bullet entered his chest and blew a large chunk of his spine out his back.

"Sniper!" Master Sergeant Fedorovo yelled and a quick glance confirmed his friend was dead.

Sirens began to cry their loud warbling warning to all on the base, but for Morozov, they were too late. His mangled body lay on the ground in a growing pool of blood, his system almost completely shutdown, except for his right index finger, which kept twitching.

The Master Sergeant stood and then ran a zig-zag course for headquarters to see if they were under a full scale attack or just a probe. Tracer rounds, some were red, orange, green, and violet, zipped low overhead. They flew through the air in a way Fedorovo found pretty, but he knew they were as deadly as hell.

Near the door of the headquarters building he found a dead guard, struck in the head by something that had taken half his skull away. He moved inside and discovered absolute chaos. Men and women were hustling around and some were even running with written orders in their hands.

He entered the combat control center and found phones ringing and orders being shouted as Colonel Ivanov stood chain smoking. He watched as the man rubbed one cigarette out and lighted another. *This is no probe*, he thought as he moved to the Commander.

"Master Sergeant Fedorovo, I need you to move near the fence at the Gulag! Colonel Kuznetsov reports the partisans have breached the fences with explosives, and most of his prisoners are gone or dead. Then check all of our other positions and help out where you can."

"Yes, sir!" he replied and then moved from the building. Outside the door he stripped the dead soldier of his Bison sub-machine gun, ammunition, grenades and other needed gear. He stayed on the main road, but jogged as he moved. Finally, a large flatbed truck zoomed by him at a high rate of speed, only to be struck by a rocket propelled grenade. It exploded with a huge fireball and screams were heard for a minute or so coming from the cab. As he ran past the truck, he could see three dead bodies sitting in the flaming seat, all burned black, and unmoving.

The run to the gulag wasn't far, and when he arrived, partisans were moving all over the compound and Russian bodies covered the ground. Angry that the Base Commander had stripped the gulag of men for his upcoming gas attack and left a minimal number of guards, the Master Sergeant ran to a Russian Captain with a radio man. Jumping in the hole, Fedorovo yelled to be heard over the gunfire, "Give me the damned radio!"

When the radio man looked at the Captain for approval, the officer took a round through his chest that splattered blood on everyone behind him. He collapsed unmoving to the bottom of the hole. The radio man handed the radio to the Master Sergeant.

"Base operations! I need anything you have in the air to drop what it is carrying on the gulag and do it now. Repeat, the gulag has been overrun, so hit it with what ever is in the air."

"Stas, is that you? This is Petov, so best of luck, my friend. On the way, but get your head down."

The Master Sergeant stood and screamed, "Get down, now!"

Two fast moving jets began an even, slow dive toward their target and at the bottom of their dives, they each released two canisters of napalm. The containers tumbled through the air, with one striking the prisoner barracks and the others in a large field. All of the canisters erupted into huge fireballs and waves of the burning liquid flew high and then dropped on those running from the flames. Soon, men and women, along with children, could be heard screaming pitifully as they stumbled around inside the fire.

From just outside the gulag wire, a missile was launched as the jets pulled up and the lead aircraft, flying too low to take any serious avoidance maneuvers took the missile right up his exhaust pipe and exploded into a huge fireball in the sky. The pilot ejected at the last second, but as he descended in his parachute, the nylon in his parachute canopy was soon burning. Between the fireball and the napalm, the Master Sergeant knew one had ignited the material. He watched in morbid fascination, as the chute began to burn and a few seconds later the pilot fell like a rock to his death.

Two Russian soldiers, in foxholes nearest the gulag, stood and began stumbling around fully engulfed in flames, their movements almost comical, if not for their piercing screams of anguish. Fedorovo stood and sent a burst from his Bison into both men. They fell unmoving.

The aircraft wreckage began to land on parts of the gulag and the Master Sergeant watched as a piece of a wing landed, along with a wheel. It rained metal for a few minutes and glancing up, he spotted the remaining jet high up.

The radio came alive, "Stas, are you still there?"

"I am here, Petov; have the next attack with guns or missiles about fifty meters from the far fence on the south side."

"Be advised the partisans have surface to air shoulder-fired missiles. The next strike will be low and fast. The pilot states he will be moving from your left to right, near supersonic speeds, so bury your asses in your holes. He will make one pass, using his Gatling gun and then will return to base to refuel and rearm. Copy?"

"He had better hurry, or the gulag will be under new management in about ten minutes."

"He is coming in hot and ready now!"

"Copy and out." Standing amid the flying bullets, the Master Sergeant screamed, "Get down now!"

Suddenly, there came a sound like a long giant zipper was being jerked down and clumps of dirt, sticks and rocks, flew twenty feet in the air. Partisans screamed as body parts were blown from torsos and a fine red mist mixed with rolling dust rose to the sky. Bodies jerked and danced as the impact of bullets threw each partisan in many different awkward directions, all at the same time. Fedorovo looked over the edge of his hole and saw a human head fly high in the air.

This time there was no missile fired and the Master Sergeant thought it was because the aircraft had flown by too quickly. A Russian machine-gun crew opened up and row after row of partisans were struck. The gunner was good, too, because his tat-tat-tat was limited to just a few seconds on the trigger. Long bursts would soon heat a barrel to the point bullets would fly in all directions.

Glancing down the slight hill, the Master Sergeant saw a huge crowd of partisans moving toward him and his men. *It does not look good*, he thought as he picked up the radio and asked, "Petov, are you still there?"

"I am here."

"I need help, my friend, and now; if you have anything, send it to me. I estimate maybe a thousand partisans about fifty meters from the gulag fence line."

"Let me check I what I have in the air."

"For God's sake, hurry!"

A minute passed and then Petov said, "I have two Black Sharks that will be over your position shortly. They will make a number of passes from left to right using machine-guns and missiles. One has you visually right now, so get your heads down!"

"Down!" Fedorovo screamed and few seconds later he heard the guns on the Black Shark firing, screams from the dying and injured, and the high pitched whine of the helicopters turbine engines. The helicopter made two more passes and then flew off to rearm and refuel. The second aircraft arrived seconds later.

"Stay down!" the Master Sergeant yelled once more as he watched the helicopter fly overhead and line up for a pass on the partisans.

Seconds later, four loud explosions were heard, along with distant screams, and when he peeked over the edge of his foxhole, he saw nothing but four clouds of dust. The helicopter was seen lining up for another pass, when a rocket zoomed from ground level, struck the aircraft hard near the engine and it began to auto-rotate to the ground in flames from the cockpit back. The helicopter landed hard on its side, near the Russians forces, and a squad burst from the trenches in an effort to save the pilots. One man was pulled from the wreckage and another exited the co-pilots compartment in flames. He stumbled a few feet and then fell to his knees. Seconds later he fell to his side, dead. Of the ten who ran forward to rescue the pilots, six, including the injured pilot returned alive.

"Here they come!" yelled someone off to the left of the Master Sergeant.

Glancing down the hill he saw partisans running toward them and they looked like ants, because the distance was great.

Picking up the phone he said, "Petov, I need anything you have!"

"I have some artillery, if you want it."

Fedorovo quickly read off the coordinates and said, "Now, read that back to me."

Less than a minute later, he said, "Okay, fire for effect, and now!" Then looking around at his soldiers he shrieked, "Get down!"

He heard the scream of the first shell and buried his head in the dirt. At times the coordinates were off and when that happened, men and women died. The explosions were loud, and glancing up he saw more bodies now on the ground. The screams of the injured and dying partisans were clearly heard on the hill.

"Petov, mix a little white phosphorous (WP) in with the shells! It will be good if you can do this!"

Minutes later the white phosphorous shells landed and the hot shrapnel burned white zig-zags into the air. As long as the WP had air, it would burn, which made it a terrible weapon to use on people. The injured could only stop the burning and lessen damage, by covering the wound with mud or removing the shrapnel. The screaming partisans grew louder and then they began to withdraw.

Petov changed the range as the resistance began to retreat. Finally, the partisans broke and ran for the distant trees, and the Russian NCO had the trees pounded by the big guns.

Finally, he called Petov and said, "Cease fire, I repeat, cease fire."

Standing, he called out, "Who is the ranking man still alive?"

"That would be me, I think, Master Sergeant." a thin and lanky Senior Sergeant said.

"Get your ass over here with the radio." He grabbed the dead radioman by his shirt collar and pulled him from the hole. He then rolled the dead Captain from the hole next and finally asked, "What is your name?"

"I am called, Alkaev. Adrian Alkaev, Master Sergeant."

" Alkaev, you are a senior NCO, so you need to start acting like one and be an example for your troops."

"We are cooks, bakers, paper-pushers, and mechanics, not combat soldiers. We were rounded up and told to defend this area. This was the first time in my life, well, that I have fired a weapon in combat."

Great, a bunch of people who have no idea how do defend themselves, the Master Sergeant thought and then said, "The radio is set to talk with someone who will try to give you air support, only keep in mind, sometimes they cannot help you. I am supposed to be looking at how the rest of the base is doing too."

"I understand and think we can hold on to what we have. We will be fine."

Master Sergeant Fedorovo nodded, climbed from the foxhole and made his was toward the fuel storage area, only he never got there. There came a huge explosion that actually hurt his ears and then he saw the fuel storage tanks cooking off one after the other; he turned away. He was too late and moved toward the flight line.

Tracers zipped through the air as helicopters were landing and taking off. Refueling and arming were taking place at the same time, which was usually not done for safety reasons, but the partisans were making a big push, so safety went out the door.

Refueling trucks were moving all over the flight line and aircraft were all over the field. Some aircraft were in flames, some on their sides, but most were waiting for fuel and bullets. One truck of fuel had the cab stitched with a row of bullets and with the driver dead, it continued on until it struck a parked helicopter getting ready for take off. The crew ran from the aircraft just before the collision and wisely so, because when they collided, a big fire ball resulted, and the flames rolled and rolled as they moved for the sky. Then ammo began going off and everyone ran for cover.

"RPG or LAW got the fuel truck," a Major who was behind the sandbags with Fedorovo said, and then pulled a flask from his coat pocket. He guzzled a bit and handed it to the Master Sergeant who downed a healthy amount.

"I have never seen this many of the resistance in one place at one time, sir." the Sergeant said.

"This is being done, I think, to make Ivanov pull his troops back to protect this base and to prevent him from using the nerve gas he has planned to spray."

"I have no idea why it is being done, but there are one hell of a lot of them. In the last staff meeting, intelligence stated there were fewer than 3,000 resistance fighters in the whole state. If that is true, sir, every one of the bastards are attacking us right now."

A bullet hit the concrete by his right leg, which made the Sergeant jerk his leg, as the projectile zinged off into space. He could not see the attackers, but he knew they could easily blow the perimeter wire and overrun them, but hadn't for some reason. *They have a reason*, Fedorovo thought. He glanced around the base and saw many fires were burning and bodies, mostly Russian, covered the ground. He shook his head at the senselessness of even being here, but he was a soldier and went when and where ordered.

A loud explosion was heard along the perimeter fence and then screaming partisans ran for the aircraft hangers. Russian machine-guns chattered, as rifles banged and pistols popped. A helicopter flew over head, banked hard and lined up for an attack.

The Americans were crossing the open field between the runway and the taxiway when a stray round bounced off the concrete, struck Master Sergeant Fedorovo in the head, and down he went. His world was instantly black.

CHAPTER 11

My squad held just outside of the airfield fence to cover the attacking forces with the new single man-fired surface to air missiles. I found them easy to use, and I'd been able to down two choppers early in the attack. I'd fired at a jet too, but it was just too fast, and by the time my rocket was airborne the jet was in a steep climb and moving double-quick. I think I missed because I'd been leading the bird and when he pulled the nose up to climb, I'd fired at that moment.

"Tanks! They've brought out the armor!" I heard Sandra yell to be heard over the noise of battle.

I knew then we'd soon be withdrawn from this battle. Oh, we could fight the big beasts, but in the long run we'd have to run off like a scared dog, with our tails between our legs. We just didn't have anything effective against them. The best we could hope for in most cases was to blow a track off and then the tank was still far from being helpless. I don't like the big brutes and never have, because unless you can hit one in the ass where the armor is the thinnest, they're hard to put out of action while moving.

"If we had enough flamethrowers, by God, we'd fight 'em!" Walsh said from beside me.

He was correct, but only to a point. A man with a flamethrower had to get in close, saturate the tank with burning fuel, and that was hard to do. Then, the crew of the tank didn't burn to death, but suffocated as the flames consumed the oxygen within the heavy vehicle. Besides, I think the whole Mississippi resistance only had three or four flamethrowers, so we'd be withdrawn.

Dolly began to bark loudly and when I glanced at her, her eyes were on the sky. I looked up, saw a Black Shark lined up to attack, and yelled, "Everyone down, now!"

The bird came in hot, spitting bullets by the hundreds as the barrels on his Gatling gun rotated speedily and sent hot empty brass flying out behind him. Smoke covered the nose of the air-craft as people on the ground began to die. Sandra suddenly jerked, screamed, and then began to flop around on the ground next to the wire. Dolly ran to her side.

I pulled out a Strela-2M missile launcher and as soon as the aircraft passed, I stood, aimed and waited for the chopper to nose up. Bullets zinged past me and one tugged hard at my shirt sleeve. I tracked the aircraft and gave the trigger a half-squeeze, which brought an Infrared engaged light on and I heard a slight buzzing sound. I was now locked onto my target, but still had to apply lead and elevation. I then squeezed the trigger.

As soon as the missile left the launcher, I fell to the ground and looked toward the Black Shark. The pilot took evasive action and even dispensed chaff, but to no avail. The missile flew into the engine exhaust and an immense explosion resulted instantly, send-ing parts of the aircraft in all directions. The largest piece I spot-ted was the almost intact cockpit and it fell to the ground still burning.

Remembering Sandra, I gained my feet and ran to her side. She'd taken something in her side and was in terrible pain. When I held her still, I saw a long sliver of metal stuck deep and wasn't re-ally sure how to treat it. I pulled a syringe of morphine from her medical bag, gave her a shot and waited for the drug to work.

"B . . . baby," she said in almost a whisper and when I leaned closer she continued, "I'll not make it. I'm bleeding internally . . . and there is nothing we can . . . can do. G . . . give me more mor-phine, please."

"I can't give you more or it will kill you."

She reached up with her right hand, rubbed my cheek and said, "I . . . I know it . . . will kill . . . me. I c . . . cannot survive." I no-ticed bright carmine blood bubbles on her sweet lips.

With tears in my eyes and pain tearing at my heart, I pulled more morphine from her bag and gave her a second shot. I felt tears rolling down my cheeks and my lips quivered in anguish as I waited for my wife to die.

Sandra, no longer able to speak, met my eyes, gave me a faint smile and then mouthed, "I love you."

My heart broke into a thousand pieces as I raised her head, and I cried uncontrollably. I loved this woman so much, and now I was being forced to kill her. She and I both knew the Russians would torture her if taken captive, and she'd been their guest once before. I felt her quiver violently once and she squeezed my hand hard, and then went limp. She was dead. I reached over, pulled the metal from her side and discovered a good twelve inches had been buried deep within her. She knew she'd not survive, and I knew it too at that second. I slowly lowered her head to the ground and stripped her of all gear. My last act was to place a grenade, with the pin pulled, under her, to hopefully kill those who tried to recover her body. The Russians were big on body count and I hoped in death, my baby would send a few of the sonsof-bitches straight to hell.

"John, we have orders to fall back and do it now." Silverwolf said as he ran to me. He glanced at Sandra, put a hand on my shoulder and added, "Come, there's nothing we can do for her now."

I stood, adjusted my gear and noticed most of the firing had stopped.

"Let's move, folks, we're going to have some pissed off Russians in a day or two." I yelled and then fell in with the rest of the group leaving.

Hours later, my heart still heavy from Sandra's death, we stopped in a forest of dense pines and oaks. The trees were huge, well over a hundred feet tall and it was full daylight. I was a mental mess and called Silverwolf to my side. He neared, squatted and said, "Are you okay?"

"No, I'm not, and until I tell you otherwise, you're in charge because you're the next ranking man." I noticed my hands were shaking as I spoke.

"I can do the job, except where are we to go?"

"Back to Pearl, and remember the housing area we were at near the shopping center, on the south side of highway 80? We're to move into the houses on the other side of Old Brandon road."

"My parents lived there until the fall. They both died there too, so I know the neighborhood well. Does it matter what street we take shelter on?"

"Ballard Street, according to Colonel Lee, and up on the hill, so we're not subject to the flooding in wet weather."

Silverwolf gave a low laugh and replied, "That whole western end of the road used to flood when heavy rains came along." He paused for a few minutes, cleared his throat and then added, "You know it's not likely most of us fighting the Russians right now will survive, right? I'm sorry as hell you lost Sandra; she was a good woman, but it's not likely in two years or less, most of us alive now will still be around. It's a deadly game we play, my friend, but know she died fighting for a principal. She died to free our country and many more will pass on before we are finally free, but it'll happen."

"Thanks, but that won't bring her back to me. I loved her, deeply, and now she's gone!" I felt the tears running down my cheeks, except I didn't care.

"Do you think you're the only one to lose somebody they cared about? Grow up, John, because there's not a person here who hasn't lost a loved one, not a single soul. Sandra was a damned fine woman and an excellent nurse, but she's dead. Do you think she'd want you sitting around on your ass, a broken shell of the man you were before, because of her death? She'd want you to avenge her death, and that, my good friend, we'll do. Now, I'll take over command until I determine you're ready to return to your position. I know her death happened less than 24 hours ago, but get over it and do the job fast, too."

After a Russian ration, which I shared with Dolly, I pulled the big dog close and realized she was all I had left of the old days. I hugged her and scratched her ears as I cried silently, feeling a deep soul hurting grief like I'd never felt before. At some point, exhaustion claimed me and I fell asleep.

Dawn was cold, with snow flying in all directions as we neared Pearl, Mississippi. It was a ghost town now, with most people gone years ago, and the once beautiful yards were now overgrown with weeds and brush.

Near the top of the hill, we located a house that must have been over sixty years old, since most of the houses were constructed in the housing boom following WWII, after all the soldiers returned home. Using Veterans Affairs funding, most bought new homes, and settled in for a comfortable life. Well, comfort, I thought, is long gone and survival is hard enough these days.

Surprisingly the front door was unlocked, so we just walked it, and I immediately felt like an intruder. The furniture was still in place, family photographs were hanging on the walls, and the fridge still had some moldy and hardened food in it. Once power had been lost, the food had gone bad quickly. Of course it'd been ransacked, like most homes, but I couldn't help but look at the images on the walls and wondered if the people in the photos survived or not. Most I knew were dead.

Silverwolf immediately issued orders. "I want toe poppers around the house, except for a straight path out the back door. From now on, no one uses the front door. I want a booby-trap placed on the front door and someone will pull guard in the living room 24/7. I also want a Claymore rigged in the yard, against the house, to cover the sidewalk and driveway. Let's move and make this place a home."

"Can we use the fireplace?" Joyce asked and then leaned her sniper rifle against the arm of the sofa.

"Maybe, if the weather gets cold enough. Now, that means it'll have to be pretty damned cold before it will be used. Let's hurry now, the snow is coming down hard, and Joyce, you can gather up some firewood or limbs to burn."

"I'll take care of the wood."

"Scott," Silverwolf said, "I want you on guard as the others work."

"I have it covered."

I stood and started to move toward the door when Silverwolf said, "You're looking better. What do you think of a fire in here?"

"Keep it small, about the size of a saucer and you should be fine. Remember, if the Russians come looking for us, and they will once over our attack, they'll pick up the heat with their infrared gear at night. Also, any patrols they have out will smell our smoke. We need a place to meet if we're suddenly attacked and need to split up."

"I'll allow a fire, because it's growing colder and as for meeting, we could meet by the old fire station, on highway 80. Say, behind it about 200 feet."

"That'll work and I agree we need the heat; it'll help the Russians rations go down smoother, too. The nasty-assed things are so terrible cold."

Two hours later, Kelly, who was on guard said, "I have movement."

There were no lights on in the house and it was dark outside. The fireplace contained a fire no larger than a cup saucer. I suspected the smoke was what brought us the unwanted attention, but it was cold out and we needed the heat. It was still snowing, so I said, "Silverwolf, I have command now and all is well. Joyce, move to the window and keep us covered. Kelly, slip your NVG's down and see what you have out there."

Minutes passed as we made our weapons ready, when Kelly said, "They're not Russians, for sure, and if I were to bet, I'd say cannibals. They look like the group that took us captive before. If so, they're fairly well armed."

"Walsh, bring the flamethrower to the door. If we're threatened or attacked give them a few squirts and then return inside. Fire is a well known way to scare some folks off."

I heard the blast of a toe-popper, followed by a loud scream. I made the booby-trap on the door safe, opened the door, and Walsh stepped outside. He immediately sent a long finger of flame from side to side. The whole area lit up like it was full daylight. Screams were heard; one man ran down the street, his clothing ablaze as the flames ate at him like a fast acting cancer. Rifle shots were heard, followed by blasts from shotguns. I moved into the kitchen, and picked up the clacker for the Claymore mine. Kerr armed the door again and then all moved into the kitchen with me. I allowed no return fire and a few long minutes later, I saw the door move slightly. The pin in the grenade was barely in, so if the door opened just a little more, it'd be pulled out and explode.

The fuse on the grenade was set to zero, which meant no delay at all. Suddenly, someone kicked the door open and started shooting. The grenade blast was loud in the small frame house, but nothing compared to when I blew the Claymore. The whole door disappeared and I heard horrific screams as ball bearings struck people outside. When the dust settled we moved forward, cautiously, because we would search the dead for gear we could use. Just outside, near where the door used to be, was a butcher's shop, with blood and meat scattered all around. Further back, an injured man tried to run, but Kerr put a bullet in the man and down he went. Between the grenade and Claymore, I counted fifteen bodies and three more had burned to death. Kerr had shot one, but I knew we had to move.

"Out the back. I suspect the Russians will be here and soon. Move toward the old fire station on highway 80 and do it now." I ordered as I looked everyone over, but saw no injuries. Each of us wore Russian NVG's, so moving at night would pose no problem.

"Kerr, you take point and Silverwolf, you bring up the rear. Let's move, folks, I see headlights on the street now," I said.

Three Russian trucks, equivalent to an American deuce and a half, stopped in front of the house and a squad of men poured from the rear of each vehicle. They approached the house cautiously, but then I heard three mines go off, followed quickly by screams of pain. I hurried to catch up with my people. The Russians would be angry.

The old fire station was just as it always was, except unmanned and deteriorating quickly. Hoses were still stacked neatly inside, firetrucks were still parked at the ready, but each vehicle was missing a gas cap and the diesel had been stolen years ago by desperate men and women. Food was long gone from the kitchen and the place was cold. *It's better to be cold than dead*, I thought as we entered the recreation room and moved to sofas and chairs. Joyce immediately pulled her sleeping bag out, as did Arwood and Kelly. Walsh was downstairs keeping watch, and I didn't have to wonder about him falling asleep this night. He'd been the guest of honor of cannibals before and then they attacked us tonight, so he would remain alert.

I walked to a far window and curled up in my sleeping bag, too. It was cold in the room and my bag was warm so I tried to sleep, but it avoided me. My mind began to fill with all sorts of things, and most were about Sandra. *Sandra, you were a good woman, baby, and I miss you*, I thought.

As I said earlier, my once stunning wife had been disfigured while a guest of the Russians, after she'd been raped by them countless times. During questioning, she'd turned defiant and it had cost her her beauty. Her ears were removed, one at a time, then the tip of her nose was sliced off. It wasn't until her lips were hacked off that she began to talk, but slowly, her pain beyond endurance. More than once she'd passed out, only to awaken in the same nightmare. We'd rescued her, or what was left of her, as soon as we could, but not before she'd been physically and mentally damaged. She'd cried the night we freed her and begged for me to shoot her, only I loved her and couldn't lay a finger on her. She was hideous with her face as it was, but over time, I grew used to it and life went on.

Most folks don't realize true love is not about looks or sex appeal, but a spiritual bond between two people. It's deeper than physical attraction, which is shallow, and disappears over time. Sandra and I knew each other better than anyone else in the world. Now, well, she's gone and I'm alone. Only a fool would have joined the resistance and expected both of us to survive, but I had done just that. I knew, beyond any doubt, she was still near me, because I would feel her presence at times.

I believe in God, but I'm a poor excuse for a Christian. I'm fighting a holy war in my mind and defending a country founded on Christianity and no other religion. There is little mention of any other religion except Jews in our nation's history, if you look at it closely. The Jewish folks I knew before and after the fall were deeply respected, and Israel was the only nation that tried to help us, but our President at the time refused help, saying, "Americans will overcome this alone."

I knew our nation was doomed when we started bowing to the demands of the Muslims and allowing their laws to be followed, their foods to be served and their customs to be adhered to. Our nation was known to respect other religions and we allowed other faiths, even if we disliked them, to be practiced. We were truly the only nation on earth where freedom of religion was practiced and enforced by laws. We are and always were a Christian nation, *always*, but the liberals had us twisted, and since they were in power we sat on our asses said nothing. Our lack of speaking up cost us many lives in the years before the fall of America, with wars with Muslim nations, then allowing them to immigrate to our country in large numbers and granting them almost instant citizenship. Following that, those that spoke English well were hired for high level government positions, which was a terrible mistake, because they were bound by the Koran to kill all non-believers. In other words, the Muslims wanted all Christian Americans dead and out of the way, and they actually had a plan organized, but the financial collapse of our nation caused many of them to return home. Those that didn't leave fast enough were hunted down by good ole boys and killed.

Then, one aspect of the collapse that always confused me is how stupid our paid politicians were at the time. Here we were zillions of millions of dollars in debt, and they allowed four million illegal Mexicans to become citizens almost overnight. Most of these Mexicans weren't doctors, lawyers, or other professionals, but minimum wage workers, and a large number were not working at all. The Liberals stated over and over that these aliens would make our country stronger by providing workers, but if that was true, why was Mexico such a poor country? They instantly qualified for unemployment benefits, but they'd not worked a minute in the United States. The treatment of these illegals brought instant resentment from Americans born in this nation and who had a whole different set of rules to live under. Then, when it became known that the illegals were getting better benefits than our nation's retired military, protests began in the streets.

Lastly came the clashes with police and riot control units. Looting became such an everyday thing the evening news no longer spoke of any occurrences of looting or rioting. At first people started sniping at police officers, blaming them for a lack of protection from looters, when in fact our society was terminally ill. Kids had grown into adults with little or no respect for each other, authority, or laws. Finally, just before the fall, folks started attacking police stations with explosives and weapons. Civil law was about to undergo a massive change, because the first thing the President did was enact Marshall Law. Shorty after that, God withdrew his blessings on America, and we fell hard as a nation.

Soon after thinking about God being disappointed with America, I entered the dark void of sleep.

CHAPTER 12

Master Sergeant Fedorovo awoke in a hospital, his head aching and his body sore. At first he was confused, then he remembered the partisan attack. He raised his right hand and felt a bandage on his head, then his eyes blurred and he felt nauseated. A few seconds later the feeling disappeared so he called out, "Nurse!"

"Oh, so you have finally awakened?" a short doctor asked as he neared the Sergeant's bed.

"What has happened to me?"

"You took a glancing blow from a bullet. You are a very lucky man, because the round was fired at an angle or ricocheted from the pavement, and it simply gave you a slight wound." the doctor said as he read from a chart hanging from the end of Fedorovo's bed.

"When will I be released?"

"Master Sergeant, head wounds are very tricky and while you may look and feel fine, we have no idea yet of the damage done internally. We will run some tests this morning and then we will discuss this again."

"Bullshit, sir. I have to see to my men. I can do as well with a bottle of vodka in my hand as I can laying here swallowing your useless pills. I am leaving."

The doctor, a Lieutenant Colonel, knew old Sergeants well, so he replied, "If you can get dressed and walk out of here, you are free to do so."

"Good." Fedorovo replied and slid his legs over the side of the bed. Standing, he suddenly was overcome with a sense of dizziness and had to sit back on the bed again. It was then his vision became blurry again.

"So, as I suspected, you cannot walk from your bed. I know you have blurred vision, you are dizzy, and your stomach may be upset. It is all symptoms of a head injury. Now, lay back down and rest."

Moving slowly back into the bed, Fedorovo asked, "How did the attack go?"

Writing on Fedorovo's chart, the doctor said, "Well, not good for us. We are still counting casualties and checking the base for damage. The last numbers I had were: We had lost over 800 men and women, dead, a good dozen or more helicopters, and almost two thousand wounded. So many were injured, we had to send the more serious cases to Jackson by convoy or helicopter."

"And the partisans?"

"That, Sergeant, is a good question. We counted only 300 bodies and found no injured, or more likely, those discovered wounded were killed. Colonel Ivanov ordered that all captives be executed on the spot and from what I have heard, he is one mad commander."

"We are going about this war wrong and will never win as things are."

"That statement could get you a room in a gulag, but I will ignore it as a result of your head injury. To challenge the government is not wise, Sergeant."

"My Grandfather used to say, 'You attract more bees with honey than you do with vinegar.'"

"So, off the record, what in the hell has that got to do with this war?"

"Sir, we should have come into this country and tried to win the Americans to our side. We should have brought food, medicines, and clothing to help these people. Instead we came in issuing orders and hanging people. When we started mass executions, or reprisals, we lost this war, because it does nothing but instill a deep determination to see us beaten by the enemy. It places hatred deep in each Americans heart for all Russians."

The doctor laughed and once sober he said, "It was exactly that the Americans tried in the Vietnam War. They had a motto, 'Winning hearts and minds,' except it did not work. No people want their country to fall in the hands of others, so they fight, and I agree, we will not win this conflict."

"To quote a doctor I know, ' That statement could get you a room in a gulag.'"

The doctor grinned and then asked, "Are you in a lot of pain? And, by the way, our conversation never happened."

"My head hurts like hell. With each beat of my heart, the pain throbs."

"Nurse!" the doctor yelled and when a young male Lieutenant appeared, he said, "I want morphine added to this patients IV, and do it now."

"Yes, sir. I will see to it right now." the Lieutenant said and then walked to the controlled substances locker.

"You will be feeling fine in just a few minutes. Now, over the next three days, I want you to rest as much as you can and that means sleep, too. I want no contraband vodka in this room, either, and I know how you Senior NCO's can be about booze. If at the end of three days, you can get out of bed and walk out of here, you are free to leave, deal?"

"Deal." Sergeant Fedorovo said.

The nurse entered the room, injected a medication into the IV and few minutes later, the Master Sergeant was getting sleepy. He was asleep before the doctor left his room.

"By the end of the day, Major Borisovich, I want to know how in the hell we lost over 800 dead and the partisans only lost 300! My whole base is in tatters, with the flight line littered with burned helicopters, my fuels and oils all gone up in flames, and over 2,000 wounded! I lost over half of my well trained and expensive air crews to what, a bunch of peasants? I want answers, do you understand me?"

"Yes, sir. My intelligent specialists suspect we were attacked by a force of well over 1,000 partisans and by hitting us at night, they had the element of surprise on their side, sir. Sir, you must stop thinking of this resistance as a bunch of peasants because they —"

"Do what? Do not tell me how to think, Major, or I will have you shot, you arrogant bastard! How *dare* you sit there and challenge my thinking!"

"Sir, with all due respect, I only meant the partisans are made up of many prior military members, hunters, and gun owners. As a result, they are, in most cases, better trained than the average Russian Private, sir."

"Horseshit! We have the best trained army in the world, Major. Let me tell you something and you would be smart to listen well; Our soldiers are the best in the world, the very best. I cannot be swayed to think these . . . these . . . criminals running the streets are better trained. Now, you had better get your thinking together, Major, and do the job quickly. I will not tolerate insubordination and if you *ever* challenge me again, you are a dead man. Have I made myself clear, Major?"

"Yes, sir, very clear." The chastised Major lowered his head.

"Now, Lieutenant Colonel Vasiliev, what can you tell me about this attack and how can we avoid it in the future?"

Standing, Vasiliev replied, "We estimate over 5,000 partisans were involved in this attack, which may be an overestimation, sir, but we suspect other resistance members were brought in from Alabama, Louisiana, and Tennessee. They must know most of our troops were gone, massed for the pending gas attack, and decided to hit us when our manpower is at it's lowest."

"And, why do they know so much about us and we so little about them?"

"We know the names of many members of the resistance, but that is about it. Not much we can do with a list of names, sir."

"Oh, I disagree, Colonel. There is a great deal we can do with a list of names. Right after this meeting, I want you to try and locate the families of all known resistance fighters. I want the families arrested and brought to the gulag as hostages. Then print posters and place them around town, threatening to relocate the families up north, after we select 50% for execution. The only way to prevent us from taking any actions is if the partisans surrender to us. Put the typical lies on the poster about how the partisans will be treated well, fed and given new clothing. Once we have most of them locked up, we will execute them."

"What of their families?"

"What of them? Shoot them, too. This is war, and all of you must harden yourselves against any thoughts that are not ruthless and cold. If a people will not bend to the will of Mother Russian, by God, we will force them to their knees. Now, I want all of you in this room to understand, my patience is short and I am not pleased. I will soon have Moscow on my ass and when that happens, I will be on yours. I want results, gentlemen, or some of you will disappear. Dismissed."

Later, as he moved down the hallway, Major Borisovich met the eyes of Lieutenant Colonel Vasiliev and in a low voice said, "Taking hostages will not work. During the American Civil War the North took the families hostage of all known partisans. The Yankees threatened to shoot some and all survivors would be relocated out of state."

Stopping, Vasiliev said, "Interesting, but what happened?"

"I am not sure of all the details, but the building they were being kept in collapsed and some of the women were killed and others injured. The North never executed any of them, but not a single partisan surrendered, and when the families were sent out of state, the partisans became more aggressive and bold. By taking their families, all the North did was strengthen the determination of the resistance."

"Perhaps our Colonel needs to read more American history."

"Maybe," Borisovich grinned and then replied, "but I will damned sure never tell him. I thought he was going to go crazy and have me shot earlier."

"He can, you know, and I suspect if we do not start producing more results he will start lining us up against a wall. I am at my wits end and not sure what can be done to produce more partisan deaths."

"Try my job, intelligence, my friend, because it is much too difficult. The Americans do not talk well and by the time we get information, say from a torture session, it is usually too old to help us. It is like we are chasing ghosts instead of human beings. What scares me the most is, the Colonel thinks the average resistance member is a halfwit, but the exact opposite is the truth. Most are between 25 and 35 years of age, with two years or more of university education, four years prior military training, most were hunters, and almost all are in excellent physical shape. But, the Colonel sees them like a peasant on the Russian plains, a farmer with no education, no prior military training, and bone tired most of the time, except he is so wrong in his assessment. The resistance is a finely tuned military force, with lots of experience, and may God protect us if they ever get their hands on the gear and aircraft we have."

"We must stop them before that is allowed to happen. I have heard rumors that China may step in and offer the Americans supplies and aircraft. If that happens, it is all over. I do not think the Russian people want a full size war on their hands."

"Uh, that is more than a rumor. Just between us, our intelligence has confirmed the meddling of China, and they have their own goals with America. Our experts suggest they want the United States to be the next communist country."

"Communism does not work. Hell, we tried it for years and even with millions of the opposition killed, the program failed. It is only a matter of time before the Chinese will be forced to admit this fact."

"Maybe, but right now, that is their goal in America. I hope to be gone before the resistance is better armed and supplied, or it will turn extremely bloody. I shiver to think of Americans having planes, tanks, and artillery in their hands, especially after all the murders we have committed in the name of retaliation."

"I hope to survive the coming week. Let us stop talking of this foolishness or someone may overhear us. We need to go to our sections and do what must be done. If you will send all the information you have on the partisan families, my teams will round them up." Vasiliev said and then started walking once again.

Of the more than 2,000 confirmed names of the resistance, only 150 families could be found with valid addresses. After locating the homes, the Russians waited, wanting to hit most of the people at the same time, so the rounding up of folks would not scare some away. Major Borisovich knew if they screwed this up, heads would roll and his would be one of the first. It took time to organize the trucks needed and the troops to collect the people, but once ready, Senior Sergeant Yefrem and his squad were part of the rounding up detail. Captain Vladlen Vanya was the ranking officer, mainly because he spoke broken English.

The first house they visited this night didn't go well.

The home was a two story building in need of painting and Vanya walked to the door and knocked.

"Someone looked out the upstairs window, sir, so give them time to open the door. I suspect they are an old couple." Iona said and held his weapon in a relaxed manner. *How much trouble can rounding up a bunch of old men and women be*, he thought.

Growing impatient, the Captain knocked again. He glanced at his watch.

Suddenly, the sound of a shotgun was heard and the blast came through the door and struck Captain Vanya in the middle of his stomach. Part of his spine was blown out of his back, along with parts of his lungs and liver. Blood spattered in all directions, with a long finger landing on Iona's face. The Captain fell to the porch screeching, as his feet kicked and his fingers clawed at the wooden surface. Pulling his medical bag, Iona pulled the fatally injured officer away from the door and started to examine him.

Two more shotgun shots were heard, which dropped two screaming Russians, but then a machine-gun opened up near the truck and bullets flew into the wood frame house. The three injured men were pulled to safety as the gun riddled the structure. Finally, silence.

There was a noise of something rolling and when Yefrem looked toward the sound, he screamed, "Grenade!"

The explosion was loud and left Iona's ears ringing. He looked the Captain over, shook his head and ignored the man's screams. Pulling his medical bag to him, he prepared two syringes with morphine and then injected both into the dying officer. In less than a minute Captain Vladlen Vanya was officially a statistic of the Russian American War.

The grenade had caused six more injuries and as Iona was working on them, Senior Sergeant Yefrem led the men to the porch. He pulled a pin from a grenade and tossed it through the hole in the door. Almost immediately the Russian grenade shattered a window as someone inside tossed it outside. The resulting explosion injured no one, but it did make all involved nervous.

Pulling another grenade, the Sergeant knew the fuse was set to four seconds, so he pulled the pin and let the spoon fly. After two seconds he threw it through the shattered window. There was an explosion and a loud scream followed. The Russian troops kicked the door in and entered shooting.

An old man in his late 60's lay on the floor, his right arm and half of his face was gone. He was moving toward on old single shot shotgun, when Yefrem shot him down the back with his Bison sub machine-gun.

There was a thin woman in a recliner. She looked to be dead. So Melor moved to her and pulled her body from the chair and tossed her lifeless form to the floor.

"No, don't touch any—" Yefrem yelled, but too late.

An explosion was heard, followed instantly by screams, and when Yefrem looked around, the room was filled with dust and blood was dripping from the ceiling and walls. He saw five men down; three from another squad, and Melor had saved some of the men by taking the main force of the blast with his body. Quickly checking himself and finding no injuries, except he couldn't hear, Yefrem stood on shaky legs.

In ran Iona, medical bag in hand, and he was shocked by the dripping blood. He moved to Melor and shook his head. Then moving to Ilyich, he pulled out three tourniquets and applied them to what remained of his two arms and right leg.

Iona said something to the Senior Sergeant, but he heard not a word and pointed to his ears. Within a few minutes, the medic had a IV in Ilyich and was giving him morphine for his pain. He then yelled for the radioman and told him he had a patient that would be dead if not taken out by helicopter.

Yefrem walked outside, sat in Captain Vanya's blood on the top step, and thought, *Damn, we have lost almost a dozen men and all by two old people. And, this is our first house! What if they all resist like this? How many men will this roundup cost my country?*

Minutes later, Iona sat beside the Senior Sergeant and looked his ears over. Pulling out a pen and a small pad he wrote, "Your eardrums have both been ruptured. I am going to give you some morphine for your pain. Is that okay with you?"

Yefrem nodded in understanding.

"Also, I want you to leave on the helicopter with Ilyich, because your days of combat are over for now, and maybe forever."

Yefrem said, "I am to leave with helicopter. The pain is less now. How many dead do we have?"

Private Iona wrote, "Too many. I do not expect Ilyich to survive. He has lost much blood. Melor is dead. Captain Vanya is dead. Two other men were shot fatally. Right now we have four dead and many wounded. How can this be? Only two old people lived here? I do not understand."

"These Americans will fight us until only one of them lives, and he will go to his death fighting too."

"Do they not fear death? To resist us means death, Senior Sergeant."

"To them, to wear the yoke of Russian dominance is a fate worst than death. They are an independent lot, Americans are, and have never been beaten in a war."

"What of their war in Vietnam?" Iona wrote on his pad.

"The military did not lose that war, the politicians did. They pulled out all Americans and left, just as they had the communists on their knees, begging for peace. It was a big mistake and after they had lost over 58,000 troops. Two years later, South Vietnam was under new ownership and the American politicians let it happen."

Iona looked up as he heard the *whop-whop-whop* of a helicopter and wrote, "The aircraft comes and you be sure to get on it."

"I will do that, Sergeant Iona. I will speak to the Colonel about your promotion. You saved lives here today and are a good soldier."

The medic smiled, nodded, and then quickly moved to his patients, wanting to load the most serious first.

The helicopter didn't land but lowered a basket, much like an American Stokes litter, and the injured were loaded one at a time. Once Senior Sergeant Yefrem was in the helicopter, the nose lowered and it moved toward Edwards.

At almost every home they approached they were met with stiff resistance and by the time they'd gotten to dwelling number five, they'd toss in a grenade, and kick the front door in immediately after the explosion. Often the occupants were in bed, since it was night time, and the grenades did nothing but awaken them, but fight back the Americans did. A dozen more dead and injured were added to the list the Sergeant in charge carried in his shirt pocket.

Finally, at home number ten a helicopter landed in a nearby street. Colonels Ivanov and Kuznetsov, the gulag Commander, ran from the helicopter. They walked quickly to the ranking Sergeant.

"What is causing all the casualties, Sergeant?" Colonel Ivanov asked.

"We are meeting armed resistance, sir, and in some cases, it is very heavy."

"You mean to stand there and tell me Russian troops cannot take a bunch of old people into custody?"

"That is exactly what I am telling you, sir. These are not a bunch of old people sitting at home waiting to die, and all have fought to the death."

"Has this house been attempted yet?"

"No, not yet."

Pulling his pistol, Ivanov said, "Watch me and learn, Sergeant. I will show you how it is done properly and it will not take me long, either. Come, Kuznetsov, and let us teach these young men how this job is to be done."

Kuznetsov pulled his pistol and slipped the safety off. He followed the Colonel up the steps to the door. Ivanov pounded on the door and yelled, "Russian army, open your door!"

A male voice answered from inside, "Kiss my ass, you communist sumbitches. If ya want our asses, come and get 'em."

"Kuznetsov, move to the side of the window and warn me of any movement inside."

The gulag officer had no combat experience, and Ivanov had just one encounter, but the junior officer moved for the window. The window had been busted out years ago and the Colonel didn't duck as he move in front of the window frame. There came a loud *twang* and Kuznetsov fell screaming, with an arrow from a crossbow in his neck. Blood, a bright cherry-red, ran through his fingers and spurted into the air with each beat of his heart, as he tried to stop the bleeding. Then he began to choke as Iona squatted beside him.

The medic pulled the arrow shaft the rest of the way out, applied a compress to the holes, and then gave the Colonel and shot of morphine. As Kuznetsov drifted off in a drug influenced sleep, Iona filled out a casualty tag that would go around the Colonel's neck.

Ivanov, angry at the stupidity of Kuznetsov, kicked the door in and was surprised to see no one in the room. A squad of men followed him and one asked, "What is that smell? It reminds me of rotten eggs."

The Colonel continued through the house, checking all the rooms and found them empty, until he got to the kitchen. An old woman of about 80 held a lighter in her hands and a man lay on the floor, shotgun in hand. As he raised his pistol, Ivanov knew he was too slow, because the shotgun fired, the Colonel was knocked against a far wall, and then the whole building exploded. If they've been more thorough as they searched the rooms they'd have found small propane tanks, the size of the containers used in a barbeque grill, with the valves open, in every room. The blast from the double barrel shotgun had supplied the fire needed to ignite the gas, which caused the resulting explosion.

Iona smelled the gas and as he started to stand, the whole building exploded in all directions. He fell on his patient and shielded him with is own body. Kuznetsov suddenly screamed and his body joined many others as sharp pointed pieces of wood struck the unsuspecting Russian troops. A large mushroom cloud of dust and flames formed in the sky directly above the building. The large blast was followed by many others as the individual tanks of propane exploded as well. Each tank that exploded, sent sharp metal shrapnel in all directions, and more men called out in pain. Then, minutes later, it was quiet.

The medic, moving to the Colonel, saw a long sliver of wood stuck in his chest near his heart. He called two soldiers over and said, "I have to remove the wood from the Colonel to treat him. I want you both to hold him down as I do the job."

"When?" the youngest looking Private asked.

"Right now." Iona replied and then grabbed the wood with a solid grip, and then slowly removed it. The Colonel screamed and kicked for a minute or so and then passed out. From what the medic saw after removing the wood, it'd gone completely through his body. Rolling his body to his side, he saw an exit wound. He pulled the man's shirt off, ignoring the 30 degree weather and plugged both holes with cotton bandages. He then wrapped the injury in cotton as well.

The helicopter was still parked in the street, so Iona slowly stood and made his way to the crew. He was suddenly exhausted and when he neared he said, "I need you to transport all our wounded back to Edwards."

"Sorry, but we are the private crew for Colonel Ivanov. We are under orders to wait for him so we can return him to base."

"Colonel Ivanov and ten other men died in the explosions that just happened. Now, both of you out rank me, but I am sure a review board will be interested in why you two allowed brave Russian soldiers to bleed to death, when they could have been saved. Your boss is dead meat."

They looked at each other and the oldest man shrugged and replied, "Load them on the aircraft, and do it quickly."

Returning to the remains of the burning and smoking house, he'd just bent over to check on Kuznetsov when the helicopter exploded, throwing debris and burning fuel high into the air. One crew member had gotten out of the helicopter alive, but his right leg was in flames. One soldier ran to him and sprayed the leg with a fire extinguisher from a truck. The fire went out instantly, but the other man could be heard screaming as he burned to death, still strapped in the left seat.

"Rocket propelled grenade!" someone yelled, and all went to ground.

"Radioman!" the Sergeant who Ivanov had given a hard time called out.

"He is dead, Sergeant." an unknown Private said.

"Bring me the radio, and do the job now. Base is going to shit when I tell them the base commander is dead, along with a good dozen other soldiers, and their gulag commander is severely injured and may not survive."

"Here is the radio, Sergeant." The Private handed the radio to the man.

CHAPTER 13

When dawn arrived, I was still tired and so was Dolly. I fed her most of my Russian ration and then moved around to loosen up my stiff body. My eyes felt like they had grit or sand in them, and my back was sore from sleeping on the hard floor. While the fire station blocked the wind, it remained cold in the place. Looking out frost-covered windows, I saw snow was still falling, but I knew it'd not last long. It was rare this far South to get more than an inch of snow and it never lasted long. I figured by mid-day most of the snow would be melted, but right now I needed to meet Colonel Lee and see if our joint attack against Edwards had gotten the results we wanted.

Our primary goal was to prevent the nerve gas attack on unarmed civilians in the state and to do that, we'd hoped to hit the Russians hard enough they'd call off the attack, and then move men back to their units in order to provide better security for all bases. Edwards Air Base wasn't the only Russian base we'd attacked, and all up and down the state we'd attacked various staging areas, warehouses, and bases. Most were considered a success, except Jackson Air Base, where we'd taken horrible losses. Of course, we'd expected Jackson to be difficult, because it was the main Russian base in the state. Of all the bases, since it was the central supply receiving port, it was better armed and defended. While the Strela-2M missiles had downed a few helicopters at Jackson, the fast movers, the jet aircraft, were based there. We learned the missile wasn't as good against jet aircraft as it was against the much slower choppers. The jets had torn our people to pieces and we'd experienced over a thousand dead and three times that many maimed and injured. Jackson was a failure, in many ways, but it did show the Russians we'd attack where and when we desired.

An hour after dawn, I said, "Saddle up, we're going to find Colonel Lee. We have carried out his plan as well as we can, but I need to know if the Russians have called off their gas attack."

Joyce, who was on guard appeared at the top of the stairs and said, "Russian truck just pulled up and I have them near the front door to this place."

"Everyone to a window, but don't shoot unless I start first. Joyce, you remain in the vehicle bay and keep an eye on them. Let me know if they enter the building or when they leave."

"Will do." she said, and then moved down the stairs.

From my window I could see highway 80 well, and one large Russian truck was parked in the driveway with its engine running. It was cold enough the heat from the exhaust of the truck looked like smoke. I suspected it was near thirty degrees, or even a little lower. I could even see the individual Russian soldiers breathing as they moved around outside.

Five minutes later, as I watched, the Russians piled in the back of the truck and they pulled onto the highway and turned toward town. Joyce walked to me a few minutes later with a poster in her hand.

"Read this. The English is rough, but you'll understand the meaning." she said.

I read the text, looked around the room and said, "The Russians are gathering up all family members of partisans and will relocate them to a gulag out of state, unless they decide to execute them. All members of the resistance are urged to surrender to save your family. We all know what will happen if you surrender, except this poster says you'll be treated well, fed, given new clothing, and assisted in starting a new life. The rest of the lies are on it, so read it." I then passed the poster to Arwood.

I wasn't concerned; my parents were dead, and I knew better than to believe a word on the poster. After about ten minutes, Walsh, the last man to read it tossed it to the floor and said, "I have family, but they live in the backwoods of Mississippi and the Russians won't find them."

"Do any of you want to surrender?"

Silence, but finally, Joyce said, "My parents were alive the last time I saw them, but they are elderly and proud of my work with the resistance. My dad told me no matter what happened to them to keep up the fight and I intend to do that."

"How do they know who is a partisan?" Silverwolf asked.

"The Russians have computers and by guessing, looking at the ages of each of us, they can then check our police and military records, if we have any. The Department of Defense will have data on all of us who served, including our DOD-214 details, or discharge papers. If you were still on active duty at the time of the fall, they'll know even more about you. Also, gun registration information, hunting license information, and even our drivers license info will have some details. If you ordered a veteran license plate, even that will be documented. Then consider the spies we've found within our groups the last few years, which I'm sure furnished as many names as possible; they'll have a fair tally of who is with the resistance. They will suspect anyone with a military background, a hunter, or registered gun owner to be a partisan."

"They'll be wrong in some cases." Kerr said.

"Do you honestly think they'll give a damn?" I replied and then added, "Walsh, pick up the poster and bring it with you to show the Colonel. We need to find the man, and as soon as possible. Looks to me like this poster may fool some members with us, and we want to avoid that if doable. I don't see the Russians keeping their words and I'm sure all partisans who surrender and their families will be murdered. Let's move toward the Pearl River and Kerr, you take point, while Silverwolf, I want you bringing up our rear."

We moved quickly, but not so fast we didn't look for mines or booby-traps. The Russians knew we were in the area, so I knew they had mines out, so we stayed off the beaten path and in the rough grasses and brush as much as possible. We'd covered about half the distance to the river when Kerr stopped and motioned me forward.

I made my way slowly to the man and squatted beside him. At first I didn't see anything, but finally I spotted a thin nylon line stretched between some brush. I waved him back, moved forward, and discovered a Russian hand grenade in a ration can, pin pulled and spoon held in place by the can. The line was secured to the neck of the grenade and the other end to a bush. The line was about six inches above the ground and all it would take is for someone to walk into the line, pull the grenade out of the can, and depending on the timing on the explosive, it would detonate. I marked the line with a stick and motioned Kerr forward.

A few short minutes later we were moving once again. It was hard to say who placed the booby-trap and while we placed most of them, the Russians did as well. With the Russians, it was usually a pressure mine or they'd spray an area with cluster bombs. While we had mine detecting gear, most units didn't carry it due to weight. If given a choice, most would carry more bullets instead and it made sense in my mind. We rarely ran across a lot of mines, which would justify the gear, and since we were usually in Russian "controlled" areas they planted fewer mines than us, to avoid injury to their own people.

About a mile later, I heard a loud noise off in the distance that I couldn't identify and at first thought it was a bulldozer. I gave Dolly to Joyce and moved forward with a pair of Russian binoculars in my hands. I quickly located the source of the noise and it was a Russian T-90A tank. The big beasts were heavy and almost impossible to knock out because of the three level composite armor that protected the three man crew. Behind the tank I counted a company of men, so they were looking for us or others like us. I instructed Kerr to lead us at right angles away from the tank.

We moved slowly in the beginning, so we'd be less likely to be seen, and I felt my apprehension mounting. Usually when hunting others, movement is what is spotted first. Then, we entered a grove of big pine and oak trees and our rate slowed down even more. We'd no sooner entered the trees than I heard the sound of choppers moving quickly overhead. It looked to me as if the chopper and tank were working together and hoping to bag some partisans. If they did, I prayed it wouldn't be us.

The underbrush was thick where we were walking and suddenly, I heard Arwood say, "Shit, I think I am on a mine! Good God, no!"

"Everyone back up slowly, but step in footprints or you may step on one, too." I said, because we were on an old game trail, which was mostly dirt. Then, turning to Arwood, I asked, "How do you know you're on a mine?"

"I felt something snap when I placed my weight on my foot. I'm scared, man."

"Hold on and let me move to you. Let me see what we have first, then you can be scared later."

I spoke and pulled my bayonet as I approached. He was just ahead of me, so I squatted beside him and gently ran the knife into the soil under his foot. I felt something hard, so I checked all the way around and felt the same thing. Slowly, using the blade of my knife, I pulled just enough soil away that I saw the Olive drab color of a mine.

"It's a mine. Kerr, do you know much about mines?" I asked.

"A little. Do you have any idea what kind it is?"

"No, I've never seen this type before."

"Let me come and take a look." he said. It was then I heard dogs barking and Dolly jerked on her leash that Joyce held.

"Damn me, now they have dogs after us."

"Go, no need to worry about me, I'm a dead man." Arwood said, but his eyes begged us to stay.

"Silverwolf, back track a ways and see what we have. Here," I tossed him the binoculars, "so you don't have to get too close. Joyce, go with him and see if you can put the fear of God into those Russians. Try to buy us a little time, if you can. Hand Dolly to Scott."

Kerr placed his head on the ground, blew some dust away and said, "I see what looks to be an Italian P-25 mine and the fuse is sticking from the top. From what I remember, if the fuse is not broken the mine will not detonate. There is no timer and detonation is instant. So, if I'm correct, the mine is not armed."

"What in the hell would an Italian mine be doing here?" I asked.

"Who knows, but that's what we have."

I said, "Now, we're going to move back about a hundred feet, Arwood, and then I want you to remove your foot from the mine and back up. Then mark it by sticking your bayonet in the ground near it."

"W . . . what if it explodes?"

"Then, don't worry about marking it for us." I said and saw instantly my attempt at humor was not appreciated.

"You'll be fine and safe. Now, let us move back."

"If I'm safe, why are you two moving?"

"Do you want the truth?" Kerr asked.

"Of course, you know I do."

"Because I just may be wrong. Nonetheless, you can't spend the rest of your life standing here, and I suspect that'd not be long with Russians on our asses."

"Damn me, okay. Move back then." Arwood said, and he was sweating hard now.

I heard two shots, within three seconds and knew something had just died and then it dawned on me, no more barking. Three more shots were heard, all from her sniper rifle and then I heard two explosions that sounded like grenades and a long burst of automatic fire.

"Move, Arwood or I'll leave you. I cannot risk the lives of the whole group for a single person."

I watched the man cross himself and then step backward — nothing happened. He pulled his bayonet and stuck it in the ground in front of the mine. It was then Silverwolf and Joyce returned.

"Had a Russian squad with two dogs. Now there are about five seriously injured Russians and no dogs left alive. I figured the five injured will require ten to twenty men to pack them out." Joyce said then added, "But, Silverwolf saw the tank swing this way, so we'd better move."

"How far off was the tank?" I asked.

"A good mile, maybe." the man replied.

"Alright, when we move forward, I want my man on drag, Silverwolf, to pull the bayonet from the ground and sprinkle some dirt on the mine. Maybe we'll get lucky and the Russian tank will roll on it. Let's move, folks." I said and then continued, "Kerr, you're my point man."

We hustled through the woods, and stuck close to the trees as much as possible, because I could still hear choppers at times. I suspected this was a Russian Killer team out looking for any partisans they could round up. Between the tank, choppers, and ground troops, they'd be hard to fight if you were boxed in tight or cornered.

We'd covered about a mile, when the grove of trees suddenly stopped. I could see the clearing was a fire lane, intentionally cut by foresters years ago, and we had to cross it. I had an eerie feeling as if I was being watched or something bad was going to happen. I thought for a moment, glassed the area with my binoculars and even sent Kerr up and down the lane, on our side, looking for ambushers, but saw nothing out of place. I then sent recently promoted Walsh over and he had no difficulties at all, so, it must be my mind is working overtime. I then had Kelly over and about half way to the next wood-line, he disappeared in a quick flash of flame and smoke, and glassing the man, I saw he was severely injured. Both legs were off, one near the knee and other up about a foot higher, and his arms were both mangled up pretty badly.

"Damn," whispered Kerr, "he's our medic, too. I can get him and pull him to the other side, if you want."

"Give it a try, but I don't think that's a mine field, but rather an isolated mine placement."

Kerr ran to Kelly, looked around and then yelled, "Looks like a motion detector mounted at an angle from the far line of trees to yours. We need to all get over and now, because I think either fast movers or choppers will visit us."

"What about the mines?" Scott asked.

"Don't worry about mines. If a jet shows up, there is a good chance he'll drop napalm on this place and I'd like to be long gone when that happens. All of you, move across the clearing, and do it now!"

Kerr had placed Kelly over his shoulder and was running to the trees.

We all made it across the clearing and one glance at Kelly told me all I needed to know about his medical condition; it was fatal.

"All of you move forward about a half a mile and wait for me. Silverwolf, you cover me as I treat Kelly. Once back with the others, you take drag." I watched as they began to move.

"I have you covered, but hell, he's a mess. I'd overdose him on painkiller and let the medication kill him without pain."

Kelly was on his back screaming as blood spurted from this legs and arms. His chest and head had a number of areas oozing bright ruby-red blood and his bodily fluids smelled of copper and human waste. I reached into his medical bag, pulled out two vials of morphine and injected him in the neck, twice. As he died, I stripped his body of any gear we could use, which was little because his equipment was as riddled from the mine as his body. A few minutes later, he gave a loud sigh, quivered violently and died.

"Damn, I hated to lose him. Not only was he a good medic, but a good man to boot." Silverwolf said and shook his head.

"Good people die, my friend." I replied and immediately thought of Sandra.

"We'd better get moving."

"Slow trot, and I know any mines will be marked. If we find any, after we pass, we'll clear them of warnings and maybe bag us a Russian or two."

Less than a mile later, we caught up with the group, hadn't seen any mines and it was then I heard a chopper nearing. Choppers are strange aircraft and the noise of their blades can echo which makes them difficult to place at times. This was one of those times.

"Everyone on the ground now." I ordered as I heard the aircraft more clearly now and it seemed to be right overhead. We all fell to the ground and most of us crawled to a bush or in the brushes to make a smaller target.

Glancing up, I saw the chopper come lower and the gunner was searching the ground carefully. I considered using a Strela-2M missile on his ass, but worried about overhead limbs and branches. I finally just lowered my head and waited. A few minutes later, the aircraft moved on.

"Stay where you are, because sometimes they'll back up and try to catch partisans moving." I warned.

Finally the engine and blade noises of the chopper moved on, so I stood and said, "Let's move. I want Scott on point and Kerr bringing up the rear."

We'd covered about a half mile, when Scott dropped back and reported, "I have a couple of squads of Russians moving right for us. I'd estimate we have five minutes or less before they get here."

"Everyone under cover and we'll try to let them pass us. If you hear me shoot, then join the dance." I said and then prayed, *Please Lord, let them walk by us without seeing us and don't let them have a dog.* I pulled Dolly into some blackberry bushes and had her lay down with me.

CHAPTER 14

Cigarette smoke filled the small conference room as Lieutenant Colonel Vasiliev stood in front of the group and said, "With the deaths of both Colonels Ivanov and Kuznetsov, I am both the commander of the gulag and the base commander, by orders from Moscow. Major Sokolov, as the troop commander, you are to also run terrorist operations, temporarily, until replacements are sent. My position is also temporary until replacements can be found. As of this day, a soup kitchen will be provided to all civilians who live in the town of Edwards and three good meals will be fed to all. I also want any stored civilian clothing taken to the same spot and issued to those who need garments. We will try to win their hearts now, if we have not already ruined any chances to do so. Any questions?"

"What of the civilians in the gulag? We have many people who were breaking no laws, but were simply collected as bodies for executions or reprisals. Do we keep them or let them go?" Major Sokolov asked.

"Screen each closely and if they are not a registered gun owner and have broken no laws, then let them go. Do the same with those collected that we know are family members of partisans."

Master Sergeant Fedorovo asked, "Have you coordinated the prisoner release with Moscow, sir? They may have ordered the prisoners rounded up and if you release them, well, you know what will happen." He'd finally walked out of the hospital, but did little except drink vodka for his pain, and paperwork.

"I appreciate your concern, Sergeant, but I have given my orders, and I wish to see them carried out. Major, you will also see the civilians are fed and present them with good food. I want the prisoners in the gulag fed as well as our own men are. Any other questions?" Vasiliev said.

Silence, but many thought the Lieutenant Colonel was committing professional suicide and it was only a matter of time before he disappeared or was recalled to Moscow to answer for his actions.

"Now, this meeting is over and I want my orders carried out immediately." The man turned and walked into his office.

Master Sergeant Fedorovo stood beside the Junior Sergeant in the serving line at the old market place in Edwards. So far, only a handful of Americans had come to eat, but the old Sergeant suspected most distrusted the Russians. It is too soon, he thought. *Hell, just last week we were executing them and now we offer them free food. They probably think it is poisoned.*

A tank sat in the square, with a squad of infantry men, who were checking people by age and arresting anyone that might be old enough to be in the resistance, but they'd be released if nothing was found on the Russian computer systems. One man started to run and a quick burst from the tanks machine-gun brought him down. He now lay face down on the cobblestone street, a pool of blood under him, and his unseeing eyes open.

The Master Sergeant saw few military or fighting age people present. He did see many slip food into their coat pockets, obviously to either eat later or to take home and feed someone else. He knew it was likely some partisans were being fed with the Russian food, but that was not his concern. He was here to provide security for the cooks and food servers, and he was doing his job well.

Feeling the urge to pee, the old Sergeant walked behind the tank, unbuttoned his trousers and a few seconds later, moaned with relief. He was just about completed with his business, when he heard a loud yell to stop in Russian, followed by the *tak-tak-tak* of the machine-gun crew. He quickly stepped around the tank and was moving for the food serving vehicle, when there came a loud explosion, and he was knocked off his feet. Laying there for a bit, still in shock, he felt himself all over and other than his ears ringing, he felt nothing wrong or any blood. He stood, and then turning to the serving area, he watched as flames and smoke rose to the sky. It was then the screams of the injured were heard. Bodies were all over the street, along with body parts.

About 20 meters away, a young blonde woman lay on her back, her eyes blinking, and blood pooling under her back. She suddenly screamed and when the Master Sergeant glanced in her direction, a young Warrant Officer was pointing his pistol at her. The man fired twice and each time a bullet hit home, her body jerked. Finally, she lay unmoving, as the light in her eyes went out slowly.

"Medic!" someone yelled and two men ran for the flames.

Fedorovo moved to a senior cook and asked, "What happened?"

"The beautiful woman came for food and had a briefcase in her left hand. She placed it on the ground as I served her. I moved to the truck to get more beef, and it was then I heard the shooting. I am not a combat troop, so I stayed behind the van until the explosion. My wait was a short one, too."

One medic, a private said, "We have four, one is a civilian, that need a helicopter if they are to live. One man has lost both arms and legs. The others will die if they are not cared for by the hospital soon. We have ten dead, but only three are Russian. Those in line for food were blown to pieces."

"I will make the call, so relax." Master Sergeant Fedorovo said and then yelled, "Radioman?"

"We do not have one, Sergeant," a young Lieutenant said, "but my tank crew has already contacted base, using our radio, and a helicopter is on the way."

"Thank you, and how long did they say?"

"They said the aircraft was starting engines when my driver finished speaking with them."

"Medic!"

"Master Sergeant?" the man asked as he neared.

"Separate those who need to be airlifted out, from those who can be taken by truck to the hospital."

"Just the Russians, right?"

Oh, that is a good question, he thought and then said, "If we are to win the hearts of the Americans, we need to take all to see a doctor."

"What of the dead?"

"Leave the Americans here, because I am sure someone will come for their bodies. Place our dead in the truck. I do not think it matters much to the men who were killed how soon they get to a base. However, treat all the dead with dignity."

"I will see to it, Sergeant."

Hearing the chopper approaching, the Sergeant walked to the tank and the driver had his head out of his hatch. Seeing Fedorovo, he asked, "He wants smoke so he can see the wind, and where do you want him to land?"

"I will have smoke for him and have him land in the center of the town square. It is big enough for two or three helicopters. How far out is he?"

"Three minutes before he gets here, or that is his guess."

"Corporal!" he yelled at a young man, "Stand by to use a smoke grenade and get in the center of the square."

"Will do, Sergeant."

A few minutes later, the helicopter flew overhead, circled and then hovered above the square as the Corporal popped the smoke grenade. Using his hands, the man then slowly worked the aircraft to the ground. As the engines continued to run, the wounded were loaded through an open side door. As the pilot watched the Corporal, he began to slowly rise into the air.

From a side street, behind the helicopter, a partisan stepped out, aimed his Strela missile and fired.

"Missile!" Fedorovo screamed to the tank driver, but he was too late. The missile struck the aircraft in the engine and then exploded, throwing helicopter parts, dead bodies, flaming fuel and debris of various sizes in all directions. The aircraft rolled to it's side and then struck the ground hard, where it exploded, killing the Corporal and all inside the helicopter.

The tank started almost immediately and the commander yelled to be heard over the engines, "Gather men behind me and let us see what is down that street the missile came from."

The tank driver went around the huge fire from the helicopter and then moved to the narrow street the partisan had used. Fedorovo didn't like the situation, because the houses were too close to the street, and a few were two stories and dangerous in his view. The tank commander was up and partially out of his hatch, manning a machine-gun, and while the rest were closed, just one grenade dropped down the hatch and all would be killed.

Moving to the rear of the tank, he pulled a telephone from a box and started speaking to the man. It was then he heard shots and saw two Molotov cocktails and a grenade fly out of the hands of partisans. The outside of the tank immediately burst into flames and the grenade went right down the hatch. The driver's hatch flew open and the driver madly crawled out but was afire, as the grenade exploded. The tank commander, who was half way out of his hatch was blown into the air. Fedorovo realized the weapons operator never had a chance.

As soon as the Russians kicked the door to the building open, the Master Sergeant moved forward and wrapped the burning driver with his coat to put the flames out. He heard gunshots, an explosion, and then more shots.

The tank was in flames now and the Master Sergeant yelled, "Everyone away from the tank before the ammunition and fuel explodes. Move, people!" He stood, placed the wounded driver over his shoulder, and ran for the market place.

The Soldiers, three fewer now, ran behind him. When a Sergeant neared, the Master Sergeant asked, "What happened?"

"The stairs were booby-trapped and there were only two of them. They were hard men to kill."

Nearing the market place, he lowered the injured man to the grasses, ignoring his screams and looked toward the street. A few minutes later, he heard an explosion and saw flames and smoke rolling toward the gray sky. *The tank has just blown up*, he thought and shivered at the thought of being trapped in a tank with a fire. Minutes later there came a series of horrific explosions as the fuel and ammunition exploded as well. Smoke, dust, and debris flew through the air in all directions over the buildings.

Vasiliev was mad, but not overly so, with the disaster of the food serving. He'd lost well over a dozen men and since he'd filed his report with Moscow, threats were already coming in by emails and phone calls. He was in his office, feet propped up on the edge of his desk, as he sipped a small glass of vodka. He should have known the food idea wouldn't work, not the way he'd planned it. The civilians needed to come to the gate to get foodstuff and from now on, he'd keep his people away from civil projects. Food and clothing would be issued, after the civilians were searched, and then allowed in a warehouse near the gate. He'd place a tank by the door and a company of men to protect the place. He saw no reason the Americans would not flock to get the free food and clothing, thus improving relations with both countries. *If* he could only keep Moscow off his ass long enough to complete his ideas.

"Colonel, we just got a call that a squad of our men have located a large number of partisans in a group of trees and his estimates are over 400 of them." Major Borisovich said as he stuck his head in the door.

"Where are these trees? Did you find them on the map?"

"No need for a map, sir, it is in the trees on the south end of the camp. One of the infrared equipped helicopters picked up the body heat. There were so many, he returned to base and reported a gear malfunction. Testing proved there was nothing wrong with his equipment."

"Right now? How in the hell did that many resistance members get so close to us without being spotted?"

"Intelligence thinks they entered the trees last night and spent the day there, planning to attack us tonight."

"What is the weather forecast for tonight?"

"Uh, cloudy, overcast, cold with snow. The snow is to hit shortly after 2000 hours, sir. Why?"

Glancing out the window, the Lieutenant Colonel asked, "What time is it?"

"1900 hours, sir. Why did you want the weather forecast?"

"The worst the weather is, the better the conditions are for an attack. I want the whole base on alert, and do it *now*! But quietly, because I want no sirens or lights all over the place. Get the men into position and quietly, too. Alert Base Operations and tell them I want all aircrew on immediate alert for base air defense. Now move, Major!"

As the Major scurried from the room, Vasiliev grew concerned. He was a well trained officer and this was not his first combat command, but partisans didn't fight by the book. They reminded him of the American Indians he used to read about as a kid. The Natives were experts at hit and run and they very rarely attacked in mass to overwhelm their enemies, but slowly wore their enemies down by killing a few here and a few there. Or, they'd meet a small group of their foes and battle until a couple were dead and then end the fight. Like partisans, they didn't have unlimited manpower, but the Lieutenant Colonel did and he would use it, if attacked. The man stood, moved to the tea pot and poured a cup of tea and then added a little vodka. This night, or so it looked likely, he'd get little sleep.

He contacted all the members of his staff and placed them on alert and recall. Recall assured him the men would be in position when the attack happened. He took a sip of his vodka and tea, and thought, *But, when and where will they strike?*

By 0130, the suspected attack had not happened, and Vasiliev was thinking perhaps it was all a mistake and the infrared gear was messing up again. He walked from the office, lighted a cigarette and moved down the empty hall. Lights were on in many offices, but he stuck his head in Major Borisovich's office and said, "I am calling it a night. Keep the troops ready the rest of the night, except I think it will be a quiet evening. If you do need me, however, I will be in my quarters."

"Of course, sir, and enjoy the remainder of your evening." the Major replied.

Like all the troops, he was wearing full combat field gear, including a helmet and while the damned thing was heavy, he had to set the example. Just outside the building, he took his helmet off, ran his hands through his dirty hair and curse at how filthy he felt. He'd just put the steel pot back on his head, when he felt a sharp impact to his head, the helmet went flying and he was knocked to ground. *Sniper,* he thought. *I need to lay still and not move, or they will put another bullet in me. I did not hear the shot, so they are using a silencer with the rifle.*

The door flew open, five men rushed out, a Sergeant squatted and said, "He has been shot in the head!"

The young Sergeant's face suddenly had a black dot appear, right above his left eye, and then the back of his skull flew apart as a long finger of red blood shot from the hole. He blinked once, quivered, and then his lifeless body fell over the Lieutenant Colonel's. Two privates grabbed the Colonel and pulled him inside. As they worked, two more men, attempting to move the Sergeant's body were struck by the sniper. One was struck in the center of his back and his chest exploded, sending bone, flesh, and blood onto the wooden wall. He screamed, grabbed for his wound and then his body shook violently as another bullet struck him in the lower belly. He began to shriek and jerk violently as the second man tried to pull him into the door. The uninjured man took a bullet to the throat, and almost instantly a fountain blood shot from his injury. Choking on blood, he fell, half in and half out the door. In less than three minutes, both men were still as blood ran from their bodies, making small rivers of red as they flowed toward the steps.

Vasiliev, once inside, sat up and leaned against a wall. He felt dizzy and sick to his stomach as he raised his right hand to feel his injury. While he'd bled a lot, it felt to him as if the bullet had only burned his flesh. He lowered his hand and it was covered in blood.

"Help me stand and we will go out the back door. I must get to our command post and direct operations from there. I want all in the building to leave at the same time."

"Not yet, sir. I need to bandage your injury." the Major said. He pulled a dressing from the Lieutenant Colonel's first aid kit and tore it open. Once completed he added, "If you had not been wearing your helmet, I think you would be dead right now. It ran a farrow around your skull, just breaking the skin."

"Let us move, because I am needed."

The Major helped him stand and placed the Lieutenant Colonel's arm around his neck. They then walked down the hall-way, knocking on doors and emptying rooms. Vasiliev figured the sniper couldn't see on the other side of the building and he was right.

At the command post, Vasiliev immediately took control and other than sniping, no one had attempted to breach the perimeter fence. Before his death, Colonel Ivanov had had the fence charged with electricity, to assist in base security, so maybe the fence would keep them out. *It is unlikely*, he thought, *because they blow one hole in the thing and it will all quit working.*

"Sir! One of our helicopters, uh, Delta One Six, claims move-ment toward the fence line now." A young man wearing a headset yelled out to be heard over the normal voices. It instantly grew quiet.

"Tell Delta One Six to wait until the partisans reach the fence line, then engage the enemy. Alert all helicopters in the air we are about to have guests. Make sure our defensive positions all know we will soon be under attack. Notify Base Operations and tell the commander I want everything that will fly in the air. *Now!*"

"Yes, sir."

"Pulling a full bottle of vodka from his desk drawer, Vasiliev poured a water glass half full and then chugged about half of it down. He sipped the rest as he said, "Damned doctor wanted to put me on morphine for my head wound. I have to be able to think, so vodka will keep me functioning until this is over."

"Delta One Six is engaging the enemy now, sir!"

Raising his glass high, the Lieutenant Colonel said, "Gentlemen, the game begins."

CHAPTER 15

I heard the dog before I ever saw it and the animal was sniffing our trail hard. I had Dolly laying beside me and she wanted a piece of that animal badly. I could clearly see the Russian troops approaching and suddenly the dog handler stopped, looked around and then said something. I saw the troops bring their weapons to the ready position.

I'd guess there were a hundred Russians and seven of us, so it didn't look good to me. I waited until the group was right in front of my Claymore mine and then squeezed the clackers. A loud explosion echoed through the trees, followed by screams and shouting. The dog was still alive, his handler down and then the animal broke free. I saw dirt kicked up all around the animal and he was moving right for my position, so I released Dolly.

Silverwolf blew another Claymore and more screams were heard. All of us began tossing grenades as fast as we could pull the pins. Finally, Walsh stood with the flamethrower and squirted his liquid death down the trail. He was advancing toward the Russians when I saw him suddenly explode into a walking ball of flames. His screams were a much higher pitch than the Russian wounded and I know I smiled when a long burst of fire from one side or the other, dropped him to the trail. I pulled my pistol and as Dolly and the dog fought, I waited from them to give me a clear shot. Finally, they separated, each dripping blood from their mouths and I fired one round into the dog. The Russian dog dropped instantly, dead before he struck the ground.

I called Dolly, looked her over and saw some injuries on her face and neck. I put my whistle to my mouth, gave three loud blasts, the signal to retreat and began to back away from our enemies. We'd agreed to meet a half mile down the trail and off to the right about a 100 yards. Knowing the Russian troops would be supported by choppers, I moved slowly and stopped to listen often. Abruptly one chopper flew over; I heard it's machine-guns open up, so I kept moving.

Twenty minutes after I reached the agreed upon spot, Silverwolf arrived limping and Scott was helping him along. I waved as they neared and once beside me I asked, "Where are the rest?"

Silverwolf said, "Walsh was killed when his Flamethrower tanks blew, Kerr was struck in the head and is dead as hell. I don't know about Joyce."

"Joyce was in a huge Pine behind me and I saw a chopper cut her to pieces. As we retreated, she was taking shots at the Russians. I knew for every shot, a man died, but then a chopper showed, and a door-gunner chewed the tree to pieces. A minute or so later, I saw her body fall from the tree. John, there is no chance she's alive; hell, she must have fell over a hundred feet anyway."

"I agree, if the guns didn't kill her the fall did. How badly are you hit?" I asked looking at Silverwolf.

Grinning, he said, "A piece of shrapnel from one of my own grenades hit the leg. It went through the meat and missed the bone, so I'll live. It hurts like a bitch though."

I handed him a white pill from Sandra's medical supplies and said, "This will kill your pain for a couple of hours. Now, we need to be moving quickly, and keep moving until dark. Once dark, we'll stop long enough to have a cold supper, then continue to Colonel Lee. I suspect we'll reach him at some point later tonight. Scott, help him until the pill kicks in, then he can use a limb as a cane." I wiped the blood from Dolly's back and discovered most of it was not hers. She had one scratch down the middle of her back and that was it. I wiped it down with a bit of rubbing alcohol and while she didn't like it, she didn't move away from me. I knew it had to sting her a little, but she trusted me.

Scott asked, "How many Russians do you think we killed?"

"I have no idea, but not as many as you think we may have. Our only advantage was the Claymores and I suspect we may have killed a couple, but injured a good half dozen or more."

"Surely we killed at least a dozen or more."

I gave him a tired grin and said, "No, not even close, or if we did it was pure luck. But if you're worried about it, you have my permission to go back and check."

"Ain't no way in hell."

"Okay then, let's kill the chatter and get moving. I'll take the point and you help Silverwolf. In about twenty minutes his pain will go away. At that point he should be able to walk with the aid of a cane and any green limb will work fine as a walking aid. Let's move."

We moved through the woods slowly at first, until the pill started working, and then much faster. I was disturbed by the loss of my three people and all were my friends, except I'd learned in this war to adjust to loss. I'd lost my best friend, his wife, and my wife, and eventually I'm sure, it'll cost me my life. Except, what choices did I have? What is the value of this nation, even in human lives, if that's the price to be paid? Millions have already died, more would die, and the dying would probably continue well after the Russians were removed.

Our evening meal was cold Russian rations and creek water. I didn't like the idea of drinking the water, but Silverwolf assured me the enemy hadn't poisoned the water yet, but not long ago, they'd sure as hell used gas on a bunch of people down near the Louisiana state line. I was not very trusting of water sources and told both of them so.

After our meal, I gave another pain pill to Silverwolf and off we went. Even with the pain killers I knew he was hurting, but if I gave him morphine, Scott and I would have to pack him and I didn't like that idea. It's hard to respond fast if needed when you're carrying an injured man. Snow began to fall and I felt the temperature dropping fast. Still, while wanting to stop for the night, I needed to get back to Colonel Lee, and replace my dead people. I would not be able to complete my missions if not manned at 100 percent, and removing the Russians from my nation was my key concern. Nothing else in life mattered right now; nothing.

Colonel Lee moved around a large map, nailed to the side of a building and said, "Tonight we will strike Edwards Air Base. Our primary mission is to show the Russians we can hit when and where we want. Intelligence indicates they currently are short the base and gulag commanders. One we know was killed, but the other we don't know for sure yet. The acting commander has ordered the return of all troops and called the poison gas attack off. Now, this new acting commander is an interesting individual."

"Interesting in what way, sir?" a voice from the back asked. All officers and senior Sergeants were assembled outside and most were sitting in the dirt or grasses.

"Not long ago, he attempted to open a free soup kitchen in Edwards. We found out about it, of course, and took it out, along with over a dozen men and a tank. It cost us three lives, gentlemen, but well worth the price."

"Sir, I don't see the purpose of attacking Edwards, just to show them we can."

"We'll use snipers, probe a bit, and who knows, we might get lucky and overrun the base." the Colonel said and then took a long drink of his pine needle tea.

I asked, "What about my squad, sir? I'm down to two people, including me, with a third, but he's injured."

"John, I have replacements for your unit, so relax and see Top. Later today I will furnish more information about when and how we'll move toward the Russian bear."

As the man turned to move, Top yelled, "Tennnn Huuut!"

Everyone jumped to their feet.

"At ease!" the Colonel said as he rounded the corner of the building.

"John!" Top yelled and then waved at me.

I moved to him and he said, "I have nine replacements for you and all are experienced men and women. Your sniper is a woman called Mary, with over eighty confirmed kills, and she's a hard woman. Scott is to remain here and work for us. The Colonel thinks the man's language skills and intelligence will better serve our purpose if he's placed at headquarters. If nothing else, he can monitor Russian radio conversations."

I shrugged and replied, "Fine, he's yours, but I'd like to have Silverwolf back once healed. He's a good man in the bush."

"Hell, he's an old cowboy from way back is why he's good in the woods. I'll keep him on the roster and assigned to you. Now, come with me and let me introduce you to your new people. By the way, I'm sorry to hear about Sandra, she was a brave woman."

I nodded, not wanting an emotional conversation and replied, "Now, let's meet this new group of mine."

The group was a mixed bunch of prior military and law enforcement types. My sniper, Mary, was a prior USMC nurse and I was glad, because I needed both skills in the unit. I introduced myself, exchanged a few words with each of them and answered any questions they had. More or less, we just made small talk. Bill Hale, my medic, was a prior Army combat medic, with two tours behind him in the sand box, so my grin grew wider. Top swore they were all good people and they seemed to be. One, Ellis Perry, a country boy from the delta area of Mississippi, had a slow speech but a fast mind and had Army EOD experience. My smile grew even wider as I moved from person to person talking with them.

Finally, I said, "I want all of you to get some food in you and rest. We have a mission coming tonight and we all need to be well rested. I can't give any details, but we're going to grab the Russian bear's balls with our teeth."

Asa Gunn, a tall man at around six feet and four inches, closely cropped hair, said, "Well, I cain't help ya much there since I wear dentures, but if you need something blown up, by God, I can do the job."

Everyone laughed and then Charles Black, short, soft blue eyes and long shoulder length hair, said, "It doesn't matter to me.

When I volunteered to help push the Russians out of Mississippi, I donated my life and really don't expect it back alive or in good shape."

"So," Bill Hale, another tall man, with piercing gray eyes asked, "you're only fighting for our state then?"

Black said, "How well do you remember the years before the fall? Everything I'd been raised to think was proper in life was suddenly declared wrong by the Liberals. We had the rag-heads killin' each other, folks in Africa killing each other, folks were changing their genders overnight, gays and lesbians were marching in pride parades, abortions were way out of hand, black folks were killing white people and cops, and they even attacked the Confederate battle flag. All of these changes were not only suddenly socially acceptable, but fully endorsed by many."

"Well, I'm a black man," James Morgan said and then continued, "born and bred in Mississippi. I have to admit that flag was hated by many folks, and most of them were of my color."

"But, why, is what I want to know?" Black said and then slowly shook his head. "Don't you realize Old Glory had much more slave blood on her cloth than the CSA battle flag? Hell, slaves were brought to this country and spent years suffering under the stars and stripes, but the Rebel flag flew for only four bloody years."

"I never said I hated the flag, and I didn't. Only, many saw it as a symbol of racism, or the KKK. I've never told anyone, but also I've never hidden the fact, that I used to teach American History at a Mississippi state university. I think you'd be greatly surprised at just how ignorant the average American was when it came to our history. Why? First, many had absolutely no interest, and then, the north won the war so they wrote the history. I had students tell me the war started over the north's desire to free black men and women, and while the thought is nice, that wasn't the case at all. The primary reason in my eyes was state's rights, but most historians will never agree. Then, when Lincoln saw he would win the war, he decided to remove the slavery thorn from the government's ass. But, don't you see, after he was assassinated, writers, newspaper reporters and others suddenly started telling their readers what a noble man Mister Lincoln was and how he fought a bloody four year long battle to free the slave, which is pure bullshit. Lincoln fought the war for one reason and that was to preserve the Union, but slavery was certainly an issue. Now, enough talk about slavery and battle flags, we have enough to do these days."

"Well, by God, I want it known right now, I'm gay and proud of it. You'll have no trouble out of me and I'll do my job. Remember, just because I'm gay doesn't mean I find any of you attractive, which I don't. You'll find I'm no different that any other man, except my sexual orientation is different," Fox said.

Black met his eyes and said, "I'll tell you right up front, I don't like you or gays."

I could see trouble coming and said, "That's enough of this bullshit. As long as any man or woman does their job in this unit, they'll be treated with respect and dignity, regardless of their sexual preferences, religion, race, or other differences. And you two, I'll tell you both right now, any problems and I'll go to Colonel Lee and we'll take legal action, understood?"

Both men nodded, so I walked away.

At dark we moved as a small group to the trees near Edwards Air Base, and I was surprised at the number of partisans already in place. Choppers were heard coming and going and we'd moved in so close that I felt safe. The only way we'd be detected was if one of the choppers flew over our position with his infrared system on, and I suspected most would turn the system off as they neared the base.

Our late night supper was cold Russian rations, washed down by either creek water or cold tea from the meal container. I hated eating them cold, because I knew I'd get indigestion from all the fat in the meal. Then, we posted guards and went to sleep.

The next day was boring as we remained in the trees and tried not to move much, but that's hard to do for almost ten hours. I spent the day cleaning my gear and talking with my new squad individually, so I got to know each better. I spent a lot of time with both Black and Fox, just to make sure I could depend on them, and had an uneasy feeling about the two. However, we were all grouped together to attack an air base and the attack would happen. I just hoped neither of them would cause me trouble, but I'd know in just a few short hours.

At exactly 0130 I heard the light *poot* sound coming from the sniper rifles, which were all armed with silencers. I moved to Mary's side and asked, "What'd ya hit?"

"Nailed a Lieutenant Colonel coming out of a building. Looked like a clear head shot. Oh, wait, here come more."

"I'll leave you alone, because you know what you're doing." I said, and then moved back to the rest of my squad.

"When do we go?" Silverwolf asked.

"You'll not come along because your injury hasn't completely healed yet. You'll stay back here with the Colonel and provide his security. All of headquarters will remain behind, so you'll be with them."

"John!" the Colonel called out, so I moved to him.

"Take a half-dozen men and start using the Russian missiles on choppers and jets taking off and landing. I want the flight line a flaming mess when we attack. The more y'all bring down, the less that will be in the air later trying their damnedest to kill us."

"Yes, sir." I replied, and hoped we were able to down enough aircraft to make a difference. Choppers were dangerous to folks on the ground and as a weapons platform, they were deadly. I rounded up the men we'd trained and had them spread out and cover our forest as well as we could.

I took Hale and Perry with me to help spot the birds, because a fast moving aircraft can seem to appear out of an empty sky at times. Less than five minutes later, a slow moving chopper flew right in front of me and I let the missile fly. I watched as the explosion took place and saw one man thrown from the aircraft, just before it slammed into the ground and exploded. Unlike most crashes, I saw no survivors walking around in flames or heard any screams.

Two additional choppers went down by missiles fired by others and it was then the base siren began it's warbling tone in warning. Then a tank came driving down the perimeter road and I saw a bright spotlight on top sweeping the area. I heard three light *poofs*, the light exploded into many pieces, and I knew our snipers had turned the light off for good.

Then three lighted Molotov Cocktails flew through the air and exploded on the tank. The fire was followed up by a hit from a Russian RPG-7, and the tank began to smoke. It was then the hatches came open and the three man crew tried to escape, but they failed to clear the hatches before they were killed. All three Russians were slumped over, half in and half out of the tank. A partisan ran for the driver's hatch and threw a grenade inside. Seconds later it exploded, so I moved away to avoid the big beast when it blew.

I'd just returned to my squad when the tank exploded and the blast knocked a good hundred feet of perimeter fencing into the sky. We knew the fence was charged by electricity, but not any longer. Colonel Lee yelled and onto the air base we ran. At that point, the noise was unbelievable, with grenades exploding, hundreds of guns going off, screams of the wounded and even aircraft noises. I glanced up, and spotted a chopper with the door-gunner firing. I raised my missile but before I could even lock onto my target, the bird exploded into thousands of pieces sending flames, smoke and debris all over the place. The main cabin of the chopper fell and I clearly saw the pilot and copilot dead in their seats as flames danced on and inside the wreckage.

I fell to the ground as a Russian machine-gun opened up and sent a long line of lead through a small group of partisans in front of me. As I laid on my back, I looked up and the sky was filled with tracers, both incoming and outgoing. I heard a loud scream followed by an explosion, and when I looked toward the sandbags, the machine-gun was tilted on it's side and smoking. I counted three Russian bodies sprawled on the ground, each with a fatal wound.

A man in front of me suddenly fell back with half his head missing, struck the ground and his body began to quiver and jerk as he died. I stepped over him and kept moving forward. A young Russian face suddenly appeared in front of me and I squeezed the trigger of my Bison, running bullets from left to right and down he went. A long trench was alongside the flight line and in a zig-zag configuration. The Russians had machine-guns located with interlocking fire, but some of our people were in the ditch, clearing the guns out. The fighting was close and personal now, with gun butts, knives, and even rocks. I saw one Russian drop with an entrenching tool in his neck.

I pulled my pistol and moved forward. A bulk of a man ran for me, his upper chest and arms covered in blood, while around him lay three partisans. My pistol barked twice and his eyes grew huge; he stopped, looked down at two bullet holes in his chest, and then fell to his knees. I fired one more shot and his head exploded as the round struck him almost between the eyes. Blood flew from the back of his head as he collapsed to the dirt in the bottom of the trench. I stood for a second, watching blood running from his head melting the freshly fallen snow as it ran downhill.

CHAPTER 16

A bullet zinged into the command post, struck a radio, and then ricocheted. A nearby radio operator screamed and fell from his chair to the floor. Blood was spurting from a severed artery in his leg and his eyes were open wide in fear. He twisted and shrieked as his feet kicked and his nails raked the hardwood floor.

"Medic!" Vasiliev screamed as he squatted beside the injured man and pinched the artery closed. He then said, "Lay still, Sergeant, if you want to survive this injury."

A medic appeared and began working on the radioman. A few minutes later two men with a litter arrived and packed the injured man from the command post. The Colonel saw blood dripping from the stretcher and for some reason, it made him shiver. Then glancing at his blood-stained hands, he suddenly had a feeling of doom fall over him like a veil. Shaking it off, he moved back to his chair to monitor radio transmissions.

"Sir, the partisans are in the aircraft hangers!" the radioman suddenly said.

"Call Major Borisovich and order a counter attack on the hangers, and do it now!"

"Yes, sir."

Suddenly there came a huge explosion and it was followed by a number of lesser detonations. The radioman was talking in an excited voice and turning to the Colonel, he said, "The gas storage tanks have just gone up in flames and most of our petroleum, liquids and oils!"

"Damn me! Moscow will have my ass for this." Vasiliev exploded from his chair, then moving to the radioman he said, "Do we have any jets in the air?"

"At last count, six, sir."

"All one flight?"

"Yes, sir."

"Let me speak to the flight commander."

"Give me a couple of minutes, sir. I have to change frequencies to do this."

"Do what is needed, but hurry."

"Yes, sir."

The Colonel paced the floor until the radioman said, "Use my headphones, sir."

"Flight lead, this is Lieutenant Colonel Vasiliev and I have a mission for you."

"Copy, you have a mission for us, sir. Go ahead."

"What are you loaded with, as far as munitions?"

"Napalm, rockets and some bombs, sir."

"I want you to drop napalm on the fence lines on the south side of the base, and then hit the fuel storage area with rockets. Any Gatling guns?"

"Yes, where do you want them?"

"As close as you can get them to the hangers without damaging the structures."

"We will try our best."

"Radioman, I will be outside watching this, so if I need changes made, I will call out to you. Senior Sergeant, I want you and five of your men to come with me; the snow is falling harder now, so be sure of your targets if you shoot." Stepping outside, he was appalled by all the damage and fires he saw. The fuel tanks were sending flames hundreds of feet into the air and the hangers were aflame as well. Abruptly, the southern fence line was a huge ball of rolling fire and he knew the jets were attacking. Gatling guns, with their loud cough were heard over the other weapons fire and, using his binoculars, he saw partisan after partisan blown to pieces. Two rockets were seen to leave one jet and they head straight for the fuels area. When the second jet released his, most everyone looking saw they were low.

"Get down, *now!*" the Senior Sergeant yelled and a second later, Lieutenant Colonel Vasiliev's world turned black.

He heard noises, but could not open his eyes. He smelled blood, smoke from burning rubber, and death. He tried to move, only his limbs refused to work for him and a few seconds later, he entered the black void of unconsciousness.

When he next heard something, he discovered he could open his eyes, but when he looked around, he was with partisans and not Russian troops. He heard English spoken.

Then a voice asked in Excellent Russian, "Colonel, do you know where you are? Open your eyes, because I saw you looking around a few minutes ago."

Vasiliev opened his eyes, saw Corporal Scott and said, "Your Russian is excellent."

"So is yours, sir. Do you have pain?"

"No, but I am a bit confused about how I got here and where am I?"

"You were discovered moaning in your command post, the building destroyed, by one of your own aircraft I must say, and most around you were dead. You were captured because you are an officer. Right now, you are in an interrogation center."

"W . . . what will happen to me?"

"It depends on how well you answer our questions, sir."

"But, the resistance keeps no prisoners of war."

"Would you believe me if I told you we have exactly five prisoners and each is a high ranking officer? They are Majors or above and will be kept until the end of this conflict, then exchanged."

"Or used for reprisals, right?"

"That could happen as well, yes, sir."

"What are the extent of my injuries?"

"You have a concussion, three fingers on your left hand have been broken, and your right ankle is lightly sprained, but not broken. You are also missing about half of your left ear and you have some minor facial injuries."

"Then, I take it I am in no danger of dying?"

"Oh, but you are, if you do not answer our questions during your interrogation."

"I see." The Colonel lowered his eyes and then quivered.

"Colonel, we have people here who can no longer work as fighters, because they have been maimed during questioning conducted by your people. They are the lucky ones, but let me assure you, they love to question Russians. They learned much about torture from being guests of your army, sir, and they will demonstrate later just how effective they can be."

Two men neared and Scott said, "Pack the stretcher to cell number 6. He is to have his ankles in chains and his collar chained to the wall. If he makes a run for freedom, kill him."

Seeing Vasiliev looking at him with questioning eyes, he repeated the orders in Russian.

"Colonel," Scott said, "you will now be taken to our guest lodging, where you will be given a blanket, some chains, and fed twice a day. By the way, our troops are only fed twice a day and they will be eating the same food you will, Russian rations. I do hope you enjoy your stay with us and if so, please recommend us to your friends."

Meeting Scott's eyes, the Colonel said, "I will cut your heart out for this one day."

"Maybe, sir, but I doubt that, seriously. The first place the interrogators start working is on a prisoners hands, arms and legs. I suspect by the time they finish with you, you will not have enough use in your hands to even write your name."

In English, Scott said, "Take this man to his cell."

Vasiliev discovered his cell was about five feet wide and eight feet long, with a ten foot ceiling. He was chained to a wall, but given enough chain to use a large empty can as a toilet. He was surprised to find the place heated and his blanket almost new. A one gallon plastic container was near the toilet can and it held what looked to be drinking water. He saw an uncovered light, which he was to discover, burned 24/7, and he was fed through a small siding slot in the metal door. His bed was made of concrete and in the middle of it was a Holy Bible in Russian. He moved to the bed, tossed the Bible to the floor and then tried to sleep, but it did not come.

I need to get out of here and the sooner the better. If they start the torture and discover I am the commander at Edwards, they will likely kill me, he thought.

He spent the remainder of the day reliving his childhood years in his mind and tried to remember the smallest detail. It was after he relieved himself in the metal bucket he heard a voice whisper in Russian, "Who are you?"

Unsure if it was a Yankee trick or not, the Colonel replied, "I am the admin officer assigned at Edwards, and you?"

"I am Major General Unetsov and I have been a prisoner for over three years."

"Who is the ranking officer, sir?"

"That is Lieutenant General Stepan Sokoloff, and he is a good man."

"Inform him I am going to try and escape, if I can."

"It will only get you killed, but if you must try, do it before the first interrogation or they will cripple you. None of us have the use of our legs or hands as we once did."

"I am sorry, sir." Vasiliev said.

"It is war and these things happen. It would be better to have died in battle than to be a prisoner and Moscow will be hard on us when we return."

"I am only a Lieutenant Colonel, sir, so I know little of Moscow or its workings."

"Mark my words, escape and you will be a hero; be released as a prisoner when this all ends and you will end up in a gulag."

"I hear you, sir."

Silence for a good five minutes.

"Sir?" Vasiliev asked.

"Yes, Colonel?"

"If I can get away, what should I tell Moscow?"

"Give them our names. We have two Colonels, Petya Mihaylov and Artem Kozlov. There are three Generals; myself, Colonel General Ivan Popov and Lieutenant General Stepan Sokoloff. Tell Moscow we have told the Americans nothing. I fear for our families if Moscow does not think we are resisting and we are. But, every man has his breaking point and all of us have experienced ours."

"I will tell them, sir."

"Oh, and Colonel?"

"Yes, sir?"

"Good luck, because you will need it. If you get away from this camp, head due north and you will run into the Jackson Air Base. There lies safety."

"Yes, sir."

"Enough, someone comes."

He heard keys jingling and voices speaking low, but he knew no English. He'd seen a few old American movies on television, but he understood none of it and the movies had subtitles. A key was inserted into his cell's lock and he waited for the door to open. He suspected two men, but what if there were three or more?

Two bored looking and young partisans entered his cell, and he pretended to be asleep or passed out, so one would come near him. His eyelids were barely open.

"Hey, get up!" one yelled and neared him.

His pistol is on his right hip, the Colonel thought.

When he didn't respond the man bent over to shake him. When he touched Vasiliev, he threw the chain over the mans neck and pulled it tight. As soon as he felt something snap, he clawed for the pistol. Since most of the weapons were Russian, he knew how to use the gun. He fired one shot, dropped the other guard, and then taking the man in his arms by his head, a quick snap broke his neck. He raced against time as he pulled the keys from the dead man's pocket and attempted to find the proper one to unlock his chains. Soon he was free, but knew he'd have to fight his way out; he'd been too slow. He moved to the downed guard and stripped him of his Bison sub-machine gun, ammo and two grenades. He'd already taken a knife and ammo from the man with the broken neck.

He then stepped into the hallway and heard General Unetsov say, "Good Luck! Remember us! Return for us! Return!"

When he stepped outside, he was surprised to find it dark, with the moon showing that half the night was gone. He stayed in the shadows and at one point saw a squad of men running toward the cells. He watched for search lights, but saw none. *Damn me, I am sure they have night vision gear they have stolen from us. I need to use more caution. I must return.*

He had no idea when he was away from the camp, because there was no fence or guards. *I must keep my calm about me or I will perish*, he thought. *Keep my eyes open for mines and booby-traps, too.*

He moved slowly, fighting the urge to run, to run as fast as he could. He knew he had to maintain control or he'd end up dead or captured again and one equaled the other, in his mind. What the General said was true about Russians who became prisoners of war going to gulags, because most had in the past. *If I go to a gulag, most of my family will disappear*, he thought, as he moved slowly through some thick brush, keeping his noise to a minimum.

The night passed slowly for him and near sunup, he grew hungry and tired, but he kept moving. Knowing his survival depended on him either reaching safety or being found, he started to hunt a hole for the day, and then realized, Russians ruled the land during the day. So, he continued to move.

The land was rough, swampy and marshy areas all around, and at night the temperature was cold enough he felt the need for a fire but didn't want to stop, and he had no way to start one anyway. Each bad section of land he had to walk around, which was difficult, made his progress north much slower. He knew the partisans would be after him; after all, he'd killed two and they'd want revenge. His fear suddenly grew larger, but he forced it down and continued to move.

As he walked he looked for food, but the plant life he saw was unfamiliar, and he'd not risk a shot at any animal. He'd been hungry before and knew he'd not starve to death. He did drink water from a fast moving stream, but wasn't sure if it was smart or not.

He knew he should purify it, but the only way he knew to do it properly was to use chemical pills, bleach, or by boiling. He had no pills, was fresh out of bleach, and he suspected if he got a fire burning the smoke or smell would get him caught. *When I return, I will have the hospital give me a physical and see if I have picked up any parasites. They will know how to treat me*, he thought.

As he moved, his aches and pains grew greater and by mid morning his head was pounding. He had to stop for a bit to allow his double vision to return to normal. It was then he decided to stop every hour for ten minutes, or longer if needed, in hopes his pain would lessen. His first break was for thirty minutes, so his pain level would drop.

He fought the urge to vomit, but wasn't sure if it was caused by bad water, his injuries or fear. He continued to move. He'd neither heard or seen any sign of pursuit, but suspected he was being tracked. *Keep moving north until you can move no more*, he told himself as he watched a sluggish snake slide toward the water of a nearby swamp. He knew little of this country, except there were poisonous snakes and alligators were wild, but other than that, he knew nothing.

It was mid-afternoon when he heard the sound of a helicopter. His head came up and he listened closely. It seemed to be nearing his position, so he moved toward a wide open field, hoping to get picked up. He was still dressed in a Russian Lieutenant Colonel's uniform so he suspected he'd be picked up quickly.

Five minutes later, the helicopter flew right over him, made a lazy circle and then flew over him again, but lower this time. He saw the gunners in the door watching him closely. He waved and screamed, unaware his voice would not be heard over the roar of the aircraft engines. Finally, the aircraft neared him from the front and when he moved slightly to the left to avoid flying debris, he saw the barrels of a Gatling gun move with him. They'd locked onto him and he knew a false move on his part would get him killed.

The helicopter started to lower and finally when the wheels touched ground, a man left the aircraft, and neared him. He was shoved to the ground, searched and then handcuffed. He offered no resistance and was then led to the helicopter.

Once on board, his injuries were checked, cleaned and wrapped. The medic looked at his eyes with a light, shook his head, and then reaching into his bag pulled out a white pill. He then handed a canteen to the Colonel.

The ride to the base was short, less than twenty minutes and when they landed, an ambulance was there to take him to a hospital. The pill made him sleepy, but he remained awake as he was taken to the medical facility, which confused him, because it was a tent and not a building.

Looking up at a Private carrying his stretcher, he asked, "Where am I? Why is the hospital not in a building?"

"Sir, two days ago partisans attacked us and most of the solid structures were destroyed. The hospital burned down, killing most of the patients, so this tent will have to do for now."

We lost the hospital? What else did we lose? Most of the permanent buildings are gone? I wonder if that includes the aircraft hangers? I will wait, because a Private will know little, he thought.

He was removed from the ambulance by stretcher and placed on a table.

After a few minutes, a doctor neared and said, "Hello, Lieutenant Colonel Vasiliev, we were told you were killed in the command post and your body was not recovered. Where have you been, sir?"

"I was a prisoner of war, but escaped."

"Are you in much pain?"

"A little and my head has most of it right now."

"I will fix your pain, but Colonel, you may wish you had stayed with the partisans. Headquarters sent a new acting commander, uh, a Colonel Igor Staslov, and after he arrived he spoke poorly of your defenses and action during the attack, sir."

"Oh, and how could he have done better?"

As a medic started an IV, the doctor said, "Sir, I am not a soldier, but a doctor. I have no idea about things of war, because my goal is to stop the suffering of our wounded. I am a healer, not a killer, so you will need to ask the Colonel yourself."

"Can you remove these handcuffs from me?"

"No, sir, I cannot. We have orders if you were found injured, that we were to secure you and take you prisoner."

"Prisoner! I am the damned commander here! I demand you release me this moment, doctor, and that is an order."

The doctor nodded and the medic inserted a needle into his left arm. As his world faded, he heard the doctor say, "Colonel, with all due respect, sir, you are no longer a commander. As a matter of fact, Moscow has ordered your immediate arrest. Now, rest and sleep, because you are safe with us for right now."

CHAPTER 17

Colonel Lee was ashen as he leaned forward and asked, "What do you mean it looks as if a Russian Colonel has escaped, Sergeant? The man is either here or gone, so which is the case?" The Colonel was so angry, I thought he might climb on top of his desk if given any more bad news. I noticed his office was bare, with the exception of a large Mississippi map on one wall.

Sergeant O'Brien stood at attention and said, "He escaped, sir, after killing two guards."

Lee's eyes narrowed, but he didn't speak, not for many long minutes. Finally, he asked, "Are we at least out looking for him?"

"Oh, yes, sir. We have ten squads after him, but so far they've found little."

"Sergeant O'Brien, you will investigate this issue and prepare a personal briefing for me to be conducted at 0700 in the morning. I want to know the who, what, when, and where of this entire escape. I can tell you right now, Sergeant, I am not a pleased man. Lieutenant Colonel Vasiliev was the overall acting commander of not only Edwards Air Base, but also the gulag, and chief of anti-terrorism operations for this area. And now you tell me the bastard is free to kill more Americans."

"I'm just the senior enlisted guard of the Russians, sir. Lieutenant William Johnson is the officer in charge."

"In the morning, have Lieutenant Johnson *and* you here. As the two senior men, I want answers and, by God, both of you better provide them, or heads will roll. Dismissed, Sergeant."

As soon as the Sergeant walked away, I neared Colonel Lee and said, "So, our last fish got away, huh?"

"Yes, but it will do him little good. The word our spies have is he's facing legal charges for his poor defense of the base and, I think, being made a scapegoat. The odds are he'll either commit suicide, be shot, or return home to a gulag."

"How can our spies know this when the man hadn't escaped yet? Colonel, I don't care what they do to the man, because he killed two of our troops. While I respect the Russian as a soldier, his welfare is not my concern. I came to you to see if you have other missions or plans I need to be aware of, sir."

The Colonel gave a dry chuckle and said, "The Russians marked him dead, body not recovered, but there were thoughts of him being taken prisoner. I don't care personally what they do to him either. I was letting you know his status. Now, we are still licking our wounds from the attack on Edwards, which overall was a victory for us, so there are no other big operations planned at this time. However, if you're itching to get at the Russians, you can always hit a train for us. I'll allow you a company of men and women to complete the task. Give me a few hours and I'll have the time and place for the train I want you to hit."

"Time?"

"Yes, I don't want you to hit just any train. We need you to take out a supply train, because we always need supplies, guns and ammunition. We have spies in most places and if I can discover the usual time for a supply train, I'll let you know. How'd your squad do during the attack?"

"No problems with them, not that I could see. Mary had four confirmed kills as my sniper and I'd like to recommend Private Gunn for promotion to Corporal. He's a damned one man army."

"Promotion granted and instantly, because we need good people. Now, if you'll excuse me, I'll get someone to finding a train for you and I've some paperwork to do. But, John?"

"Sir?"

"Just between us, my health is declining quickly and you may have to step into my position faster then either of us thought."

"I'm truly sorry to hear this, sir. Are you in a lot of pain?"

"No, I have medication, just stating facts. Will you be ready to assume command?"

"Oh, yes sir, but I dislike the circumstances."

"As do I, son. Now get out so I can get some work done."

"Yes, sir." I saluted and left his office.

Tonight it's cold, well below zero and a light snow. I hate cold weather, which was the reason after I got out of the army, I'd moved to Mississippi. Occasionally the weather would get cold, but it never lasted over a couple of weeks until this year. I glanced at my watch, saw it was 2000 and knew the train would be along soon. Mary neared and then lay down beside me.

"What's on your mind?" I asked, knowing she came to me for a reason.

"Do you think the explosives on the track will cause the train engine to go off the track?"

"Uh-huh, I do. I've been blowing up Russian trains for years. Oh, the explosives might not do the job, but it'll sure as hell blow the tracks up and that means the engine will continue to move forward off the track. Eventually, beyond any doubt, it'll stop moving, and most roll on their side. Why?"

"Do you want me to take the engineer out?"

"No, not really, and it's not because I'm soft. Most of the engineers work for us, providing departure and arrival times. They're civilians, forced to work for the Russians."

"Oh, I didn't know that."

"They know we'll attack their trains, so at the first sign of trouble, they usually jump from the engines and lay on the ground. I try not to hurt them, but some have been killed. It's a deadly thing we do."

Silverwolf said, "The train's coming, see?" He pointed by I saw nothing.

"I don't see it." I replied.

"Do you hear it?" he asked.

I gave a dry chuckle and then said, "No, I don't hear it either."

"Trust me, boss," he smiled, "it'll soon be here."

We were about fifty meters from the tracks and I had Gunn with the Claymore, just about where the second car would be on the train, but he was up closer. The second car was a flatcar, with a number of soldiers, maybe ten to fifteen. Usually, a senior NCO was in charge of the men on trains, unless they were carrying a valuable load; then an officer would be present.

Finally, I saw the single glaring eye of the train as it moved through the darkness toward me. I glanced at Silverwolf and he smiled. I could never figure out how I couldn't see or hear what he did, while my eyesight and hearing were excellent.

"Down, and wait for the blast." I said as I prepared to blow the rails. I had about half my folks down about a hundred meters, to hit the rear of the train at the same time we hit the front.

When the train was close I blew the charge, smiled, and saw the train continue on. Close to ten feet later, the engine teetered and then fell to it's side, just as the Claymore went off.

Shouts and screams of pain filled the air as soon as the sound of the blast cleared. My people opened up with a line of lead death the length of the train. Bodies fell from the train with screams and then I yelled, "Charge!"

We came out of the brush and trees screaming as we each picked a target. I moved to the train engine, saw the engineer out walking around, dazed. I struck him hard to the head, which knocked him to the ground. This way, he'd have a goose egg on his head to show the Russians when they came.

One car of Russians was putting out a lot of fire, mostly automatic. I moved slowly along the sides of the cars, pulled the pin from a grenade and tossed it inside. I heard screams in Russian, followed by a loud explosion. Two men either jumped or were blown out the door and landed in bloody heaps on the gravel, dead. Corporal Hale ran forward and tossed another grenade. After it went off the cries of the wounded ceased.

"Gunn!" I yelled.

"Yo!"

"Get me a count of all dead, both sides, and injured. Any Russians caught alive or with minor wounds will return with us. Kill their seriously injured. I'll not have them get patched up so they can fight me another day. Let me know the overall status of our wounded as well."

I started hearing pistol shots and knew Gunn was on the job.

Silverwolf neared and said, "Looks like a train full of rations, bullets and winter uniforms."

"Take it all and have the men with bicycles put a full load on, and what we can't take, destroy. Also, check every car for any cash or anything we might have overlooked."

Minutes later, Private Perry walked to me and said, "I found two boxes, but they're locked."

"Lead me to them."

Dead Russians littered the ground outside and the floor inside the car. I noticed one man was a full Colonel, so whatever it was, it had value. I moved to the boxes, found them locked, and shot the locks off. I then pulled the containers open and saw the international sign for radiation. I then flipped the internal tops off; they were like a huge briefcase, and inside I saw what looked like a war head.

No, this can't be, I thought as I met the eyes of Perry.

"What is it, sir?"

"I think you just found, I pray I'm wrong, two tactical nuclear warheads."

"What's that?" he asked.

"Nuke bombs."

"Oh, shit, not good." he said and then slowly backed away from me.

I'd just shot the locks off too, but I had no idea what it took to make one of these things go off. I suspected a code or key had to be used before launch.

"Get five men, Private Perry, and they're to take turns packing these back to the camp. At no time are these to be left alone. Do you understand?"

"Y . . . yes, sir. I don't have to stay with 'em, do I?"

"Keep them in your sight at all times."

"Yes, sir."

I pulled Silverwolf aside, told him what I found and then he replied, "We need to return now. Once they know we have these, they'll come and they'll not be happy. I'm sure they'll do whatever it takes to regain control of them, too."

I nodded, turned toward the train and yelled, "Let's move, folks! We're leaving in five minutes."

The attack had gone well. I wondered if what I'd found would be of use to us, or if I'd just reduced the ability of the Russians to use two small tactical nukes against us for a few days. So far, they'd used poison gas, mass killings and other abuses against us, so nukes were just another tactic to them. I thought nukes would be used by them if they felt they could gain something by using them. Worried, I pushed my people hard to return.

When I returned, Colonel Lee was in his sleeping bag and not looking good. A Russian IV was in his arm, he looked weak and frail, but he was able to talk.

"So, how do we activate the nukes?" I asked.

"I have no idea, but the special group I have made up of scientist and engineers should be able to come up with a way. But, for God's sake, don't use it against them first."

"Oh, trust me, sir, I have no desire to start a nuclear war with Russia, because it's a war I can't win."

"Smart on your part, but if they start, I hope we'll be able to retaliate to a limited degree. Placing one near the Jackson Air Base and Vicksburg port would show them we mean business."

"What is the rumor I hear of the Chinese offering us arms and supplies? Is there any truth to this?" I asked.

"They've already started airdrops to some groups of the resistance. So far it's been explosives, some clothing, some weapons, ammo, RPG's, and rations. Most of the rations taste like hell, well, to an American. The meals consist of rice, meat, noodles, and veggies. In a pinch they'll do, but I heard Russian rations are better, so you know the Chinese meals must really suck. The key here is they're starting to assist us, but my question is why? What's in it for them?"

"They're enemies of Russia, so that may be enough," I said and then continued, "or they want something in return. We have no central leader, so if they want something, they'll have to wait."

"Back to the tactical nukes you found. We need to learn how use them, activate them, and protect them."

"True, but your team of experts will soon have that information. How are you feeling, sir, and don't give me some bullshit and say fine."

"I'm weak and I'll grow weaker. According to the doctor we now have, I've got about six months to live. I figure, when I'm too weak to do much, I'll load myself up with explosives, we'll attack the Russians in Edwards and when you pull back, I'll stay behind. Once I have enough Russians around me, I'll detonate the explosives and take some of the bastards with me."

I nodded, but didn't reply. Colonel Lee was a good man and I'll hate to lose him, but I fully understand his hatred of the Russians.

"We also collected some rations, ammunition, and winter clothing from the train. I have it being issued to our combat units first. Any left over will be issued based on individual need."

"We need to relocate and do the job soon." he replied.

"Oh, I've given that some thought. I'm not sure Colonel Vasiliev could find this place again, but to be safe, you're right, we need to move."

"Any suggestions?" he asked, and whatever was in the IV must have been working, because he was starting to look better and stronger already.

"South of here is an old farm house; has two floors, and it's surrounded by oak and pine trees. There is a storm shelter, long porch, barn and a number of out buildings."

"I want you to get us moving, and the sooner the better. It's not likely the Colonel remembers how to get back here, but it's time to move. I never like to stay in one place over a month and we've been here twice that long. I've found the longer you stay the more likely you are to be discovered."

I turned and yelled, "Top!"

A few minutes later, he stuck his head in the door and asked, "Yes, sir?"

"Get the troops to start boxing and bagging things, we're going to move. I want double guards on the prisoners, but not the two American prisoners we have." I said.

"What of them?" Top asked.

"They've both been found guilty of spying for the Russians, so they'll die here."

"I understand, sir." he replied and I could see he had more to say, but for some reason he didn't.

"In case you're wondering, I'll do the executions myself, and by pistol. They should be hanged, in front of all the troops, but we don't have the time for that. We suspect the Russians are going to pay us a visit."

"I suspected the Russians were the reason, sir. I'll get them ready to leave."

"Good, and they have one hour." I said. Top nodded and then walked away.

"And when will these executions take place?" Colonel Lee asked.

I pulled my Russian pistol, looked it over and replied, "Right now."

"Good and remember, they both confessed, so it's not murder."

"I know, sir. Let me take care of this and I'll return to assist you to your new office."

"Don't worry about me, I'll have the medics move me. You get the nasty job done and then see to the move."

"Yes, sir. Right now, I'll send a squad to the location to check it out and they'll be back in a couple of hours. We'll be moving toward them, so we'll run into them as we move."

"I need some sleep, so see to my orders, and thank you for your help."

I gave him a pat on his shoulder and said, "We're all in this together, sir, so rest."

He nodded and I walked toward the door. Once outside, I called for Silverwolf.

"Yo!"

"Come with me. I have two American prisoners to execute. Once that's done, take the squad and move to the old Egger place. Make sure it's secure and then move back toward us. We'll be moving for the place so keep your eyes open. We need to relocate, and now." I said and then moved for the prisoners cells.

The jailer opened the door to the hallway and led me to the Americans.

"They're in cells six and seven, sir." He then handed me the keys and left.

I handed the keys to Silverwolf and nodded as I pointed to cell six. He opened the cell and the man looked up at me. I could see the fear in his eyes.

"Are you Berry Smith?" I asked.

He nodded and then asked, "What do you want?"

"Mr. Smith, you were found guilty by a court of law and sentenced to be executed. The time has come for you to pay for your crimes."

"No, please! I don't want to die."

"Secure the prisoner, Sergeant." I said to Silverwolf, who grabbed the man's chains and pulled him to his knees.

As I pulled my pistol, he continued to beg. I finally said, "You have one minute to pray and I suggest you do so right now."

I was watching my watch and when a minute passed, I put the barrel of my pistol against the back of his head and pulled the trigger. The shot was loud in the small room and the man's head exploded, throwing blood all over the cell floor. Silverwolf released the chains and the body fell to the floor where it jerked and quivered.

"Next cell," I said.

We moved to cell seven and the prisoner was an older man who simply nodded. He'd heard our shot and knew we were coming. When I walked in, he knelt and said, "I've already spoken with the Lord."

"Are you John Windsor?" I asked.

"Yes."

"You were found guilty by a court of law and sentenced to be executed, sir."

"I was, so let's get this over with." he said as his eyes met mine.

I raised my pistol, fired one shot into his head and quickly walked from the room, with Silverwolf close behind me.

CHAPTER 18

"All stand, please." a Sergeant said as he looked around the courtroom. Most of the men outranked him, but he felt, as the bailiff, he held some power.

"Be seated." Major General Leonid Anatoli said as he sat down.

"Case number 097864, Lieutenant Colonel Pasha Vasiliev is accused of disobeying orders, conduct unbecoming a field grade officer, and dereliction of assigned duties."

"Colonel, I am Major General Anatoli, and these charges are most serious. How do you plead?" the General asked.

Major Yuliy Motya, the Colonel's defense counselor, stood and said, "Not guilty, sir."

"Would the prosecution and defense approach the bench? I have some things to say for your ears only."

When they neared, the General said, "Let us save some time here, gentlemen, because Moscow wants Vasiliev found guilty. Now, counselor," he said as he glanced at the defense counselor, "in a few moments, you will ask me for more time to prepare your defense. I will grant it, but you must get your client to agree to plead guilty. If so, I will see he gets a light sentence."

Motya nodded.

"Now, return to your seats."

As soon as Motya was back at his table he said, "Sir, I feel I would be doing my client an injustice, if I did not ask you for additional time to prepare his case. Therefore, the defense requests ten days."

"Disapproved; however, I will grant you five days. This court is adjourned until five days from now when it will start in earnest."

As the General started to stand, the Sergeant yell, "All stand."

In his room, Vasiliev listened to his attorney and finally said, "I did nothing incorrect and I followed my orders; there were just too many partisans and they were well armed. Have you ever been in combat, Major?"

"Uh, no sir, but the issue here is someone in Moscow thinks, essentially, that you are a coward. They think you were terrified during the attack."

The Lieutenant Colonel laughed and said, "Any man in combat is scared, Major, but I am no coward. A real man fights his fear and moves in battle, does what is required, sir, which I did."

Wanting to switch the conversation, the Major said, "You realize you are not to leave your quarters or use the phone, correct?"

"Hell, I have an armed guard just outside my door and where am I to flee, sir? Those on this base want my ass and so do those outside the base. I hope you gave my list of the POW's the partisans have to the commander."

"I did." Motya replied, but didn't say that the commander had thrown the list in the trash.

"They seemed to be honorable men."

"Look, plead guilty, and I will get you a light sentence. If you fight this, well, you could end up being shot."

"I am a man of integrity, sir, and I refuse to admit I did anything wrong during the attack. No, I will fight this to my last breath. You and I both know Moscow is looking for a scapegoat and I'm the man."

"As you wish, Colonel. Do you have enough Vodka? If you need anything, just let me know and I will bring it to you. You are still a Lieutenant Colonel in the Russian army at this time and will be treated like one."

"I have drink and I am treated well enough. I am sure when I am sent to a gulag, no one will care about my comfort then."

"Plead guilty and I will see if I can get the gulag time reduced or avoided completely."

Vasiliev glared at the man and replied, "That will never happen. I suspect the judge called you to his bench today to tell you I will be found guilty. He wants a guilty plea, so I do not take up his valuable time, but by God, I will take his time. I will never plead guilty to something I did not do. If blame must be placed somewhere, then blame Moscow."

"Your words are treasonous, so watch your tongue." Motya said, his eyes large in surprise. He suspected the room was bugged, so he had to say something.

"Why? They plan to either kill me or put me in a gulag for life anyway. You and Moscow can kiss my ass. So, why do you not run back to comrade Judge and tell him I will have my day in court? I want the record to show I did nothing wrong."

"I cannot guarantee your safety if you do not plead guilty."

"Can you guarantee it if I do?"

Silence filled the small room.

Vasiliev smiled and said, "I did not think you could. Now, leave and let me eat. There is something about law and lawyers that ruins my appetite." He stood, moved to the door and opened it. The guard outside turned to face him.

"It is okay, Private, I am only shooing a skunk from my quarters."

"Sir, think of what I have suggested. If you fight the system, you will lose."

The Colonel laughed and said, "If I do not fight the system I will lose. Now, get out."

Motya left without another word and once the door was shut, Vasiliev moved to the cupboard and pulled out a quart of Vodka. Pouring a water glass half full, he sat on the sofa and tried to think. He saw no way to avoid punishment, none. While he did have professional contacts, none would put their careers on the line for a man accused of being a coward.

I must think, he thought and then took a big gulp of his warm drink. It was his first drink of the day and the strong alcohol caused him to cough and his eyes to water. He decided to get drunk this night, because in the near future, strong drink would be denied him.

Major General Anatoli was sipping a much better quality of vodka than Vasiliev when there was a knock on his door. The General nodded to his enlisted servant, a Corporal, and the man moved for the door. He pushed a button near the steel door and asked, "Who is disturbing the General at this hour?"

The guard outside the door said, "It is a Captain from the message center. His name is Arkhip and he has a priority message from Moscow for General Anatoli's eyes only."

"Has he been disarmed?"

"He is clean of any weapons, Corporal."

The General's aide pushed a button near the door, a buzzing sound was heard and then the clicking of the door unlocking. He pulled the door open and said, "Enter, sir."

Arkhip entered, snapped to attention and said, "I have a priority message from Moscow, sir. It is for your eyes only."

Wearing a robe, cigarette dangling from his lip, and a glass of vodka in his hand, the General said, "Well, bring it to me and then be gone."

The Captain moved to the General, handing the message to him, and then left.

Taking a big gulp of his drink, Anatoli opened the sealed envelope, removed the message and began reading. He read the message, folded it, and placed it back in the envelope. He then broke out laughing. *The fools in Moscow have no idea what is going on over here, none!* He thought, then he gulped the rest of the drink.

Standing, he said, "Corporal, I am going to bed now. Make sure I am awakened at 0500, because I have a full day of court tomorrow. In the mean time, call the base commander and tell him at 0730 hours, I want to see Lieutenant Colonel Vasiliev and his legal counsel in my courtroom. Do you understand?"

"Yes, sir, and I will call the commander as soon as you are in bed, sir."

At 0730 hours, Vasiliev and Motya were seated at the defense table waiting for the Major General to arrive. The Lieutenant Colonel was nervous, expecting to be taken out and shot. He still reeked of Vodka and vomit, from his night of heavy drinking.

"All stand!" the Sergeant yelled.

"Be seated, please." the General said as he moved to his chair.

Sitting, he paused a few minutes and then said, "Lieutenant Colonel Vasiliev, you will now stand."

Shaking, his stomach in knots, Vasiliev stood and stared straight ahead.

"Last night in my quarters, I received a Top Secret message pertaining to this case. A military review board has reviewed your case after a thorough investigation, and have decided you not only acted properly on the night of the partisan attack, but valiantly. Effective immediately, all charges against you have been dropped. You are to be decorated for your bravery in the near future, and you have been promoted to the permanent rank of Colonel."

"Am I free to leave, sir?" Vasiliev asked as he stood in shock. The last thing he expected was to have the charges against him dropped.

"Oh, yes, and my aide will escort you to your new quarters. However, please allow for the formalities of this court to complete, before you leave, sir."

"Thank you, sir. I will wait."

"You are a very lucky man, Colonel, and never in my thirty years in the army have I seen this happen. If you are a practicing Christian, you need to say a prayer of thanks." Then, looking around the courtroom, the General added, "This case is dismissed."

Motya looked that the Colonel and then asked, "Well, is that not a surprise?"

"It is to me, but I think Moscow decided the Russian people need a hero and I am awfully glad they chose me. Only in Russia, can a man be close to a firing squad, then be proclaimed a hero five minutes later."

Standing, the lawyer extended his hand and smiled.

Vasiliev grunted, met the man's eyes and said, "Avoid me, Motya, because I have little use for men with no backbone."

Before the lawyer could reply, a Corporal neared and said, "Colonel, you are the new base commander here and if you will follow me, sir, I will take you to your quarters."

As he walked away, he turned, pointed his finger like a gun at the lawyer and said, "Stay away from me, Major."

Motya felt a shiver go through his body.

Master Sergeant Morozov was standing in Colonel Vasiliev's office early the next morning and the Sergeant was almost completely healed. His earlier injuries pained him at times, but the pain was managed easily by a few sips of vodka. The senior NCO was standing about three feet in front of the officers desk at attention.

"Master Sergeant, do you understand your mission? I know my directions are vague and I do not know for sure where I was being held, but the partisans have five of our senior officers and they must be rescued."

"If you are sure it was in this area, we will find the camp, unless they have moved. With your escape, it is not likely they remained there."

"I want you to take three dog teams and look for them. It is absolutely essential that we rescue the officers. Now, what I am about to tell you is not to be spoken of outside this room, understand?"

"Yes, sir, and I have a security clearance."

"This pertains to your mission too, or I would not bring it up."

"Then I have a need to know, sir."

"A few days after the attack on the base, two tactical nuclear weapons were taken by the partisans following an attack on a train. These weapons are small, just big enough that a man can parachute in, set the timer, and then get safely away. The blast is small, but sufficient to destroy a city, lets say, the size of Saint Louis, Moscow, or Jackson."

"Sir, they are useless to the partisans if they cannot arm them."

"That is true, if these were a bunch of peasants, but they are not." The Colonel opened his top desk drawer, pulled out a bottle of vodka and two glasses. Nodding toward his chair, he asked, "Drink?"

"Oh, yes, sir. Once in the field, I will not get much vodka." He moved to the chair and sat.

"My intelligence section is positive they have a number of learned men with the resistance and some are known scientists. I feel over time they will be able to arm both weapons."

"Oh, that is not good, because they could kill a lot of Russians, sir."

Pouring two crystal glasses full of the clear alcohol, he handed one to the Sergeant, and then said, "I can assure you, if you happen to recover the tactical nuclear weapons, of a promotion, medal and an immediate return to Russia, Sergeant."

"Sir, I lack the formal education to be promoted to a higher rank."

"The message I have from headquarters is the man who is responsible for the recovery of the weapons will be immediately promoted to the rank of Captain, regardless of his current rank. In your case, since you are a Master Sergeant, I am sure I can have you promoted to the rank of Major, or maybe even Lieutenant Colonel, due to your obvious intelligence and combat experience. It is something to think about during your mission."

"But what of my limited education?"

"This is a war, Sergeant, and I think education means much less than experience. I do not know much more than what I just told you. So, I want you to lead a group of men, along with a Lieutenant Ioann Oleg, after the partisans. The Lieutenant will be on his first mission, so he will be more or less useless to you, but he will be in charge, on paper. I will personally brief him that he is to listen to you and agree with your suggestions. In other words, he will be there for show, while you will be calling the shots."

"When do we leave, sir?"

"We had to borrow some helicopters from Jackson, but as of right now, you will leave at 0400 in the morning. You and a company of men will be inserted near a swamp that is slightly north of where I think the camp is located. Then, moving due south, you should find the place. I want hourly radio reports or when something important is discovered or happening. I have a squadron of fighter jets on standby to support you, along with ten Black Shark helicopters. We must recover these weapons at all costs."

Knowing the conversation was over, Morozov stood and saluted.

Returning his salute, the Colonel said, "Good hunting."

The Master Sergeant nodded, did an about face, and left the office.

That evening, right after supper there was a little knock on his door. Morozov moved to the door and opened it. Unlike the junior enlisted, his quarters was actually a small prefabricated structure with many luxuries denied the common soldier. The lower grades slept in tents, while the Master Sergeant actually had a bathroom and bed.

A small squirrely looking Lieutenant asked, "Master Sergeant Morozov?"

"Yes, sir. Please enter my humble quarters, sir."

The man was small, maybe five feet four inches, about a 54 kgs, with short blonde hair. He wore thick glasses with military issue black frames and he looked about fourteen years old.

"Have a seat, sir. Drink?"

"Uh, no thank you, Master Sergeant. I do not drink." Oleg sat in a wooden chair.

Pouring himself a drink, the Sergeant asked, "So, what can I do for you?"

"I am here mainly to meet you and let you know I have no combat experience. I will have to depend on you a great deal during our mission."

"I will keep you out of trouble, sir, and try to save lives. How old are you?"

"Twenty, why?"

"How did you finish a university so quickly?"

"During my secondary school years I attended a military academy and when I entered college, they gave me two years of college credits. Then, once I finished the university, I was made a Junior Lieutenant."

"Do you speak any languages?"

"Some English. I took the language at the both the academy and university. I have never spoken to an English speaking person, so I have no idea if I can do the job well or not."

"If we take prisoners, you might come in handy in the field."

"We will see."

"What was your major at the university?"

"Arts; I am a painter of sorts."

Arts? For God's sake, the partisans will eat this man for breakfast, he thought and then asked, "Do you have all your gear packed, sir?"

"All but my chemical biological gear."

"Leave it. We are the only ones with the capability to release either, and it will not be done while we are on this mission."

"Because of what we are looking for?"

"Yes, sir, and I take it the Colonel has briefed you?"

"Oh, yes, and made it clear that you are really in charge. He has a lot of respect for you and your skills."

"Well, no disrespect intended sir, but I have been in the army longer than you have been alive. So, I know a few things that can keep us safe and alive."

"Good, because I hope to learn much from you." The officer stood and made his way to the door.

Morozov moved to the door and said, "Enjoy your evening, sir."

"You as well, Master Sergeant."

As the young officer walked away, Master Sergeant Morozov thought, *If he is alive twenty-four hours from now, I will be surprised as all hell. He is like a big baby.*

CHAPTER 19

We moved quickly and by dark, were in the new building. I immediately had a squad of carpenters building cells for our prisoners, and selected a private office for Colonel Lee. As I was setting his office up, Silverwolf walked into the room and said, "Our men on drag and two fellows I left near our old headquarters state Russians are all over the place, with an estimated strength of a company. I ordered them to come here in a roundabout way and for two men to shadow the Russians as they move."

"I think they're looking for the Nukes."

"They can't know we have them."

"No, but obviously the escaping Colonel remembered where we were located. It's a damned good thing we moved. I want all trails and roads to this place heavily mined and booby-trapped. I want snipers planted in trees, with assigned areas of responsibility for shooting. Rush the job too, because if they have dogs, they'll trail us easily enough." I said, and then scratched Dolly's ear. She was closer to me now that Sandra was gone. She was all I had to remind me of the old life.

"I hear you, and John, Colonel Lee is looking so much better now than earlier. I honestly thought the man was dying on us."

"He is, but slowly and over time. John, we don't have time for small talk, so get people working on the mines and such. Thanks for your help, too."

"Will do." He turned and left.

As I was moving some books, the Colonel entered and said, "Good news, I guess. Our scientists say the nukes can be activated with a magnetic key and code. They've managed to reset the code and a key is being made. I pray we never have to use a tactical nuke, but we may."

"How are you feeling, sir?"

"Weak and like hell warmed over. Thank you for putting my office together, because I can't do it. I suspect within a month, John, I'll be forced to turn command over to you. You're intelligent, have the needed skills and experience. You'll have to make some rough decisions, son."

"Oh, I know it, and don't really want the job. I've seen a lot of good commanders come and go, but count you and Willy two of the best."

"Thank you, I'm flattered."

I then explained about the Russians and Lee thought for a moment and then said, "Once we know the trail they are using, we need to set up an L shaped ambush and take 'em out. I'm positive they don't know we have the nukes, so I doubt that is the reason they are after us. Most likely the Colonel remembered where our camp was, is all."

"Sergeant Fox!" I turned and yelled from the Colonel's door.

"Yo!"

"Gather up all the fighters you can find, pull some Claymore mines and be ready to move in an hour."

"Yes, sir!"

"That's taken care of, and now I need to sleep." he said and moved toward his cot.

"Colonel, as soon as the ambush is over, I'll let you know what happened. It may be, and I think it will, we'll have to move again, but further."

The Colonel, now suddenly looking old and worn out, sat on his cot, ran his fingers through his hair and said, "Once we move, if need be, I'll turn command over to you. My legs feel heavy, I have trouble breathing, and I have little strength. I can't keep moving like this and maintain a clear head to run things. Each move costs me both mentally and physically."

"I fully understand, sir."

"See to the ambush and I wish you good hunting."

I knew I was being dismissed, so I said, "Thank you, sir, and I'll keep you in my prayers." I walked from his office.

The ambush was ready, and if things went well, we'd kill all in the group. But in combat, things rarely go as planned. I grew nervous as their point man walked by us, scanning as he moved, but my folks lived in the woods and were experts at camouflage. A good fifty yards later the whole group showed up and there were a shit-pot full of them. I looked, but didn't see any officers but suspected they'd mingled with the private solders, so they'd not stand out.

Just when the first of the group neared our last Claymore, I clicked the clackers in my hands and blew a wide path in the middle of the group and then heard three more mines explode. Bodies flew apart, as screams and shrieks filled the air as men were knocked off their feet. A cloud of bright red floated over the trail and then our other individual weapons opened up. A machine-gun raked the trail up and down a number of times throwing clumps of dirt and body parts high into the air. Periodically the gunner would shoot a few long bursts into the grass around the path. More screams were heard and overall there was little resistance. Three grenades exploded on the trail and then silence, except for the moans of the dying and the screams of the wounded. I waited almost an hour, and during that time, an occasional shot was heard from my side as a wounded man tried to crawl into the brush.

"Jonas and Burns!" I yelled finally.

"Yes, sir?"

"Yo!"

"Take your squads, go slowly, and check them out. All of us will cover you as you move forward. I want no survivors, understand? Now, move!"

"Just don't shoot my ass." Jonas said, laughed, then added, "Come on guys, let's check 'em out."

Silverwolf asked, "What of the point man and the drag man? Those two that got away."

"Take Washington's squad after the point man and have Airhart use his squad to find the drag man. Tell him to try to bring his man back alive, but take no chances. If we get lucky, maybe we can find out what they were looking for, if anything."

"Yes, sir." Silverwolf replied and then disappeared into the trees to find Washington and Airhart.

From the trail I heard gunshots, screams, and then a loud yell, "They're getting away!" Followed by a hell of a lot of gunfire. It grew quiet once again and at times I'd hear a pistol shot. I suspected wounded Russians were being shot. I heard a shout, "To the right!" Then a grenade exploded and someone yelled, "Got 'em."

Twenty minutes later, Jonas appeared and said, "All are dead, with the exception of two and they're both wounded. From the bright red blood we found, fatally too. We can track them if you want."

"Do that, because I want no survivors. Was the radio in good shape?"

"Sure and Private Baker has both of them now. But why?"

"Some of our electronic gurus have found a way to change the radio frequencies, so we can use them on a different frequency than the Russians. Radios will make our lives safer and missions much easier. Get on the trail of those two Russians and now."

"Will do, and I'll meet you back at headquarters."

There sounded a single shotgun blast some distance away.

Jonas said, "I think one of the wounded Russians now has a new injury."

"Get right on it, Jonas," I said with a slight grin. I like the man immensely.

I watched as he left with his squad, heading for the sound of the blast.

"Everyone move forward and strip the dead of any gear we can use. We need to hurry, people, because the Russians will come looking for these troops. Once they find them, they'll want our asses; now, move!"

Early the next morning, just as the sun was coming up, Jonas, Airhart and Washington returned, looking rough and missing a woman from Airhart's group. The three leaders walked to me, as their troops moved to find a placed to eat and then sleep.

"We killed three out of four, but one, a Sergeant, got away from us." Airhart said.

Jonas laughed and said, "The sonofabitch must have been an Olympic runner too, because the boy was fast. The way he moved through the trees and brush, I know he's torn to hell and back. Plus he's wounded, but I can assure you, he wasn't injured in his legs."

"I need everyone's attention. One Russian survived the ambush, so we need to pack up and get ready to move. We need to hurry too, because if this Russian is picked up by a chopper, we're all dead meat." I yelled, not angry at all, but needing them to understand how important moving from here really was.

"Sir, Colonel Lee wishes to speak with you." one of the administration troops said.

"Tell him, I'll be right there."

"Yes, sir."

Turning to the three leaders, I said, "Get your people up and ready to go. I can't risk all these lives by staying here and while I know your people are tired, it beats dead all to hell."

All nodded and Airhart said, "We tried to catch him, sir."

"It's not your fault, or anyone's, it's the way the cards fell. Now, get your people ready." I said and then walked to the Colonel's office. He looked weak and pale, and his eyes were closed.

"Sir?"

"J . . . John, take command. I'm afraid I don't, uh, I don't have as much time . . . left as I thought. I want explosives, uh, explosives placed . . . around this house and under . . . my cot."

"Why?"

"When I go, I'll . . . take some . . . of them with me. Do it."

"Yes, sir." I said, and then yelled, "Sergeant Morgan!"

"Yo!"

"Come to me, I have a task for you." I looked down at the shell of the man he used to be. Colonel Lee, like his ancestor, was one hell of a man and I was proud to have served under him.

"Yes, sir?" Morgan asked.

I explained about the explosives and he asked, "I suppose Colonel Lee wants to be able to detonate the whole thing, right?"

"Yes, he does."

"I'll be done in a few minutes." He moved from the room and was gone close to ten minutes before he returned. He slid something under the Colonels cot, and handed the man something that looked like an on and off switch.

"Sir," The Sergeant asked, "can you hear me?" He was squatted by the bed.

"I hear . . . you . . . fine."

"See this toggle? If you move it in the other direction, this whole place will go up in flames and smoke. Do you understand?"

"Damn, son, I'm . . . weak, not stupid."

I said, "Thank you Morgan, I appreciate you doing this for the Colonel."

Ignoring me, Sergeant Morgan snapped to attention, saluted the Colonel and said, "It's been a real pleasure to serve under you, sir."

Lee smiled and said, "Dismissed. Get the hell out of here!"

When Morgan left, I saw the old man wipe the tears from his eyes.

"Is that all, sir?"

"Yes, it is and John, kill as many of those Russian sonsofbitches as you can. See to your troops."

I turned and left the room, made sure the house was empty and hurried to catch up with my people. I'd gone about a quarter of a mile when I heard a loud explosion and saw a small mushroom cloud behind me, reaching for the clouds. I stood for a couple of minutes, with Dolly at my side, and watched the smoke. Colonel Robert E. Lee was no more.

In the next few weeks, we grew quiet and I pulled most of the squads in and kept them from bothering the Russians. They hunted for us and more than once they flew over our safe house, but most of my troops were resting indoors, using the barn or house. By keeping them inside, I reduced the chances of anyone being picked up on infrared gear. I met with my leaders and we discuss potential targets of opportunity or some that would hurt or cripple the Russians. I'd noticed since our attack on Edwards Air Base, there were less choppers in the air. We must have put a lot of hurt on them.

Now, I'm more like Willy than Colonel Lee, and I would be going out with my men and women to see how various attacks worked. I feel a good commander should participate in attacks at times, to know what the troops experience.

Also, as the most experienced man, Silverwolf was promoted to Captain and given the responsibility of four squads. I was happy for the man and while it provided no pay, there was respect given by me and others. He was an intelligent man and his Native American bloodline gave him a great advantage in the field. Once he entered the woods, he was one with nature and the man moved like a ghost, especially at night.

I was standing by a table, glancing at a state map, when Dolly suddenly growled, and looked toward the door. Corporal Hale came in and said, "I just got word from a man who works on Edwards that Moscow has ordered one thousand people from the gulag killed in retaliation for our attack on the base. He claimed they're pissed, mainly due to the number of aircraft lost and personnel killed."

"They should know by now, mass killings won't stop us. Did he have any other information?"

He lowered his head and eyes and then said, "Yes, he did. He said all those murdered would be women and kids, no older than twelve. He added that three others selected to die were Colonels in the resistance too."

"The Colonels I'm unconcerned with, they knew the risks, but killing women and kids is barbaric. How are they to be killed?"

"He said they were to be transported to an empty school or warehouse and then the whole place was to be soaked with gas and then burned down, with them inside."

"Is Edwards the only base doing the killing?"

"Actually, the killings will be done close to Jackson Air Base, but the prisoners will come from different gulags. The reason we learned of it is the Russians are sending a few hundred from the gulag at Edwards."

"Good God, what a hideous death! We need to prevent this, if we can."

"Colonel," Hale said, "that's not all."

"Oh, so you have more good news?"

Shrugging, he said, "They have transport aircraft landing there now, night and day. According to our source, they're gearing up to use chemicals, most likely nerve agents, in the whole state. They have no concern about killing innocents and figure if they kill just five of us, it's worth the expense."

Dolly liked Hale and moved to the man, who stood scratching her head.

I thought for a moment and then said, "Lawdy, I don't think this chemical attack report is accurate. They just tried this shit a couple of months back, so I don't think they'll try it again this soon. I can see it's just as Willy once said, 'Russians are brutal in war and they're like animals.' The killings using fire may very well happen."

"Well, I don't see where we can stop either situation from happening." he said.

"I don't know, to tell you the truth, but let me think on this a while." I said as I moved to a small portable desk all the previous Colonels had used. I sat in a metal chair, threw my cap on the desk top, and started thinking.

"Hale, tell Captain Silverwolf I need to speak with him."

"Yes, sir." he said and left the room. I sat there working my mind and inattentively scratched Dolly's ears.

Five minutes later, the two men entered and I said, "Both of you have a seat. Silverwolf, I want you to take a squad and get as close to the airbase at Jackson as you can tonight. I want you to circle the base and check security closely. Also, look for any prisoners you may see. I know they are gathering a thousand civilians and three Colonels from the resistance, according to our intelligence, to kill in retaliation of our attack on Edwards. Hale, you provide him security."

"Wow, that's a lot of people." Hale said.

"They are all to be women and children too, so that makes it worse."

"Holy Jesus, no. Why?" Silverwolf said, his eyes wide in disbelief.

"I told you, retaliation for our attack." I said as I leaned forward and met his eyes.

"I can't imagine killing like that. Have they no hearts?" Hale asked, but we ignored his question.

"Look, I want to prevent it, if we can, and we may be able to do so. I suspect we'll lose some of the prisoners, but that can't be helped. I figure a ten to twenty percent loss rate, depending on how strong the base is." Silverwolf said.

"Right off the top, I think we'll lose closer to a fifty to sixty percent because the Russians will shoot at them as much as us." I replied.

"Damn." Silverwolf said.

"Look, it'd beat burning to death, and even ten lives saved are better than none. Now, your mission tonight is a sneak and peek, no combat if it can be avoided. If you're seen, consider the mission a failure. Any questions?"

"I'll need to take some mine detecting gear, because the fence line is sure to mined at the weakest points."

"Get all you need and good luck." I stood, mainly so they'd know the discussion was over, and then shook their hands.

"John?" I said to Silverwolf.

He was about to leave and had his back to me, but he turned and asked, "Sir?"

"Don't rush this mission, and be my eyes. I really need this information; if we can save these folks depends on what you learn this evening."

"I'll give it my best shot, sir."

CHAPTER 20

One minute Master Sergeant Morozov had been talking to the Lieutenant and the next he was in hell, with bodies being blasted apart and blood flying in all directions. Men screamed as metal balls, bullets, and shrapnel tore into their bodies. In the matter of the few minutes, all the men were down, with most dead. The Sergeant looked at the Lieutenant and most of his head was missing from the chin up. Blood, now running over the dirt path, covered him. When he tried to move, his left arm didn't function well. Looking down, he noticed most of it from the elbow down was missing. He quickly took the Lieutenant's belt and secured the arm, using the belt as a tourniquet. Then, moving slowly, he backed into the brush.

His heart was pounding, and he knew from experience he was lucky to have survived the ambush. In pain and shock, he crawled for about a hundred meters and then stood. He was in some dense oaks, so assuming he was safe, he stood. A bullet instantly clipped the tree beside his head, splinters stuck in his cheeks and he took off running. It was a good half mile before he pulled off his coat, cut a long wide strip from the bottom and wrapped his arm. He moved about two kilometers and crawled under the limbs of a huge pine, to lick his wounds.

I need morphine, but if I take it, I will fall asleep. I know one of the radiomen was talking while killed, so a rescue force will be sent for us. It is likely they heard the explosions and the gunfire before the man with the radio died. I need to watch for the symptoms of shock and blood loss. But, at least I am not bleeding like before, he thought and pulled out a flask of vodka, which was all he would use for pain. *I have to stay awake, so I can be picked up when they come.*

Over the course of an hour, the Master Sergeant grew weaker. Finally, when he'd about passed out from the loss of blood, he heard a flight of helicopters nearing. He scooted back against the trunk of the tree and waited. He'd give them time to land, unload and reach the rescue scene, then he'd fire his Bison. Oh, this pain is getting to be too damned much, he thought as he pulled his last flask of vodka from his shirt pocket. He glanced at his watch and waited.

After exactly fifteen minutes had past, he raised his Bison and sent a long burst into the air. Then, minutes later, Russian troops discovered him.

An IV was quickly started, morphine given and his injury better dressed. He was packed to a helicopter and taken to Jackson Air Field and then to a hospital. He woke up two days later.

His eyes hurt when he opened them and his skin itched from the morphine. He blinked rapidly to clear his foggy vision and then raised his head. He was in a private room, due to his rank, and a few minutes later an orderly walked in.

"Well, Master Sergeant, how are you feeling?"

"Son, get me a doctor, now."

"Yes, sir." The orderly flew from the room and returned about five minutes later with an old major.

"Are you in pain, Sergeant?"

"No, but where am I and what are the extent of my injuries, sir?"

"Your left arm was in bad shape, so it was removed. You had a number of shrapnel wounds to your back, arms, and legs, which will heal in time. You are now missing your left earlobe, and as far as I am concerned, you are lucky to be alive."

"When will I return to Russia?"

"That depends on transportation arrangements. You will be transported home, discharged, draw your full retirement pay, along with a disability payment each month. I see no reason you cannot live in comfort the remainder of your life."

The Master Sergeant grunted as he thought, *You do not care how I live or where. You, because of your position as a doctor, will be well taken care of. I am just another number to you and your staff.*

Shortly after the doctor left, Vasiliev entered the room and walked to Morozov's bed. Handing him a paper bag he said, "In that bag, you will find the best vodka in the world. Now, I am sorry you will be medically retired, Taras, but your injuries disqualify you from further service. Oh, and I have told the doctor the vodka will be in your room, so leave it on the table."

Giving a light smile, the Sergeant asked, "May I have a small drink, sir?"

Picking up a drinking glass from the table, he handed it to the Sergeant and asked, "Did you learn anything of the partisans at all?"

"Sir, about three miles further, straight as an arrow, they are living in a vacant farm house. I saw it myself when we scouted. I would guess their strength as maybe two companies of men and women. It is heavily mined and I spotted one sniper in a tree, so there are more."

"Of course, no sign of the tactical nuclear weapons?"

"Oh, no, sir." He took a drink of his vodka, smiled and then added, "But you know if they have them, they are inside and guarded closely." He then took a big gulp of his drink.

"Master Sergeant, I have you leaving on a plane in the morning and it is actually the first flight out. You will be returned to Moscow, where you will be given a medal and promoted to Lieutenant, before you are discharged." Colonel Vasiliev then came to attention and saluted the Master Sergeant.

Morozov returned the salute and said, "Thank you, sir. It was an honor to serve under you."

After the Colonel left, the Master Sergeant knew the man was worried. Losing nuclear weapons to terrorists could cost a man his career or life easily. Moscow took things seriously and a smart man always remembered that point. *Oh well*, he thought, it is not my problem. *I am out of this war and will retire to the country and live as a farmer.* He took a big gulp of his vodka and smiled.

Colonel Vasiliev strutted across the room, stopped behind a wooden podium and said, "At 0400 hours in the morning, a specially trained group of Spetsnaz will parachute into the area where our troops were ambushed in an attempt to find where the nuclear weapons are kept. This will be a high altitude low opening jump and the unit consists of ten men. Their primary mission is to locate the weapons, not secure them, but if they have a chance to recover them, they will do so. Any questions?"

"Every time I have worked with Spetsnaz, they are difficult men and tend to fight a lot. They cause trouble, sir." Major Borisovich, the chief of intelligence, said.

"These have been here a week and have not left their barracks. Gentlemen, they will stay in the barracks, leaving only to complete their mission, and then fly back to Jackson when the mission is over. I am surprised, Sambor, that even my chief of intelligence did not know they were here. Looks like our security is working better now."

"Why not use conventional troops, sir?" A Captain asked.

"We just tried that, remember? And, by the way, please stand, Captain Boris, so everyone can see who is in charge of the men."

A slim man of average size and weight stood and the only difference between him and some of the men in the room was his hair was shorter. He was close to thirty, blue eyes, and there was absolutely nothing special about him that stood out. He then sat back down.

"Captain Boris and Master Sergeant Makar are your point of contacts for Spetsnaz while they are here. I expect all requests to speak to them to come through me first. Now, Captain Varlaam, would you be kind enough to give us the weather forecast?"

The young Captain turned on his computer and a map of the once United States was projected on the wall of the room. "Gentlemen, we can expect unseasonal weather tomorrow, with the morning cool, minus ten Celsius, but with clear skies. However, by noon a front will move in bringing heavy snowfall. I expect over fifteen centimeters of snowfall for tomorrow, but more is on the way. The winds will start to blow shortly after the snow arrives from the west at between 25 and 32 kilometers an hour. It is going to be a cold day tomorrow, gentlemen."

As the members of Captain Boris' group boarded the airplane, Colonel Vasiliev shook the man's hand and yelled to be heard over the running aircraft engines, "Best of luck and good hunting!"

The Captain nodded and gave a thumbs up. He was ready to go. The Colonel's breath was clearly seen in the cold morning air.

Once on the aircraft, they all plugged into the communications system. The pilot introduced the crew quickly and then said, "We will be at the drop zone in less than thirty minutes, but I will need to climb a little once over target. You will know we are close when I begin to circle the aircraft to gain altitude. At 7620 meters, you will see the jump light by the ramp door flashing red, then the ramp will lower and the light will go to all red. At that point I will have warned you, and you should be standing on the open ramp ready to leave the aircraft. When the light flashes steady green, jump. Any questions?"

"No, sir." Boris said and then glanced at his men. They were ready, and they were always ready, night or day.

The talking stopped as each man dealt with the excitement of a HALO jump. Most found the jump exhilarating and thrilling, while others, like Master Sergeant Makar did it only for the extra pay every month. He was saving for his retirement in five more years. Of all ten men, only Sergeant Vasily Geraslym truly loved HALO jumps, because he was a thrill seeker. He loved the rush he felt when his chute deployed at a little over 152 meters and he often wondered what it would feel like, if his canopy failed to deploy. He knew his death would be instantaneous, so he didn't worry about it.

Most of the men appeared to the loadmaster to be sleeping, but under the closed eyelids, each man was going over his gear, his position in the group, and his assigned and potentially assigned tasks. They were all cross-trained and, for instance, if the medic fell dead or wounded, any one of them could be designated the new medic. Their minds were active and working, but none sat in fear; after all, they were Spetsnaz, some of the best trained men in the world.

The Captain began to circle and climb as the loadmaster motioned for them to stand. Each stood and duck-walked to the ramp. Besides their parachute, each man had an equipment bag, loaded with gear that weighed around 27 kilograms, and some. The Master Sergeant had another bag of close to eighteen kilograms at his side. Each had a reserve parachute, oxygen mask, camouflage helmet with visor, communications system to talk as they fell, and individual weapons. Normal walking was out of the question.

The green light flashed on and off, so they waited.

A couple of minutes later, the light turned green, and they stepped off the open ramp and into the sub-zero winds.

Each man instantly went spread-eagle, with arms and legs extended out to help stabilize them as they fell. Makar, checked his altimeter, saw he was out at the right altitude and then glanced below out of curiosity, but saw nothing; it was pitch black. He raised his head and kept it on the horizon, his mind on the events after the landing.

He was still going over the mission when he felt the chute deploy and heard a loud grunt, which he knew came from him. He glanced up at the canopy, swung a couple of times, released both equipment bags, and then landed. Knowing the ground winds were high, he quickly released his parachute from his harness. Free of his canopy, he stood and watched the others land as he counted them.

Once on the ground, the team didn't speak a single word as the jump gear was gathered up and hidden under a rotted pine tree. The gear was no longer needed. Each man now wore night vision goggles and moving in the dark was simple. The Captain pulled out a compass, took a heading, and began walking while Corporal Renat counted paces with his beads. They'd done this exact same thing many times in training.

All members of the team knew the Americans had snipers with night vision scopes, so they moved slowly and checked the ground closely. The partisans were also known for deadly booby-traps and they were a bit harder to see with goggles on.

Private Yuliy was on point, with Corporal Ignatiy bringing up the rear. Suddenly, Yuliy pointed at the ground and squatted. Pulling his knife he pulled up three toe-poppers and put the shells in his pocket. He then refilled the holes. He took three steps forward, when he suddenly stopped and began to quiver.

Master Sergeant Makar had heard a swishing sound, then a grunt, followed by low whimpers. He moved to the point man and saw he'd tripped a booby-trap with spikes. The spikes were secured to a tree limb and held back ready to spring forward by a trigger lock. The trigger had been a thin length of fishing line across the trail and secured. Once the line was pulled too far, the trigger released the limb and it swung forward. Simple, low cost, and effective.

The designated medic, Private Yakim moved forward, glanced at the injuries and shook his head. Makar didn't hesitate as he whispered, "Morphine."

The medic knew there was no hope for Yuliy, because three fire hardened barbed spear-like points had gone completely through his chest, so he prepared the medication. Besides, there was no way they could continue their mission and pack an injured man on a litter. Each member of the team knew if they lost their mobility, they were dead weight. The team dumped dead weight.

Glancing at Yuliy, the Captain said, "Move closer to the farm house, then hide deep in the brush, because it will soon be daylight. We will watch the building today and maybe learn something."

As they moved away, Yuliy was whispering, begging them to stay and help him, but then the morphine entered his system, his pain lessened, and his head fell to this chest. A minute later his heart stopped. He was left on his knees, his body weight pulling the limb down, and blood pooling under his legs. His eyes were open, but dull and unseeing.

Soon, Private Savely, the new point man, stopped and motioned for the Captain to come to him. When Boris arrived, he was shown the house. The Captain tapped Savely on the shoulder and then the two of them moved to his men. Using hand sign, he indicated where each man was to go and he had them pair up, with him being the loner. Once in position, he camouflaged his spot well and then ate a cold Russian ration. He saw a false dawn was starting so he pulled his binoculars and scanned the house, making sure there was no reflection from his glass. He saw no one, nor anything, moving. He waited, knowing eventually they would probably step outside to pee, or head to the woods to do more serious business.

Two hours later, he'd still not seen a single person. *Maybe they are using a room in the house for bodily functions*, he thought, *but that will make the place smell.*

Finally the door opened and out stepped a man dressed in a Russian uniform except for a wide arm band on his left arm. In his hand he had some old paper, so Boris suspected the man was moving to the woods. Tossing a pebble to the Master Sergeant and Private Nika, he nodded toward the partisan. Both men melted into the brush and disappeared.

When the two Russians neared the American he was buttoning up his trousers and totally unaware he was being stalked. From out of what seemed to be nowhere, he was suddenly grabbed, gagged, and his hands handcuffed behind his back. A rope was placed around his neck and he was lead toward the Captain. The man had not had the time to offer any resistance.

Once close to Boris, Makar moved to the man and then all but Corporal Renat moved deeper into the woods. They then met with Nika and the captive.

"Move south about two kilometers and we will speak with our captive. Let us hope, for his sake, he talks and doesn't make me use torture. The Afghans taught me well how to torture a man to bring much pain and yet keep him alive." The Captain spoke in excellent English, which all members of the team were required to learn.

The captive's eyes grew large as Marka led him further away from the farm house.

Once the distance was covered, Boris sat on a log, pulled his sheath knife out and stuck it in the wood beside his leg. Meeting the eyes of his prisoner, he said, "We can do this the easy way or the painful way, and it does not matter to me."

The captive didn't speak, but his eyes narrowed.

"Bring him to me and place him on his knees in front of me." the Captain said.

"Yes, sir." Marka said and moved the man forward. He then forced him to his knees.

"Let us start with something simple, shall we? What is your name?"

"My name is Ellis Perry and that's all you're getting out of me. I'm a prisoner of war and the Ge—."

"Now, we both know that's not true, Mister Perry. See, this not a war and besides, your country no longer exists. You will be a nice man and answer all my questions, right?" He picked the knife up and let the sun glance off the sharp edge.

"Kiss my as—" Perry screamed as his left ear fell to the grass.

"There is more pain to come, sir, if you do not answer my questions."

The injured man grabbed his ear and shuddered as pain shot through him. He suddenly realized, these aren't regular Russian troops and he thought, *I don't know much and by now, they know about the farm house, because they must have seen me leave it this morning.*

"Well? Will you talk with me or do I need to get bloody?"

Ten minutes later, Captain Boris had all the information he needed, except about the two boxes. Finally he asked, "Do they have any boxes that are made of high impact plastic?"

"Two; I have no idea what is in them, but they're guarded all the time. They look like large suitcases to me."

"Where in the house are they kept?"

"Second floor, in the top left bedroom."

"Stand."

Marka pulled Perry to his feet.

"Are you going to free me now?" Perry asked.

"Oh, yes, my new American friend, and in a way you will never again feel pain or worry ever again." Captain Boris said and brought the knife blade up and under Perry's rib cage, sinking the blade in to the hilt. He then jerked the knife from side to side, viciously.

Perry shuddered and shook, gave a heinous shriek as blood spurted from his body and mouth. He fell to his knees, where Boris grabbed his hair, pulled his head back and cut his throat. The Captain then kicked the dying man to the dirt and grass. Blood spurted into the air with each beat of Perry's heart, but his body was shutting down. The fatally wounded man kicked madly at the grass, as his hands clawed at the dirt. Finally, he lay still, his eyes reflecting his fear of death.

Bending over, Captain Boris said, "Let us get back to the farm house and prepare to assault the place. We must recover the nuclear weapons."

As they moved, snow began to fall, and hard. The winds picked up, the temperature dropped, and each man pulled out his winter gear. Each wore a white fur cap, winter camouflage gloves, and white scarfs around their necks. When they neared the house, it was the same as before, no one was spotted. Boris decided to wait ten minutes and watch, but if nothing happened by then, he'd attack..

CHAPTER 21

I peeked out the hole in the window and saw the Russians, squatting in the brush. Mary, my sniper had reported them as moving into position, before dawn and saw them leading Perry away. Everyone knew Perry had gone out to do his business and when he didn't return, we knew something had happened. Until now, only Mary and I knew the man was probably dead.

"Silverwolf, pass the word there is a squad of Russians outside in front of the house, and there is a good chance they are Spetsnaz. Perry was taken prisoner and assumed dead. He is not with them now. I want everyone in position right away. Mary, when they move toward us, take out as many as you can, as quickly as you can. Don't worry about killing shots."

As Silverwolf made his way around, men and women moved to their assigned positions quietly. I heard safety's click off and then the charging handle on a machine-gun moving. My folks were ready. I expected a grenade first, then they'd come in through the widows. I moved from person to person, telling them this. I moved down stairs and waited; the minutes were long and hard on my mind. I had a squad of men upstairs with the nukes.

Then, I heard three shots from Mary in the span of three seconds and I knew a man fell with each shot. The old shutters were flung open and our guns began to speak. I saw bullets strike the men, but they quickly stood and came at us again.

"They're wearing protective armor, aim for the heads or legs!" I screamed to be heard over the gunshots.

I saw one Russian struck in the head by the old .50 caliber machine-gun and his head simply disappeared as a fountain of blood shot from his throat. He fell to the ground thrashing around. Two men were lost from view due to smoke grenades the Russians used. Since a target could not be seen, we stopped firing, but every finger was on a trigger, ready. When the smoke cleared, seven Russian bodies were laying in unnatural ways on the freshly fallen snow. Blood gathered under each.

"Cease fire, but stand ready. Mary, put a shot into the head of each Russian!" I yelled. Seven times her rifle barked and with each shot, I knew a Russian was dead, beyond any doubt.

"Now we wait." I said, "But remain in your positions."

"John, I mean Colonel," Silverwolf said, "why didn't they split up and hit us from all four positions of the house at the same time?"

I smiled, put my hand on his shoulder and said, "You can call me John in private, but Colonel around the troops. That is a damned good question and one I can't answer. Maybe Perry told them there were only a few of us here. I have no idea, but they paid for their mistake."

"Well, it could have ended differently if not for Mary, and I think she needs a promotion. She saved the bacon this time."

"Later; right now, I want you to take Jones and make sure the Russians are dead and the other two gone. We'll cover you from here."

"Sure. Jones!"

"Yo?"

"Come with me and let's check the bodies out there. Go through the pockets and take anything intelligence might want."

They walked to the door, stepped out and with their weapons at the ready, moved toward the downed Russians. In a matter of minutes, all were confirmed dead, so they started going through the pockets.

"Sir, I've checked two and nothing. No wallets, rings, identification or anything."

"See the blue and white striped tee shirts? These men are Spetsnaz and some real bad-asses. I suspect they're sterile for this mission. Now, come with me and let's see where the other two are headed."

Twenty minutes later, Silverwolf walked back into the house, kicked the snow from his shoes and said, "Spetnaz for sure and the two that got away moved east, upwind of us."

"So?" I asked.

"Why would they move upwind, unless there was to be a fire or gas used on us in some way? They were moving fast too, running their asses off."

"Shit, I never thought of that; too tired, I guess." I said and then suddenly realized our danger. "Everyone, out of the house and now! Top, make sure the two containers are brought with you! Move, I think we're due an air strike and any second now!"

As the last were leaving the build and running for the woods, someone screamed, "Jet!"

All of us ran like hell and as fast as possible. I saw one man with a nuke cast it aside and I picked it up without breaking my stride. I heard the high scream of a jet in a dive, saw it pull up and watched as two egg shaped containers rolled end over end toward the house.

There was a huge explosion, with an oily fireball that rolled inside itself, and the air around us instantly grew scarce. I knew the air was being sucked into the flames. The oily flames were tossed onto the house by impact and the farm house vanished in a few seconds, replaced by a wall of hot flames.

A second jet lined up, put his nose down and moved toward us.

"Trees, run for the trees!" I screamed.

It was then I heard a Gatling gun and people around me began to fall. Body parts flew through the air in different directions and blood seemed to hang in space, stationary. I knew then my mind was in shock. Clods of dirt flew ten feet in the air all around me as bullets zinged off rocks and metal guns we carried. In just a few seconds the Jet nosed up and pulled away. I glanced behind me and saw I'd just lost half of my people.

I kept running and when I reached the trees, Silverwolf said, "Slow down, sir, they made one pass each and then left. I'd estimate we lost half of our people."

"I . . . I'm okay."

"Where to now?" he asked as he met my eyes.

"We'll head east about ten miles then call it a day. I want you and Corporal Morgan to track the two bastards that got away and kill them."

"Morgan is dead, sir. I do have Mary. Those that aren't dead are scatter all over these woods right now."

I gave a loud yell, "Aces! I want you to form on my voice and now!"

Almost immediately people moved toward me and I looked at Silverwolf and said, "Take her, and good luck."

"Don't wait for us, we'll find y'all tomorrow at some point, but if we're not with you by noon, we'll never be there. Good luck to you too, sir." he said and then called out, "Mary, come with me!"

In less than twenty minutes, we were moving through the brush and trees, heading east. While the weather was cold, it beat being dead, so no one complained. The snow continued, and by night we had a good six inches on the ground. The winds were high, so I didn't expect any choppers out in this weather so fires were lit. After meals of Russians rations, most went to sleep. I sat by my small fire and stared into the dancing flames, wondering how Silverwolf and Mary were doing.

Mary was watching the Russians with her night vision scope and could have easily taken both men out, but the distance was great. She stood and made her way back to camp and Silverwolf.

When she neared camp, Silverwolf said, "That's close enough. Oh, it's you. I have a small fire under a large pine tree. It's not hot, but you'll not freeze to death sitting beside it. Eat if you want, because I ate shortly after you left."

"I'll do that." she replied.

As she started removing items from her pack, he asked, "Did they move or still there?"

"Still there, so do we kill them in the morning?"

"No, I want to move in close and when they're being picked up, return a Strela-2M missile to them. If we can down a chopper and kill both of them, this mission will have been successful."

"It's a big risk, but a chopper is worth the gamble." She opened the tins and placed them on the hot coals.

"We need to be in place an hour before dawn because this weather might clear, and if it does, they'll come for them."

Stirring her food to keep it from burning, she said, "I'll be ready."

They took turns guarding, not trusting the two Russians to not come looking for them, and while vigilant, the night was uneventful. Two hours before dawn, Mary woke him to make water and eat. It was lung hurting cold, with the temperature in single digits and snow was still falling. As he was peeing, Silverwolf noticed the winds were calm. He'd just started to turn, when he felt a hand go over his mouth, so he jerked his head violently and screamed. He felt a knife blade move over this throat and panicked as blood began to spurt. He was shoved to the ground and wanted to move to help Mary, but could not. He felt so weak and his eyes blinked rapidly as he wondered where all the blood he saw on the snow was coming from. Slowly, with his eyes still wide open, he entered a dark void and the world disappeared.

Mary heard the scream and knew something terrible had happened to Silverwolf. She moved away from the tree and then ran for a good mile. Finally stopping, she pulled herself up into a tree and climbed even higher. Then, once in position, she glassed the area, seeing no movement at all. An hour passed and she waited. After two hours, she climbed from the tree and made her way back to camp.

She circled the camp and saw where the two men had walked into the camp and then left later. She then looked for Silverwolf, hoping he was just wounded. A few minutes later, she found his body, gasped at the terrible condition of his throat and shuddered. He'd been a good man and an excellent soldier in the resistance. She thought, *Should I return now, or continue the mission? I think if I'd been killed, Silverwolf would have continued on, so I'll do the same.*

Mary stripped Silverwolf of all weapons, ammo, and knives he had, and then moved back to camp. Her pack she wore, but his was gone, along with the missile, so she decided instead of shooting the chopper down, she'd kill the two Russians and be done with it. She knew she could sit back a thousand yards, shoot both men, and each would be a head shot. She knew she was good.

Due to the snow, tracking the two was easy and she wondered why they hadn't chased her farther. *Must be close to time for a chopper to pick them up*, she thought as she moved over a slight hill. Every hundred yards or so, she'd stop, pull out her binoculars and glass the area in front of her. From what she remembered of their camp yesterday, it should be over the next hill.

I'll stop on the crest of this hill, camouflage my position well and wait for them, she thought. Once the rescue starts, I'll start shooting. Who knows, I may even be able to injure or kill some of the aircraft crew.

Nearing the crest, she crawled to the top, glassed the area and instantly spotted the two men. *They are deep in a forest, so how can a chopper pick them up? Maybe they'll use a hoist or rope to lift them through the trees, because they'll not be able to land here.*

She sighted in one man, adjusted her cross-hairs, then felt for wind, but noticed none. She estimated the distance to be close to eight hundred yards, so she clicked the cross-hairs a bit more to allow for the drop of the bullet once fired.

Right then she heard the *wop-wop-wop* of an approaching helicopter, so she flipped the safety off her rifle. Looking at the two men through her scope, they were preparing to leave, and she watched them placing objects in pockets, while casting other things to the snow.

The chopper was loud now and she saw it maneuvering over the two men as one Russian on the ground spoke in a small hand-held radio. A man leaned from an open door on the aircraft and using a winch, lowered a strange looking contraption on a cable to the ground. She watched as the two men extended what looked to her to be seats and then sat on the device and routed a strap under their arms. She saw one man give a thumb up and then both lowered their heads. A second later, the cable began to rise. She estimated the chopper was about 100 feet above the ground and maybe forty feet above the trees. She wanted her victims above the trees, because even a small limb, if struck, could deflect a bullet from her rifle.

When the two men on the cable broke through the trees, she took a deep breath, held it and lined the cross-hairs up on the side of the man on the left. As she released the air slowly, she gently squeezed the trigger and was rewarded a second later by a loud shot. The man in her scope suddenly jerked, blood and gore blew out his other side, and fell back limply. Blood was falling freely from the man's now lifeless body. Master Sergeant Marka never realized he'd been shot.

The second man, now with a radio in his hand, was speaking, his facial expressions animated and extreme. Obviously he knew they were taking fire from an unknown location. A second man moved to the open door, swung a Gatling gun out, and began to fire blindly.

She smiled and thought, *Son, you don't even have a target, so all you're doing is wasting ammo.* She wrote the gun off as no threat and lined the cross-hairs up on the second man. She wondered if a head shot was possible, so she raised the rifle and moved the cross-hairs to the head of Captain Boris. Taking another deep breath, she held it, unknowingly smiled, and then began to squeezed the trigger. Her shot was loud again and the sudden noise surprised her.

She saw the bullet strike the Captain a little low and to the right, which blew his teeth and chin away. Blood and bone flew through the air and when he turned his head, she saw pure terror in his eyes. *This sonofabitch is the leader*, she thought as she recognized his rank. *He is responsible for the death of Silverwolf and the others. He's likely the one who called in the airstrikes as we ran from the house, too.*

Her heart turned cold as she then shot him in both legs and when she raised the rifle, she saw him screaming, or at least she thought he was screeching; his face was badly mangled. She lined the cross-hairs up on his chest. She fired and saw him collapse on the seat. Just to make sure both men were dead, she fired two more bullets into each body.

With both men now dead, the chopper began to turn slowly, allowing the man with the Gatling gun to sweep the ground below. When the aircraft nose was pointed right at her, she was able to clearly see both pilots in her scope. She lined her sights up on the man in the right seat and fired, smiling when the bullet struck him right where his neck meets his torso. His eyes grew huge, a fountain of blood shot from his mouth, and he instantly slumped forward, with only his shoulder harness and seat-belt keeping him from falling to the floor.

She quickly moved her scope to the second pilot, saw fear in his eyes and sent a bullet into his forehead. He died at once, fright clearly seen in his lifeless eyes. The aircraft wobbled and as it turned sideways, she sent a bullet into the belly of the gunner, who she clearly saw scream and fall to the floor kicking. She squeezed off a shot at the wench operator, but missed, sending aluminum splinters into his eyes.

All of this happened in less than a minute and now, with both pilots dead, the aircraft rolled over, fell from the overcast sky, struck the trees, and finally the snow covered ground below. A huge explosion was heard, a ball of red-orange flames shot toward the sky, and oily smoke rose with the flames. A few minutes later, three loud secondary explosions were heard, and then the ammunition began to cook off.

Mary stood, glanced at the flames burning over the trees and said, "That was for you, Silverwolf, my friend. Now may you rest in peace." She placed the sling of her rifle over her shoulder, turned and moved toward the partisans.

The next morning she was still tracking the group, but had met no one. She'd known the general direction of travel and by pure luck discovered some tracks covered with a thin layer of snow. Today was warm, above freezing, so she was following tracks in the mud.

Near noon, she came upon Charles Black, the drag man, and he'd stepped from the trees, about ready to blow her away.

"Oh, it's you, Mary." he said and then lowered his AK-47.

"You're good, Charles, and that's needed. I need to move ahead of you, is that okay?"

"Sure, I see no reason you can't, but use some caution. Folks are trigger happy since the attack."

"Uh-huh, I figured as much. Talk later, I have information the Colonel needs." She took to walking faster, feeling safer knowing the group was near.

Less than an hour later, she walked to the group as they took a short break.

"Colonel?"

When she called out, I turned and asked, "Yes, how did it go?"

She told me and while I was deeply saddened to lose Silver-wolf, I'd lost a lot of special people in my life. I sat scratching Dolly's ears for many long minutes. Finally, I said, "Mary, you're a Lieutenant as of right now and if I had a medal, I'd give you one, but I don't. Not many people can down a chopper with a rifle."

She laughed and said, "It was mostly luck. If the chopper hadn't turned, well, I would never have gotten a clean shot."

"But you did and we wiped out a squad of expensive Spetsnaz, so the Russians will be pissed, as usual. They'll stay on our asses until we mingle with each others footprints and then lose them in the tracks. Colonel Bill Thomas is down this way and I want to spend some time with him and leave a nuke with him. If they both stay with us and we're killed, we'll lose both weapons."

"I understand your concern, sir."

"Get some food in you and then we have to move."

I didn't like it, but we needed to meet with the others. I don't think any single group needed both of any weapon, but especially nukes. One ambush, and they're both gone.

Ten minutes later we were up and moving again, and we'd continue to move until almost dark. The weather was warm, sun was shining and I kept thinking about the thousand people the Russians would soon execute. Right now, I could no more help them than I could myself.

CHAPTER 22

Colonel Vasiliev was livid and his eyes bulged as he screamed, "Do you mean to tell me a squad of Spetsnaz and a helicopter were destroyed by that gang of criminals? How in the hell did ten of the best trained men in the world all get killed by a bunch of washed up and retired soldiers?"

"One man was killed with a booby-trap, seven were burned to death, but we suspect they were already dead, when the MIG dropped the napalm on the farm house. The last word we had on the helicopter was they were picking the men up, then they started taking some light ground fire, and finally silence. The preliminary investigation shows all were shot and killed with a Russian sniper rifle. The pilot and co-pilot both took head shots. Also, both men being rescued, Captain Boris and Master Sergeant Marka, were shot as well. Boris was shot a number of times, which may indicate the shooter hated him for some unknown reason. In all cases, except Boris and Marka, only one bullet struck each man, but all were fatal."

"Damn me! I am about ready to start shooting people!"

"Sir, we are to burn a thousand to death in two days."

"You mean Americans, but I was thinking of Russians! This has to stop. Intelligence, Major Borisovich?"

"Yes, sir."

"Request permission from Moscow to use tactical nuclear weapons. I want to use two; one on the group in the woods that committed this crime and one on a city here. I want to show these clowns that we are nothing to be taken lightly."

"Sir, I suggest you reconsider. Keep in mind, they have two of our weapons, sir." a Colonel near the back said.

"They are useless to them without the codes or keys. Besides, Major Borisovich thinks the weapons were destroyed in the napalm fires."

"I know little of nuclear weapons, however, or how they are destroyed. I do know that if you start using nuclear weapons, the fallout in the air may endanger all of us."

"Weather, give me a forecast of when the winds will be out of one direction for a week or more, as well as the dates this should happen. I have decided, I will bomb them back to the stone-age with nuclear weapons. I will blow them away and then we will see how they react to the strength of the Russian Bear. I want the executions of the thousand moved up a day. Can that be done, Borisovich?"

"Yes, we have an empty warehouse down by the Pearl River, on the other side of Jackson, and most are there now. I started to use a school, but it was too small. I think we have less than a hundred left to transport to the location."

"Finish moving them and then kill them tomorrow, at first light. I have never, in all my years of service, seen a group of people as hard-headed as these Americans. But, I, Colonel Pasha Vasiliev, will show them the power of the great Russian army! Dismissed."

An hour later, the red phone, indicating Moscow, lit up on Vasiliev's desk. He picked it up and said, "Colonel Vasiliev, Base Commander at Edwards."

"Colonel, this is Major General Bronislav Faddey, in Moscow, and I want to know what in the hell is going on at your station that is so terrible you need to use tactical nuclear weapons."

"Yes sir, General." he replied and then explained what was going on.

Then silence.

"Are you still there, sir?" The Colonel asked.

"Yes, you idiot, but I am thinking. The use of nuclear weapons is a serious decision and one that cannot be made instantly. The global repercussions must be considered."

To hell with global repercussions, thought Vasiliev, but he said, "Yes, of course and I fully understand, sir."

"Okay, but just this once. But I am warning you, *Colonel*, if so much as one Russian soldier gets radiation sickness, I will twist your balls off. Do you understand me?"

"Oh, yes sir, and I have weather checking the winds for the next few weeks right now."

Excited, the Colonel wrote on his pad, 'use of nuclear weapons, okay with General Faddey and the date and time.'

"Good. Handle this properly, Colonel, and you will leave there a General. Screw it up and you will end up dead, understand me? You will simply disappear one night."

Vasiliev swallowed hard and his mouth grew dry, because he knew the warning was no idle threat, but a promise. He said, "It will be good to be a General, sir."

"Good, I love a man with a positive attitude. Good luck, Colonel and goodbye."

The phone clicked in his ear and he pulled a bottle of vodka out of a desk drawer, poured a water glass about half full, and then chugged it all down. *This must work out perfectly, for my sake*, he thought as he refilled the glass.

Later that evening, as a civilian janitor moved through the building, he saw the note on the Colonel's pad. Right above the words, применения ядерного оружия, нормально с Faddey, was a crudely drawn mushroom cloud and a smiley face. While not the smartest man with the partisans, he placed the note in his pocket and continued his rounds.

Knowing he would be searched on the way out of the camp, he moved to the mens room and pulling a small metal container he packed his salt in, he dumped the salt in the toilet, and rolled the note up small. He then placed the note in the container and inserted it deeply in his rectum. *Not the cleanest way to get a note out, but they never check our rears*, he thought as he moved toward the front gate.

When he neared the gate, a Russian soldier with a clipboard came out and asked in roughly spoken English, "Name?"

"Mike Wilcox."

The Russians fingers moved down the list and then he asked, "Job?"

"Janitor."

The Russian checked his name off on the list and then said, "Against wall."

"Why?"

"Search." the guard said and then motioned with his Bison.

Minutes later, the search done, the guard said, "Go."

Mike wanted to run through the raised gate, but fought the urge and walked at a normal rate. He was quickly swallowed by the darkness.

Ten minutes later, a Russian vehicle pulled up at the gate, Major Borisovich jumped out before the car was stopped and asked, "Did a man just leave here?"

"Yes, sir. He was a janitor."

"Did you check him well?"

"Of course, sir, and he was clean. Why?"

"He was seen on a security camera taking a note from the base commanders desk. I have reason to believe that note was either very important or classified."

"Sir, he had nothing on him or in his pockets. I did notice his usual salt container was missing."

"Salt container?"

"Oh, yes, Mr. Wilcox always brings his supper and a small metal container of salt. It's almost always in his right coat pocket, except for tonight."

"How big is this container, Private?"

"About the size of my little finger, sir, why?"

"You damned fool! Oh, I hope I am wrong." Borisovich said as he ran to his car.

Once inside, he said, "To the base commander's quarters and now."

"Sir, it is almost 2200 hours."

"Do as I asked and do it now."

"Yes, sir." the driver said and started the engine. As he slipped the transmission into drive he thought, *Oh well, it is not my arse that will be chewed this night for a change.*

At the commanders quarters, Borisovich knocked and waited impatiently.

A few minutes later, a Senior Sergeant opened the door and said, "Colonel Vasiliev's quarters, but I am afraid he is in bed."

"Get him up, and now, you damned fool. I will take full responsibility for your actions."

"Yes sir. Please wait."

Ten minutes later, Vasiliev appeared, looked at his intelligence commander, and asked, "What has happened now?"

"A janitor was seen on one of the security cameras in your office taking the top page off your note pad. Do you remember what was on it, sir?"

The Colonel chuckled and replied, "I wrote General Faddey's name on it and that's all, as far as I can remember. I am sure it was nothing important."

"I hope you are correct, sir, or I think the partisans will know what you are planning to do with the nuclear weapons."

"No, I would never write something like that down."

"Sorry to have disturbed you, sir and enjoy your evening." Borisovich saluted, did an about face and returned to his car.

Once inside he said, "Take me by the Colonel's office and now."

"Yes, sir."

At headquarters the guard let him enter and he rushed to the pad. At the desk he spotted it, and opened the Colonel's middle drawer to pull out a pencil. He then moved the pencil lead over the paper as he held it on it's side. Almost immediately the message was clear to him.

He placed the paper in his pocket, sat in the Colonels chair, and opened the top right drawer. He removed a bottle of vodka, pulled the cork with a loud pop, and then took a long drink. *Damn, it is almost certain Mr. Bill Wilcox is a member of, or involved with, the partisans. They now know we will use nuclear weapons, the General's name that approved the use, and the date. Shit! Oh, this is not good*, he thought. He took another long pull on the bottle and then put it back.

He returned to the car and said, "Take me to my quarters."

"Yes sir." the driver said and wished his shift was over. He had a bottle of vodka in his room calling his name.

The next morning, just as the sun came up, the Russians arrived at the warehouse near the Pearl River. A large fuel truck circled the building, as a man stood on the back with the petcock open, allowing petrol to flow freely to the ground. The truck circled twice, then left.

Major Borisovich got out of his car, nodded to a Master Sergeant and then four men with flamethrowers walked around the building spitting flames. Screams were heard inside the building and as the flames began to lick at their flesh, shrieks were heard.

One mother, obviously attempting to save her child threw him through a window, only to have him fall in the burning petrol around the facility. The child quickly burst into flames and then fell. People began to try to get out and that's when the Master Sergeant yelled, "Fire!"

Four machine-guns mounted on flatbed trucks opened fire and thousands of rounds entered the building and went through the victims. Some stood defiantly in the window, wanting to be shot rather than burned to death. Arms, some smoking and some burning, reached from the windows, hoping to grab something to help them stay alive. Finally the screams died and the smell of burning flesh grew so strong, the Russians loaded their trucks and left.

Three members of the resistance had taken photos and one now opened a door as the other two stood guard. Three people walked from the building, all burned, and coughing. One, a little girl of about five kept trying to go back, calling out, "Mommie!"

They scooped up the injured and made their way to the woods.

When Colonel Vasiliev entered his office, Major Borisovich was waiting and stood when he entered. The Colonel nodded and said, "Please sit down, Major."

"Sir, we have a serious problem." the Major said.

"Oh, I take it you had difficulties with the executions then."

"No sir, they have been exterminated, but it is about last night and the janitor."

"Oh, for God's sake, Borisovich, he got nothing of any importance."

Pulling the penciled over paper from his pocket, he handed it to the Colonel and said, "I disagree, sir."

Clearly on the pad was the mushroom cloud, the smiley face and the words, 'use of nuclear weapons okay with General Faddey with yesterdays date and time.' Colonel Vasiliev's face paled and he said, "How did you get this? I do not remember the doodling on the pad."

"Sir, first that information is Top Secret and second it is now in the hands of our enemies, I think. I do know Mike Wilcox did not come to work, and when I visited his home listed on our records here, no one was there. Someone had been living there, but things were thrown around like he had left in a hurry."

"Damn me!" the Colonel exploded.

"Me as well, sir. Now, knowing we are planning to use nuclear weapons and the fact we just executed one thousand women and children, the Americans will come for us. You had better pray, sir, they have not found a way to arm the weapons they have —or we are all dead men."

"Moscow thinks it would be impossible."

"Let me remind you sir, before the fall, this country had some very well trained scientists and engineers. Where have they all gone? Why have we found so few of them? I honestly feel the only thing that will keep them from being able to arm the weapons, maybe, is the lack of tools or equipment. I know they have men and women with the knowledge."

"Shit."

"So, the question is, do we call Moscow and report this, or keep it between us?"

Slamming his open palm down on the flat of his desk hard, Vasiliev's face turned ruddy and he asked, "Have you lost your damned mind? Hell no, we are not calling Moscow over this! I want all personnel on 100% alert. I want choppers in the air, I want teams on the ground and I want those partisans found! Do you hear me, Major!'

"Oh, I hear you, sir, but I suspect if the resistance can get within five miles of this base and detonate one of the nuclear warheads, we will all be blown from the face of this earth. So, sir, it matters little if we call Moscow or not, eh?"

"Sit down, Major." the Colonel ordered as he moved to his desk, sat, and then opened the top right drawer. He pulled out a quart of vodka and two glasses. He filled two glasses and handed one to the other man. Borisovich noticed it was a fresh bottle and not the one he'd drank from the night before.

After they both took a healthy drink, the Colonel said, "We are two smart men, are we not? Surely there must be a way to keep the Americans at bay. Oh, and by the way, you have just been promoted to Lieutenant Colonel, Sambor."

Careful, Borisovich thought, *he is using your first name.* He thought for a moment and then said, "Well the promotion is a great surprise to me, and my wife at home will love the increase in pay. Colonel, there is always a chance no one can read the Russian words on the note or by the time they find someone, we will have detonated our own nuclear weapons."

"What you say is true, but what if they *can* read it?"

"First, authorization does not mean you will use the weapons, only that you may if you choose to do so. I do not think they will expect you to detonate one in a town and the other near where we last saw the partisans."

"That's true. Yes, very true."

"However, sir, we must assume they will come for us, and I am serious. I have a bad feeling about this situation and think all non-essential personnel need to be evacuated to Jackson, just to be safe."

"I disagree, mainly because if we pull a lot of troops out, the partisans will know, so they'll attack without nuclear weapons. Everyone will stay where they are, all of us. Nevertheless, after further consideration, remove the 100% alert, because they do not need to get close to us, not if they can detonate a nuclear weapon, now do they?"

"Within five miles is what I know of the weapons. If you wish, sir, I can have a weapons expert prepare a briefing for us."

"It would be a waste of our time. Look I want everything that flies in the air and I want as many teams out looking for them as you can put together. We must find them, before they find us." the Colonel said and then threw back the remainder of his vodka.

Newly promoted Lieutenant Colonel Borisovich knocked the rest of drink back, stood, saluted and said, "Will do, sir."

Three hours later a helicopter contacted the base and reported seeing hundreds of partisans on the ground, slowly moving north. Both Vasiliev and Borisovich were contacted and then the Lieutenant Colonel had an idea. He called the Colonel and requested an immediate staff meeting, so Vasiliev told him to be in the briefing room in thirty minutes.

A Senior Sergeant yelled from the pit of his stomach, "Tennn—huuut!"

Borisovich entered the room, cleared this throat, and said, "Is there anyone in this room that does not have a top secret security clearance? If so, you need to leave now."

Two young officers stood and left the room.

The two senior officers made their way to the podium. Colonel Vasiliev said, "Gentlemen, I have dependable intelligence that the Americans are on their way here to detonate a small tactical nuclear weapon. I will now turn the rest of this briefing over to the head of my intelligence section, newly promoted Lieutenant Colonel Borisovich."

The Lieutenant Colonel then said, "Gentlemen, we have reliable reason to believe the Americans have found a way to explode one or both of the Russian made nuclear weapons they have in their possession. Approximately 45 minutes ago a force of more than a hundred partisans were seen moving toward this base."

"Sir, surely it would not take that many men to detonate a nuclear weapon."

"Excellent observation, Captain, and you are correct. It would only take two men, or even one, if in a pinch, to kill every man in this room and on this base. We feel the other men are along to provide security for the nuclear weapons and to insure it reaches it's intended target, which we feel is this base, as I said before."

"What are our options, sir?" a nervous looking Major asked.

"We have a plan, and we are sure it will work. At their present location and even their projected advance movement, they are too far away to be a threat to us right now. Also, the wind currents, if they stay as they have been for the last six months, offer us protection too."

"Protection from what," a young lieutenant asked and then added a late, "sir?"

"Nuclear fallout, Lieutenant."

The young officer suddenly looked confused and said, "Oh."

"Tonight at dark, after 1730 hours, some of our men will be loaded on a chopper, along with a tactical nuclear weapon. After making a number of false landings, the men and weapon will be unloaded and the chopper will leave, to continue making false landings. This will make it impossible for the partisans to know when the two men get off the aircraft.

They will move to the last known position of the partisans, arm the nuclear weapon and then clear the area. This weapon will be set to detonate at midnight, gentlemen."

Smiles were starting to show around the room and even a few cases of nervous laughter were heard. Feeling confident now, Borisovich asked, "Is the Weapons Commander and his Sergeant here?"

"I am filling in for the Colonel, sir, he is overseeing the arming of aircraft." a tall and lanky Master Sergeant said. He then added, "I am Master Sergeant Luka Milan."

"Sergeant, what is the blast distance for a small nuclear weapon about the size of a suitcase."

"It depends on the type, sir, and there are many in our inventory."

"Uh, how about an RA-115?"

"A little over 16 kilometers, sir."

"Oh, that far, huh?"

"Yes, sir and it is a dependable weapon too."

Colonel Vasiliev stepped forward and said, "Sergeant Milan, you will remain after the briefing, and the rest of you are excused, but remember, this meeting has been classified Top Secret."

After everyone left the room, Colonel Vasiliev asked, "Can you arm this weapon?"

"Oh, sure sir, it is simple. All I need is the key and a code. I insert the key and it unlocks a console that pops up, type in the code, and then run like hell."

"Can it be easily turned off?"

"No, it takes a different key and a new code which is written only to disarm the weapon."

"How many men will you need to go with you?"

"Go with me? What does that mean, sir?"

"It means Master Sergeant, you are about to become a hero, get a big medal, and a promotion to Captain, which will double your retirement pay. But if needed, you can consider this an order."

Realizing he was screwed, the Sergeant said, "Five men, including me. I want four to provide security for me while I arm the bomb. I will set it for midnight, but I want a helicopter to pick us up and return us to base on my call. Agreed?"

"Not a problem, and we will issue you three radios and five of the small portable ones, one for each of you. I would suggest you find your men now and get ready. I want you in the air at 1730 hours."

Grinning, the Master Sergeant said, "When we return, sir, I am sure my men and I would love a case of premium vodka."

"It will be in your quarters, and Sergeant?"

"Yes sir?"

"When you get on that helicopter, I want you to climb on as a Captain, understood? Your promotion was immediate, so you are out of uniform, sir." the Colonel said and then smiled.

CHAPTER 23

Sergeant Belton was on point and it was already dark. He was wearing Russian night vision goggles and loved them. As far as he knew, they were to move to about five miles from Edwards under the cover of darkness, and then turn east and travel to a spot near Jackson. He also knew most of the units were meeting there for some reason. He figured it was to attack another Russian base. He liked being a Sergeant, because he knew enough about what was going on to keep him happy and he didn't have enough rank to have to worry about a lot of troops. He had his squad and that was it. *With rank comes responsibilities*, he thought.

It was then he heard a chopper. He pulled out his poncho, so that if it got close he'd cover himself and maybe avoid infrared detection. It wasn't running with lights on, which told the Sergeant it was on a mission. Against the overcast sky, he saw it land in a field, close to a hundred meters away. He watched closely, saw no one get off and then it went back into the air. He heard the chopper do the same thing four or five more times. *Now*, he thought, *what in the hell was that about? It was either a fake landing or they may be having aircraft problems.*

He quickly returned to the main group and reported to Colonel Smith what he'd seen. The old Colonel looked at the oldest member in the group, Sergeant Major Henry, and asked, "Have you ever heard of that before?"

"They may be inserting a team to follow us. In Vietnam we did it all the time against the NVA and Cong. It makes it much harder for the enemy to discover where the real insertion was made."

"I'm not going to worry about it then. They know we're here, hell, they been flying over us all day. Belton, get back on point."

"Yes, sir." the Sergeant replied and then moved forward.

Almost three hours later, there came a burst of fire and Belton fell to the snow screaming in pain. Corporal Dupuy moved forward under covering fire and pulled the injured man to safety behind a tree. From what he could see with his NVG's, Belton had been shot in both legs and while it must have hurt like a bitch, he'd live.

"Sergeant Haney!" the Colonel yelled.

"Yo!"

"Take your squad and flank them."

Haney and his men no sooner neared the Russians than a mine, similar to the American Claymore, exploded and all but the Sergeant was instantly killed. He had been struck in the chest and was having trouble breathing.

The battle continued, and finally the Colonel ordered the men to pull back so they could go around the small pocket of Russians. He suspected they were some of the squads the Russians had out looking for them. It had taken time to administer to the injured and when Colonel Smith glanced at his watch, it was five minutes until midnight. He started moving and waved the men on to continue the march. Belton was being carried on a stretcher, along with Haney, who had been struck in the lungs, and they'd been given a shot of morphine for their pain.

No one saw Captain Milan and two other men moving off to the east. They left one dead and one too badly hurt to move. From his watch, it was about an hour before the explosion. He pulled the handset from the radio and called for a helicopter extraction. Twenty minutes later he was in the air moving for the airbase.

At exactly midnight, there was a super bright light to the south of Edwards Air Base and slowly it dulled. Most didn't realize the light signaled the death of over a hundred and fifty-three partisans in the first nuclear attack on the continent. The Russians had just gone too far.

"Colonel Vasiliev, I think that ends our partisan problem, at least for a while." Captain Milan said, and then laughed.

"Yes it does and by the way, that is a lot of vodka in your room for just three men."

Smiling, the Captain said, "Yes sir, it is and we earned every drop. I am sure it will last us a long time."

The End...for now.

Coming Soon,
The Fall of America: Fallout, Book #5

THE FALL OF AMERICA:

Book 1-3

Now available as audiobooks at iTunes, or at Audible.com.

ABOUT THE AUTHOR

W.R. Benton is an Amazon Top 100 Selling Author and has previously authored numerous books (over 30) of fiction, non-fiction, young adult, and Southern humor. Such notable authors as Matt Braun, Stephen Lodge, Don Bendell, and many others have endorsed his work. His survival book, *"Simple Survival, a Family Outdoors Guide,"* is a 2005 Silver Award Winner from the Military Writers Society of America. James Drury, "The Virginian," endorsed two of his Westerns, *"War Paint"* and *"James McKay, U.S. Army Scout."*

Mister Benton has an Associate Degree in Search and Rescue, Survival Operations, a Baccalaureate in Occupational Safety and Health, and a Masters Degree in Psychology completed except for his thesis. Sergeant Benton retired from the military in 1997, with over twenty-six years of active duty, and at the rank of Senior Master Sergeant (E-8). He spent twelve years as a Life Support Instructor where he taught aircrew members how to use survival gear, survival procedures, and parachuting techniques. Mr. Benton and his wife, Melanie, live near Jackson, Mississippi, with four dogs (Dolly, Newt, Benji, and Skillet) and two cats.

Visit him on Facebook
www.facebook.com/wrbenton01

The line has been crossed...

First they used chemical weapons on the Americans, then the Russians set off a tactical nuclear bomb in an effort to destroy a suitcase nuke captured by the rebels. Deadly radioactive fallout now adds to the already fierce battle to reclaim the U.S.A. and the partisans have even less to lose.

Now the rebels must decide whether to strike back in kind—An eye for an eye?

Both are available at Amazon and other online bookstores

A struggle for ultimate control

The elites have always manipulated global politics, but now a select group will launch their ultimate bid for power, *The New World Order*. They envision one world bank, only one currency, and one leader to control it all! They promise having one government will end global conflict and bring a peaceful, comfortable life to all humanity.

But with this new government comes personal costs, to free will, to self-determination and to liberty and some will find those costs too high to bear.

www.ingramcontent.com/pod-product-compliance
Lightning Source LLC
Chambersburg PA
CBHW070918190726

48292CB00004B/1014